Real Love

Alicia Wiggins

Marvelous Words Publishing

Marvelous Words Publishing
P.O. Box 28928
Columbus, OH 43228

First Edition

Visit me at www.aliciawiggins.com
Facebook – facebook.com/Alicia-Wiggins-Author

ACKNOWLEDGMENTS

This book has been a journey! Thanks to everyone who helped me along the way. Brantley, Sarah, Elliot, and Alex, you guys are always in my corner and I cannot do all the crazy things I want to do without you. To the Gibsons, Smiths, Jacksons, Hairstons, what can I say? Family is everything!

To my patient readers, thanks for inquiring and pushing me to finish this book. I hope you enjoy reading it as I enjoyed creating it.

CHAPTER ONE

DENIED.

"What the h-" Outraged, Marshall glared in disbelief at the bold word stamped across his company's proposal for the construction of the new hospital wing. The red, angry stamped lettering practically glared back at him.

He punched the intercom button on his phone. "Zen, get Chester Ryan on the phone right now!"

This had to be a mistake or one big misunderstanding. Nothing else could explain the denial. Marshall couldn't believe all of the hard work he had put into the preparation of the proposal, which now amounted to nothing more than a worthless pile of papers, and worse, the chance for his company to finally score a highly visible and lucrative project might now go unrealized.

While Oliver Construction certainly turned a decent profit, Marshall wanted to take on larger corporate projects. Restaurant and store renovations, custom home builds, and building warehouses for several medium to large businesses had been the company's bread and butter for many years and would continue to be. However, Marshall felt it was time to take Oliver Construction up a notch and the new wing for the hospital would be the project he needed to prove he could compete with the more prominent construction companies in the area.

Denied. The letters seemed to jump off the page and

scream "failure".

His intercom buzzed.

"Is he on the line?" Marshall asked preparing to verbally lash out at Chester Ryan, the councilman who had assured him that his proposal would be given the highest consideration and had all but guaranteed the bid would be accepted.

Just last week Councilman Ryan had informed Marshall that only one other councilmember's positive vote was needed before sending out the official bid approval. Yes, at the time, the hasty decision and Ryan's constant reassurance seemed a little fishy. Marshall hadn't asked questions; instead, he chose to be thankful his bid hadn't gotten tangled up in bureaucratic red tape, while at the same time hoping nothing unethical was taking place.

"Uh, Marshall, Mr. Ryan isn't available."

"Isn't available? Where the hell is he? You tell the paper pusher who answered the phone that Councilman Ryan needs to make himself available right now!"

The light on the phone's intercom went out. Seconds later Marshall's secretary, Zenobia Bryant, stepped cautiously into his office, closing the door behind her.

"Marshall, I know you're upset about this but you need to calm down."

"Calm down? Zen, are you looking at the same thing I'm looking at?" he asked, waving the proposal in the air. "How could we have gone from being five months away from breaking ground to sitting here holding a worthless pile of paper? Under the circumstances, I think I am pretty calm. Now, if I can't get in touch with Ryan, *then* I might not be so calm. As far as I can see somebody's got some explaining to do and if Chester Ryan won't talk to me on the phone, then he'd better be prepared to talk to me in person."

"That's what I came in to tell you. I'm not able to get in touch with Councilman Ryan because he's out of the office. He's on emergency medical leave, something to do with his heart. According to his office, he's going to be unavailable for the next nine weeks."

"*Nine weeks?*" Marshall struggled to keep his temper in check.

"Give or take."

"You have got to be kidding!"

Zenobia tried to keep her voice calm. Having worked for Marshall for nearly five years she knew from experience he had a short fuse. Right now, she wanted to avoid reaching the end of that fuse. "Look, I left a message with the mayor's admin. I'm sure he'll get back with me today with the name of the councilman's replacement. Until then you're going to have to take a deep breath and calm down until we can get some answers. There is nothing we can do until then."

Marshall knew Zen was right. How could he be upset with Councilman Ryan for taking ill? In reality, maybe he was upset with himself. Deep down he knew he should have asked more questions or at least did a better job of deciphering the volumes of information contained in the bid packet. His brother, an attorney, would have happily helped him with all of the legal terminology contained in the documents, but Marshall hadn't thought it necessary to consult his brother. This wasn't his first bid on a contract, but this certainly would have been his largest and most challenging project.

Now, in addition to possibly losing out on a prime opportunity, Marshall had a feeling that he may have allowed himself to be taken advantage of. Ryan knew Marshall's company had never managed a project of this magnitude. Marshall thought he had at least done the basic homework on the city's bidding process, but he had also trusted someone whom he suspected had a secret agenda. Yes, there were a few things in the bid proposal that he'd overlooked, but Ryan had assured him those items were minor and the final decision would be based on the lowest bid and the shortest estimated time to completion, although now that didn't seem to be the case.

At this point, the only thing Marshall could do was to try to fix this mess.

"We can't afford to sit on this, Zen," he said more calmly.

"I know, Marshall. I'm all over it."

"Do you think we should call someone else on the council? What about calling the mayor directly? He might have some insight into what happened."

"No. I think you should let me do my job, so you can do yours. As soon as I hear from the mayor's office, I'll set up an appointment for you to talk to the person who is in charge of handling the bid reviews."

Marshall placed the bid packet face down on his desk. He couldn't bear to look at it another second.

Leaning back in his chair, he rested his hands behind

his head and sighed heavily. He had confidence in Zenobia. She had worked magic before. This time he hoped she still had a few tricks up her sleeve.

***

"I put the tickets in your inbox."

Trenay made a face. "I know the hospital's benefit is a worthy cause, but do I have to go? I'd be more than happy to let you go in my place," she said, hoping for any excuse to stay home instead of attending yet another black-tie event.

Trenay's assistant Cristina tried to sympathize with her boss. She knew Trenay would prefer a root canal to attending the fundraiser even if it was billed as one of the year's premier events. "You already know why you have to go. I can't even begin to tell you what a great opportunity this is for you to meet and greet some of the city's most influential people. More importantly, I'm sure the mayor will notice the absence of one of his favorite appointees."

"*Shh!* Don't say that too loudly. There are enough people around this place who already think I was given this opportunity instead of earning it the old-fashioned way. I don't want my attendance at this event to look like favoritism or anything else that will take the focus off of the good work this office has been formed to carry out."

"Who cares what a bunch of lazy, narrow-minded bureaucrats think? I certainly don't. However, if you do, send them my way and I'll help to re-formulate their narrow-minded opinions."

Trenay had no doubt her assistant would come to her defense without a moment's hesitation. In fact, she had already done so more times than Trenay knew.

Generally, it irritated Trenay that she had to constantly prove herself over and over to her critics, although lately, she had begun to find it less annoying. For the first time in her career, and finally, at thirty-six years old, she felt really good about the work she was doing and had very little time or patience to give much attention to her detractors.

In keeping one of his campaign promises, Mayor Joseph Hanover had created a new office, which made the responsibility of overseeing and enforcing green building practices in Ohio's capital city a priority. At the time, appointing a virtually unknown young woman, who didn't register on anyone's political radar until he brought her to the forefront, had raised more than a few eyebrows.

Where did she come from? What were her qualifications? Could she possibly be the mayor's mistress? Those were just a few of the questions swirling around following her appointment.

Trenay had tried her best to ignore the innuendos that she was Mayor Hanover's mistress, long lost illegitimate daughter, and several other preposterous accusations that held no validity and which most reasonable people eventually ignored. However, after one of the local, more credible magazines ran a story about Trenay and the new office, citing her impressive credentials, family ties to the northern Ohio area, and her goals for the new office, some of her former naysayers quieted down a bit. Unfortunately, some feared their jobs would be in jeopardy or that they would lose out on city contracts because of the new green standards that had to be met. Basically, that particular group amounted to a handful of people who didn't know asbestos from apple peels and were okay with the outdated building practices that awarded contracts to companies who were oblivious to destroying wetlands and green space instead of renovating existing structures or working with the landscape, not against it. With those companies, the only green that caused them concern had to do with pure profit. Mayor Hanover wanted a change from those outdated practices and attitudes. He worked tirelessly to prevent urban sprawl and decay and wanted his city to be a model of growth and self-sustainability.

As far as Trenay was concerned, those who were most afraid of losing their jobs or contracts should be. She had some very strong opinions about conservation, renovation, and responsible building. She had also uncovered and worked diligently to put a stop to some very outdated "old boy" type of contract award practices. Already her office had fought to award bids to at least two minority and female-owned businesses who, despite their obvious qualifications, had been previously overlooked on several of the city's key projects.

"By the way, I had to add some of Councilman Ryan's appointments to your calendar."

"That shouldn't be a problem. As soon as I heard about his surgery, I knew some of the staff would have to step in to rebalance the workload."

"Well, I hope this rebalancing act doesn't mean we're going to be working extra hours," Cristina cautioned. "I only agreed to take some of his easier reviews and appeals because we were expected to, but we already have a lot on our plates, especially you, who for some reason thinks it's your job to save the world, one unbleached, canvas grocery bag at a time."

"I know, Mother Hen. No lectures. I promise we won't bite off more than we can chew."

"Good. With that said, I hope you don't mind, I had to squeeze one of those appointments in for today at three-thirty." Before Trenay could protest, Cristina continued. "I'll pick up your outfit for tonight's benefit and drop it off at your house. I spoke with Gina and she can fit you in at four forty-five for your hair and nails. And, I've arranged for you to be picked up tonight by six-thirty at your place. So despite your obvious reluctance to attend tonight's benefit, and because I know you would rather stay here and work until the wee hours of the morning, you have no excuses left. Cinderella *will* be going to the ball."

Trenay groaned, conceding defeat. "If you only knew how much Cinderella would rather stay home and work."

CHAPTER TWO

Trenay checked her watch. She had ten minutes before her last appointment, just enough time to print a copy of the report she wanted to review for an upcoming meeting. Having a hard copy of the report would allow her to review it over the weekend and make revisions if necessary and have it ready first thing Monday morning. Since she needed to print the graphs and charts in color, she had to use the network printer at Cristina's desk. Not the fastest printer around, but it did the trick.

As she waited patiently for the document to finish printing, Trenay flipped through the Parkgate Mall file on Cristina's desk to see if the revised specs had been added. This development could potentially be the one project that would be a shining example of her office's recommended green building practices working well for everyone involved. If she could only get the developers to work with her office and not against her in terms of complying with some of the practices she had put into place. Hopefully, the company's project manager would be reasonable and open to change. In her opinion, it would be a win-win for them all.

"Excuse me."

Startled, Trenay turned toward the voice. Cristina often accused her of getting so wrapped up in her work that she was oblivious to everything else around her. This was one of those times.

Trenay quickly closed the file and turned her attention to who she assumed to be her three-thirty appointment.

"May I help you?" she asked, hoping the brooding stranger might actually be lost and not her appointment after all. Although he didn't look shady, he seemed agitated and upset. God only knew what dealings this person had with Chester Ryan.

Typically, cute secretaries were like putty in his hands, but today he had other more serious matters on his mind – the fiscal health and wellness of his business. On the other hand, by laying on a little charm he might be able to get some information out of this tall, sexy honey as to why his bid had been denied and what he could do about it. But then he thought better of it. Marshall needed to talk to someone in charge. He didn't have the time or patience for finesse today. He especially wanted to avoid wasting time with someone who didn't have the authority to get him what he wanted.

"I'm here to see Trina Bradley," he said, attempting to look past the woman into the back office. He hoped her boss would come out to see what was going on and save him from having to explain who he was twice.

"Trenay Bradley," she corrected.

"Yes, well tell *Trenay* Bradley Marshall Oliver from Oliver Construction is here to see her."

Trenay quickly picked up on the dismissive tone but refused to react. Retrieving the finished report from the printer, she took extra care leafing through the stack of papers, making sure every page had printed correctly.

Tapping the stack on the desk once, then twice, she also checked to make sure each page had aligned correctly before retrieving a report cover from Cristina's supply stash and securing it. She leafed through the papers once more before placing the report under her arm and pushing Cristina's chair neatly back up to her desk. She could feel him glaring at her but the rude stranger would simply have to be patient.

"Look, *honey*, I'm in a bit of a hurry. If you don't mind, could you let Ms. Bradley know I'm here?"

Hmm…condescending and dismissive. Well, Ms. Bradley knows you're here and she'd like for you to leave.

Slipping into the mode she reserved for difficult or rude people, Trenay faked a smile, extended her hand, and said sweetly, "I'm Trenay Bradley. How can I help you?"

Realizing his mistake, Marshall decided it would be best to apologize and quickly move on to the reason he came to the office in the first place. "I'm sorry. I thought you were," pausing to look at the nameplate on the desk, "Cristina *Veal-a-leel*."

Trenay successfully suppressed a chuckle at the phonetic butchering of her assistant's name.

"It's Cristina *Villarreal*," she pronounced correctly. "Please, let's go into my office."

Marshall followed Trenay's lead while at the same time unintentionally taking notice of the sway of her hips in the figure-flattering skirt. He quickly chastised himself – for several reasons – for even noticing. One, he had business to take care of. That came first. Second, this woman was annoying. She knew he thought she was the secretary, but instead of clearing up the mistake right away, she made him waste even more time while he waited for her to shuffle papers. Third – well, he didn't really know the third reason. Everything that mattered at this point simply went back to the bid for the construction of the hospital's new wing, but he did have a thing for a woman wearing a well-fitting skirt and high heels. And Trenay had the figure, complete with long shapely legs, to pull off the look with attitude, not to mention she had thrown him off his game, at least temporarily.

Quickly regaining his composure, Marshall squashed the inappropriate images of Trenay that had somehow sprung up in his imagination.

Removing the rejected bid from his briefcase, he placed it firmly on Trenay's desk. Pausing for effect, he wanted to give her a moment to prepare what he expected to be a rehearsed speech that meant nothing more than "we picked the lowest bid".

Trenay picked up the papers and briefly scanned the first few pages. She recognized the bid for one of Councilmen Ryan's pet projects. Ever since she had come on staff one of her goals had been to get the council members to listen to her ideas regarding responsible building. She explained to them in no uncertain terms that the city would no longer approve projects to build on green space when there were buildings in perfect condition sitting vacant due to a company's demise or relocation. Strip malls overshadowed by shiny new malls lay vacant, adding to an ever-growing problem of "ghost" neighborhoods – areas of the city where once-thriving businesses and neighborhoods now contained boarded-up buildings and vacant homes.

While the new wing for the hospital didn't fall under this category, she had concerns over the number of residents that would be displaced because of it. The land where their homes sat would have to be purchased to allow for the hospital's expansion. Trenay had an idea to revamp another area close to the proposed expansion site into a place where the displaced residents could move. Her plan would benefit all parties and revitalize an area that sorely needed help.

Chester Ryan had dismissed that idea and almost all of her other ideas as unfounded, expensive, and a waste of the taxpayer's money. His idea of growth for the city was to build, build, build. She often wondered if he was getting kickbacks for every inch of undeveloped land he approved for new construction.

"I worked for almost six months preparing this bid. My firm followed the bidding guidelines and submitted very detailed specs. And I know for a fact that we came in under Crawford and Sons."

Trenay didn't bother to ask how he knew his bid came in lower than the firm who likely would be awarded the contract, but she could be fairly sure Councilman Ryan had something to do with leaking the information.

"Mr. Oliver, your bid rejection had nothing to do with how much it would cost your firm to build the expansion."

"Then explain to me why I'm looking at six months' worth of hard work reduced to a pile of paper with a big red *DENIED* stamp across the top."

Trenay took a deep breath. *An angry customer. Nothing more, nothing less.* That's who she told herself she was dealing with. Citizens were customers and should be handled as such. Well, Marshall Oliver may be a customer, but she had serious doubt as to how she could handle him.

"Look, Mr. Oliver–"

"Marshall. Mr. Oliver is my father," he said attempting to sound much calmer than he felt.

Okay, maybe his bark is worse than his bite. Regardless, she wanted to get this meeting over with as quickly as possible. Why couldn't he simply be tall, dark, and handsome, instead of tall, dark, handsome, and rude? *It would make this meeting a lot more interesting.*

"Your bid rejection had everything to do with the fact that it did not meet the green standards set by this office. I believe we stated the reasons in the letter that should have been enclosed when we returned the bid."

Marshall looked at Trenay as if she'd just switched from speaking English to Pig Latin. "Green what?"

"Green standards for responsible building," Trenay repeated calmly but becoming increasingly irritated as he continued to stare at her with a blank expression. Surely, Chester Ryan had explained this to him, but knowing the councilman, he had probably glossed over this information, dubbing it nonsense.

"Let me explain. Using natural lighting and energy-efficient materials, managing post-consumer waste, properly filtering and diverting your job site water runoff, those are a few examples of responsible building." Trenay pulled out a folder from her drawer. She handed Marshall a small stack of papers that were stapled together and featured a recycling logo on the cover. "For this project and every project going forward, this office is looking for contractors who demonstrate that they have already successfully adopted, or are willing to adopt, the Leadership in Energy and Environmental Design, or LEED for short, of the Green Building Rating System methods." He still looked puzzled, so Trenay continued with her explanation, pretty sure, this was the first time Marshall had seen or heard any of this information. "Essentially, my office encourages the acceleration and adoption of sustainable green building and development practices through the creation and implementation of universally understood and accepted tools and performance criteria. We also provide education on those tools and performance criteria for companies unsure of where to start or exactly what they should be doing – like your company."

Green standards? Recycling? Responsible building? This simply could not be happening. Despite her well-rehearsed explanation Marshall struggled to decipher everything he heard Trenay saying. The only thing he managed to get out of her little speech was that his company's bid had been rejected because of some little known environmental loophole. Regardless, he wasn't about to lose out on a prime construction project because some environmentalist wanted to push her *save the earth* agenda.

Funny, she didn't look like a tree hugger; in fact, she looked the exact opposite of what he expected one to look like. He'd be willing to bet that she didn't have a cache of furs and jewelry like his ex-wife Tiffany, but he had a hard time picturing this pretty lady living the restricted life of a *greenie.*

Marshall placed the papers Trenay had given him into his briefcase hoping to move past all of this green building nonsense. She seemed like a nice lady and maybe she would listen to reason. Leaning forward, he smiled and said as calmly as he could, "Look, Ms. Bradley-"

"Trenay. My great aunt's name is Ms. Bradley." She smiled, hoping to relieve some of the tension that had followed Marshall into her office and still loomed.

It didn't help.

"Councilman Ryan never mentioned anything about this responsible building requirement even though we already follow some of these guidelines, like using energy-efficient materials when it's economically advantageous. So we're not completely in the dark ages. Although, I have to say I honestly cannot recall seeing this specific information in the bid announcement. I have been in the construction business for twenty years. My company has a reputation for fair business practices, professionalism, never skimping on quality, and adhering to all building codes and procedures. We don't use inferior products or materials and in the past five years, we have met or beat all of our deadlines, all while staying within or under budget. Now, if we promise to compost our lunch scraps and recycle our plastic water bottles, would your office reconsider our bid?"

Trenay had to take a minute before responding. She needed to maintain her composure in light of feeling this man seemed to think the rules did not apply to him. And even more annoying, he seemed to think she should wave her magic wand and make everything okay or at least tilt in his favor. It was clear that he was used to getting his way and she couldn't help wondering if his impressive size and booming voice intimated most people. Well, she wouldn't be giving in, no matter how rude, intimidating, angry - *or handsome* - he appeared.

"I'm sorry you missed the information in the bid announcement regarding my office's policy, *Mr. Marshall.*" She made sure to place extra emphasis on his name. "I'm also sorry that Councilman Ryan chose to downplay this part of the bid requirement." Just like he downplayed everything she or her office proposed. "However, the bottom line is Oliver Construction only meets one or two of the basic requirements, at best, this office has set for responsible building."

Trenay glanced at her watch. If she didn't leave in the next ten minutes, she wouldn't make the benefit on time, and she needed to make an early appearance so she could then slip out as quickly as possible before getting unmercifully cornered. Besides, she couldn't think of anything more she needed or wanted to say to Marshall Oliver.

"Thank you so much for stopping by. My office has additional information on green building and even some upcoming seminars on the practice. If you'd like, I'll have my assistant send the information over to you."

Trenay rose slowly from her desk.

Marshall never took his eyes off her as she gathered

papers from the filing cabinet.

She clicked her mouse two or three times, waited a few seconds, and grabbed her purse. Walking over to her door, she smiled and waited for Marshall to join her.

Marshall turned in his chair, speechless. He had been dismissed. He didn't know whether to be ticked off or impressed that she had such gall. He tried to maintain a calm game face as he walked over to the door and shook Trenay's extended hand. Typically, he had a knack for charming his way in or out of most situations, but with Trenay, he would have to use a different tactic. She clearly was immune.

Realizing that he had reached an impasse with her, Marshall knew when to stay and fight and when to wage battle another day. This one would have to wait until another day. Beginning tomorrow, he would have Zenobia file an appeal.

She may have won this round, but Trenay Bradley had not seen or heard the last of him.

CHAPTER THREE

"Stop fidgeting."

Marshall scowled and stopped tugging at his collar.

"Can you at least try to put on a happy face? People will think something is wrong with you."

"There is something wrong with me, Zen. I don't want to be here. I don't know why I let you drag me to this thing. I would rather be back at the office working on our appeal."

"Marshall, I told you, I'll get to it first thing tomorrow. The fact that I'm willing to come in on a Saturday should entitle me to some fun tonight. Do I need to remind you how much I like my Saturdays and how much I detest working on what I consider to be a sacred day? At the very least you could allow me to have a little fun, even if you would rather be a party pooper."

Marshall continued to brood as he watched Zenobia walk onto the dance floor with a guy she had been flirting with for the past fifteen minutes, when she wasn't scolding him for being in such a sour mood. Sorry that he had allowed himself to be pressured into attending the benefit he refused to try and hide his misery any longer. Why should he? Being at the event didn't seem as if it would benefit him in the least.

He needed a drink. At least if he had to be at this stuffy event then he would do it with his senses numbed.

"Scotch and soda, please. Heavy on the scotch, light on the soda. And make it neat."

Waiting impatiently while the bartender fixed his drink, Marshall scanned the myriad of faces in the crowd. He recognized the mayor and his wife, several members from the hospital's board of directors, and a few other people he'd had business dealings with over the years. No one impressive. Most of the people in attendance looked like the kind of people who attended these types of events regularly. Tuxedos, overly made-up women in unflattering, tight dresses, watered-down drinks, and bad band music were things he would like to stay as far away from as possible even though Zenobia reminded him that this could be a prime networking opportunity. *Whatever.* He didn't see one person that he wanted to spend the evening networking with.

Leaning against a wall near the bar he listened as the band played a rather pathetic rendition of Prince's *Kiss* as people crowded on to the dance floor. He hoped Zenobia would soon get her fill of the tall stranger she had been dancing with for at least two songs. But much to his dismay it appeared the happy couple had no intention of leaving any time soon as they moved closer to the center of the dance floor.

At least somebody is having a good time.

Marshall downed his drink and ordered another. After leaving a nice tip, he thanked the bartender and resigned himself to find a secluded spot to wait out Zenobia's dance marathon and to nurse his second drink. Since they had come to the benefit together, they would leave together.

No matter how much fun she seemed to be having despite his misery, he couldn't and wouldn't leave without her. His parents had raised him to be a gentleman, no matter the circumstances or his temperament.

Standing away from the dance floor and in a spot where he hoped he would be left alone, Marshall continued to watch the partygoers. Despite the cheesy band, everyone seemed to be having a good time. *Everyone except him.* He was still fuming from his earlier meeting with Trenay Bradley. He really wanted to continue being angry with her, but if he was honest with himself he would have to admit that some of the green building practices she talked about were something he had been thinking about for a long time. Before he bought out his partner, they had incorporated a few of the practices into their last projects – as he tried to explain to Ms. Bradley – but Oliver Construction was nowhere near where it needed to be. To ramp up to his competition and eventually gain an edge, he would also need to make that move, and quickly.

When he thought about it, in recent years some of the more lucrative and visible projects were being awarded to the companies that were known to be environmentally responsible. These days information was everywhere about carbon footprints, green living, and conservation. The movement had become more than just a slogan to print on t-shirts and bumper stickers. It had even seeped into his family's way of thinking.

Recently when his eighteen-year-old niece Kyra dropped by his house for a visit she had asked where she could put her empty juice bottle.

"In the trash," Marshall had remarked offhandedly. From her reaction, he might as well have said, "Throw it in the nearest lake or river and kill a few fish while you're at it." What followed was a full-fledged speech on global warming, the ozone, carbon footprints, and environmental ignorance. Who knew all of this environmental consciousness would have such an impact on his business's bottom line?

Unfortunately, he had been ignoring the inevitable trend for too long now and it was about to cost him a pretty lucrative piece of business.

Time to learn some new tricks, old dog.

Checking his watch, he decided to give Zenobia five more minutes. Maybe if he stood near the dance floor she would see him and realize he was ready to go. If not, he would have to find a spot to wait out the rest of the evening.

Casually making his way around the edge of the dance floor with his vision fixed on Zenobia to catch her eye, Marshall practically collided with someone approaching from the opposite direction. He narrowly missed spilling the rest of his drink down the front of her dress, and he quickly apologized. "I'm so sorry," he began and then stopped short when he recognized who he had almost run into. Trenay Bradley. *Speak of the devil.* The devil in a sexy, black dress.

"That's oka-" Trenay started then stopped when she recognized Marshall.

"Ms. Bradley."

"Mr. Oliver," she replied coolly.

Marshall stood just inches away from Trenay as he tried to pretend as if it were no big deal bumping into her out of the blue. Unfortunately, his efforts were in vain.

Thoughts of leaving early, boredom, and having to carry on tedious conversations with several uptight, conservative women from earlier in the evening quickly became a passing memory. His attention right now was squarely focused on the beauty standing before him wearing a black form-fitting evening gown that somehow managed to hug every curve and accentuate every one of her assets. Try as he might, Marshall couldn't utter a single word. He could only stare in admiration.

Cascading curls framed her face and shimmering earrings practically touched her shoulders. Marshall knew very little about makeup but what Trenay had applied was just the right amount to compliment her smooth dark skin perfectly and seemed to make her big, brown eyes sparkle. A touch of color and shine on her lips all but dared him to sneak a taste.

Trenay's dress was sleeveless and showed long, lean arms. Again he noticed how her curves were accentuated as the fabric of the dress wrapped her body in a hug. A deep slit at the side showed enough of her shapely leg to make him wish he could see more. Even her toes were sexy, perfectly polished, and peeking out of high-heeled shoes. She looked put together, classy, and, he noticed with more than a modicum of appreciation, drop-dead gorgeous. And while he respected the skirt and heels she'd been wearing earlier in the day, he formed a whole new level of appreciation for the total package he saw now.

Not sure if he could blame the two drinks he had consumed in rapid succession or the fact that his basic male instincts were canceling out the anger and frustration that he'd felt earlier, he somehow allowed Trenay's smoldering beauty to waft over him like glaze poured over warm pound cake. *Did she look as delicious underneath that dress?* He wondered.

Marshall was completely off his game once he recognized who she was. She didn't know why but it appeared to have taken a second or two for him to recognize her. But once he did, he then proceeded to look her up and down, from head to toe. Under normal circumstances, Trenay would have been offended by a man's open and rather unconcealed appraisal of her. Seriously, he had done everything but lick his lips! But she couldn't muster up the necessary level of indignation to be properly offended. In fact, she felt quite the opposite. For reasons she would never admit to herself or anyone else, Marshall's appreciative and almost lustful head-to-toe perusal was more than a little bit flattering.

Regardless, she still intended to give Cristina a piece of her mind when she came into the office on Monday. No, she wouldn't wait until Monday. Cristina would be getting an earful tonight!

The outfit she had picked out for tonight's affair had been elegant and tasteful. Cristina had even been with her when she picked it out from a small boutique in the Short North. Cristina only needed to pick it up from the shop where it was being altered. But no! Instead of her original outfit, Cristina had dropped this dress off at her house in its place.

She wondered exactly when her assistant had decided to switch outfits. The two of them had gone shopping days ago during their lunch hour to pick out something appropriate for tonight's benefit. After trying on several variations of what she had considered suitable for the benefit, Trenay had let Cristina talk her into trying on a sexy, body-hugging black evening gown with a split up the side that fell about an inch or two short of being scandalous. Even though her friend swore she looked "delicious" in the dress, Trenay was not convinced and opted instead for a pantsuit, feeling more comfortable in the complete cover it offered. Cristina had tried very hard to get Trenay to at least buy the dress and keep it in reserve just in case such an occasion came up where she could wear it. Declining her friend's offer, Trenay confessed that she didn't think she had the curves to carry off wearing such a sexy dress. Never one to miss an opportunity to give flattery where flattery was due, Cristina quickly retorted, "Sexy is an attitude, *chica*, not a size and you've got more than enough attitude to light this dress on fire."

Well, it turned out Cristina was right. Having nothing else suitable to wear, since the pantsuit was MIA, Trenay did her best to ignore her body's imperfections and donned the dress and all the accessories that magically came with it.

She had to admit, stepping out of her comfort zone just this once was giving her a bit of an ego boost. Since arriving tonight she had received several admiring glances,

Alicia Wiggins

an offer to dance, and one rather inappropriate offer from a very inebriated deputy fire chief. This type of attention was something she wasn't used to. She even had to suppress her embarrassment, then amusement, when her driver practically tripped over himself helping her out of the car when she inadvertently exposed a good portion of her thigh.

"I'm a little surprised to see you here," Marshall said, finding his voice.

"You are?" Trenay asked. "Why is that?"

Marshall looked out over the crowd and replied, "Green Peace demonstrations and save the planet rallies seem more your speed."

"Is that right?" she asked wondering if she should bother to let him know the type of person, she really was.

"Maybe."

"Well, there's a lot more to me than meets the eye," she replied, wondering why she would even bother explaining herself to him.

"Obviously," he said with another appreciative glance.

Blood rushed to her face and she suddenly felt warm all over. He needed to stop looking at her that way.

The band had just returned from a break and people were milling back on to the dance floor. Before they knew it both Marshall and Trenay were being moved by the crowd. Finding himself standing across from Trenay on the dance floor Marshall smiled and extended his hand.

Realizing he wanted to dance with her Trenay looked skeptical at first, then she looked for a way to escape.

"It would take more effort to weave through the

crowd to get off the dance floor than it would be sharing a dance with me."

Trenay looked around once more and the crowd continued to box them in. He was right. There wasn't a good way to escape. She nodded reluctantly. "Just one dance," she conceded.

Without wasting time, Marshall took her hand. For the entire song, they danced together in a tiny space on the dance floor. Fortunately, for Marshall, they had gotten boxed in even more and were now in the center of the dance floor where they ended up dancing for two more numbers.

While they danced Trenay struggled to think of as many mundane tasks as she could – things she needed from the grocery store, an email she wanted to write to her parents, picking up treats for her two cats – anything besides how nice Marshall looked, the scent of his cologne, and how well he danced. Most men she danced with either swayed from side to side casually looking around the room attempting to personify their coolness or they thought having sex and dancing were synonymous, as they groped, gyrated, and humped to the beat.

Marshall just had to be different!

He never took his eyes off of her as he occasionally spun her around in their little space or put his hands on her shoulders as they moved together to the beat. For a guy his size, she figured six-two, six-three, and solidly built, he moved with ease. Even his tux moved with him and didn't appear stiff or awkwardly fitted. His tux fit him so well she instinctively knew it had been tailored for him.

When the song ended and the band began to play a ballad, Marshall saw a strange look on Trenay's face. For some women slow dancing with a strange man was out of the question. Judging by the look on her face, Trenay might be one of those women. He grabbed her elbow, weaving her through the crowd off the dance floor and toward a set of doors that led out on to the balcony. Looking around they saw a few people gathered in one corner smoking. Marshall found a spot away from the smokers where they could have a little privacy.

"I hope you don't mind. It started to get pretty crowded in there," he replied.

Unintentionally or not, Marshall had given her an out from slow dancing. *Whew!* She had dodged a bullet. Her body pressed against his…she didn't even want to imagine what that would have been like. "No, that's fine. I needed some fresh air anyway. Besides, it's a beautiful night. Way too nice to be stuck inside."

"Yes, especially for May, not too cool, not too warm. Just right."

Marshall continued to make small talk while he tried to figure out if Trenay had attended the benefit unescorted. She wasn't giving up any clues one way or the other. Realistically, he should have been concerned about whether or not she had a date three songs ago. Being confronted by some brother who felt a need to mark his territory was something he wanted to avoid at all costs.

He looked over at the entrance a few times to see if he noticed anyone searching for her but after a while, he let it go. It didn't matter who had accompanied Trenay,

Marshall knew he wouldn't like him. In his opinion, whoever had escorted her tonight deserved to lose out to him. Any man who wouldn't guard such a beautiful woman deserved to go home by himself.

"Would you like a drink?"

Throughout the evening, Trenay had smiled, shaken more hands, and chatted up more people than she cared to remember. It felt as if she'd spoken to everyone at the benefit, as a representative from the mayor's office there were still a few more people she needed to say hello to before the end of the evening, but they would have to wait. She decided to accept Marshall's offer for a drink. At least with him, she didn't have to be "on" and she needed a break from all the schmoozing.

"Yes, thank you. Riesling, please. Oh, and could you make sure it's from one of the Ohio vineyards?" She'd already had two glasses, but one more wouldn't hurt, she reasoned. Besides, she had a driver. Even if she did get a little tipsy, she would get home safely.

Marshall came back a few minutes later with her wine. "So tell me, Miss Brad – Trenay – are you here this evening out of obligation?"

"Wow. Does it show that much? This is one of the mayor's pet causes. I'm here because he and his wife purchased a table and they needed bodies to fill it. What about you?"

Marshall shrugged. "It's a worthy cause." He neglected to tell her that he, too, had purchased a table. Most of the bodies that filled the table purchased by his company, besides Zenobia, were people on his crew who he knew rarely, if ever, had a chance to attend an event such as this. Not only had he provided the guys on his crew the means to attend tonight's benefit, but he had also footed the bill for their tuxes.

"I guess I misjudged you," Trenay remarked candidly.

"How so?"

"My first thought was that you were here strictly to make business connections. Shaking hands, exchanging business cards, setting up tee times, that kind of thing."

"Could you blame me if I did? I'm a businessman. I tend to use social events to meet people and make business connections. But tonight's a little different. No business cards. No tee times. I'm strictly here to support a worthy cause."

Trenay looked skeptical.

"Contrary to popular belief, I do care about causes other than my own."

That remains to be seen. After their meeting earlier, she had decided that *not* having to deal with Marshall Oliver ever again would be okay with her. Even while giving him the benefit of the doubt and knowing his company had lost out on a prime project, he had shown the kind of bad attitude, which led her to brand him a world-class jerk. She also had to keep in mind that there are two sides to every coin and maybe she shouldn't be so quick to judge.

"I hope I'm not keeping you from your date."

Marshall smiled and took a sip from his drink. Her coy way of asking if *he* was attending the affair alone. He decided to string her along. "She won't mind."

Trenay frowned. *She won't mind? What kind of woman*

wouldn't mind her date flirting – and she didn't think she was stretching the definition – with another woman? And what kind of man would do that to someone he cared about?

"What about you?"

"What about me?" Trenay asked with a little more attitude than she intended.

"Do I need to watch my back tonight?"

If he only knew, Trenay thought. Not only had she attended this affair by herself, but she also attended most events unaccompanied or with Cristina. Things were less complicated that way, particularly in the relationship department.

The last serious relationship she'd had dated back to her college days. After graduation and entering the real world, she and her then-boyfriend took jobs in different parts of the country and in very different fields. She immediately set about building her career and connecting with people who could help her learn the things she needed to know in the often-male dominated world of construction, which left very little time for a social life. It didn't take long for her relationship with her boyfriend to slowly fade into oblivion. They had parted with no hard feelings.

From that point on, she continued to immerse herself in her work, concentrating on building her career more than her social life. However, *Mr. Playboy* here didn't need to know any of that. Why would he be interested in whether or not she had a date anyway? His concern should be about *his* neglected date, not hers.

Before she could come up with a clever response to

his question, a tall, beautiful woman with short, neat dreadlocks walked out on the terrace toward them.

Marshall's date?

She spotted Trenay and smiled warmly.

"Marshall, who is this pretty lady you have cornered out here?"

She stopped in front of Trenay and Marshall. Tall, very close to six feet, and elegant, she wore a beautiful champagne-colored dress with matching stilettos. Her skin was flawless and her smile warm and seemingly genuine. Everything about her had an air of elegance and sincerity – the way she spoke, how she practically glided when she walked, and even her smile. For some reason, she didn't seem to mind her date chatting up another woman.

Trenay returned the smile. Not waiting to be introduced and feeling the need to head off any misunderstanding, Trenay quickly extended her hand.

"I'm Trenay Bradley. I'm here representing the mayor's office," she added for effect, not sure why.

The woman looked at Marshall, smiling coyly. "Miss Bradley, I'm Zenobia Bryant, Marshall's assistant. I hope he hasn't been boring you with business matters and giving you a hard time about rejecting our bid. I don't think I've ever seen Marshall so -"

"Uh, Zenobia, are you ready to go?" Marshall knew if he didn't stop her she'd say something to embarrass him or Trenay, or both of them.

"That's what I'm here to tell you. I met up with some old friends and one new one," she said and winked at Trenay. "We've decided to go to a new club over on Main

Street. Care to join us?"

Marshall shook his head. He wasn't in the mood to do the club scene tonight. "No thanks, Zen. Not feeling it tonight."

"Trenay?"

"Oh, no, thank you." Trenay didn't add that she wasn't much of a club-goer. Besides, her long day had begun to catch up with her. She was getting tired and wanted to head home soon. In retrospect, she probably shouldn't have had that last glass of wine.

A hot bath and a few chapters of the mystery she started reading the night before would be the grand finale to her evening if she didn't fall asleep first.

"Zen, how are you getting home? Now you know my daddy raised me to be a gentleman. And a gentleman always sees a lady home."

"Marshall, I'm a big girl. I'll give you a pass this one time, okay? You don't need to worry. My friends will see that I get home all right." Turning to Trenay, she added, "It was very nice meeting you, Trenay. Don't keep my boss out too late," she added with a smile. "By the way, *fierce* dress."

Trenay blushed.

Marshall cleared his throat as the two of them watched Zenobia become absorbed in the crowd on the dance floor.

"She seems nice."

Marshall smiled. "She is. I honestly don't know what I'd do without her."

Trenay finished her drink and decided that it was time

to say hello to a few more people then she could make a gracious exit. Beginning to feel the effect of her third glass of wine, something told her she needn't spend too much more time talking to Marshall, especially with him casually leaning against the railing staring at her like she was a slice of chocolate cake.

"Is there something wrong?" she asked.

Marshall shook his head and took a sip from his glass. "No. Why do you ask?"

"Because you're staring and it's making me uncomfortable."

He smiled, pushed away from the railing, and sat his glass at an empty table.

Nice smile, she decided. *Nice eyes, too.* His heavily lashed eyes seemed to sparkle mischievously under the tiny twinkling lights that decorated the balcony. *Why hadn't she noticed his eyes before? Nice lips, too.*

"You know, Trenay, you never answered my question."

"What question?" she asked, wishing she had eaten more than a few pieces of cheese and fruit. She knew better than to drink and not eat.

"Your date for the evening?"

Back to that. "Not that it's any of your business, but I'm here alone."

"I see," Marshall replied thoughtfully.

Letting her curiosity get the best of her, she asked, "You see what?"

Grabbing her left hand and lifting it he said, "Well, you're not wearing a ring and you're attending this event alone. That tells me that you're not only cute, smart, environmentally conscious, and can wear the hell of that dress, you're also unattached."

Pulling her hand away, Trenay shook her head. At this point, she wasn't sure what she regretted more – the wine, allowing herself to spend so much time chitchatting with Marshall, or the sexy way she felt when he looked at her with open appreciation and obvious lust.

"I don't see how that is any of your business."

Marshall looked thoughtful as if making an assessment. "I'm the kind of man who likes to know where he stands. In this case, where you're concerned, it just clears the path, that's all," he replied after a moment.

"Clears the path for what?"

At that moment, strong hands grasped her upper arms pulling her forward. Before she even thought about protesting or asking Marshall what the hell he was doing, soft lips covered hers, sending a shower of tingles shooting throughout her body from head to toe, leaving her speechless and for the first time ever, breathless.

Almost as quickly as he had initiated it, Marshall ended the kiss. He released her, smiled, and walked toward the entrance to the ballroom. When he reached the door, he turned, and in a voice that could melt butter, he said, "Good night, Trenay Bradley. Pleasant dreams."

CHAPTER FOUR

Under normal circumstances, Marshall would have paid very little attention, if any, to the article about the Little Lamb Childcare Center's grand opening, except the picture accompanying the story had caught his attention. Several people appeared in the shot cutting a giant ribbon at what the article described as the opening celebration. One of the people in the picture was Trenay Bradley.

The story highlighted the construction of the childcare facility using post-consumer waste, featured a state-of-the-art heating and cooling system, and used shredded tires instead of mulch for the bed of the outdoor playground. Even the dining area had containers for recycling milk and juice cartons and other waste from the children's mealtime.

Marshall folded the newspaper and placed it to the side. Leaning back in his chair he allowed himself to daydream, just for a moment. Thinking about last Friday's benefit and the time he spent with Trenay, their conversation, the obvious flirting, and the kiss they shared. *The kiss.* He smiled. The look on her face after they kissed spoke volumes. Driven purely by impulse, slight inebriation, and a serious case of lust, Marshall knew he really should be thanking his lucky stars she hadn't slapped his face. However, now thinking more rationally about her reaction, he had to say he was more pleased than confused. Even though the kiss had been brief, there was a clear distinction between how it began and the way it ended. In the beginning, Trenay seemed hesitant, almost cautious, but then her reaction changed, in a good way. He recalled the feel of her body pressing into his as the kiss went from an act he initiated to a shared action in which they both freely and enthusiastically participated.

Allowing himself a few more minutes to reflect on that night Marshall tried his hardest to recall every single detail. *Her body.* Holding her close he remembered feeling the warmth radiating from her skin. *Her scent.* Seductive and inviting. *Her eyes.* Beautiful, sparkling, and hinting at something he couldn't quite put his finger on. *Her lips.* Full and sweet, like wine and equally as intoxicating. Everything about that evening and especially those few private moments with Trenay at the end of the evening were etched into his memory.

Marshall smiled and picked up the newspaper again to take another look at the picture. Talk about not judging a book by its cover. Trenay could have easily fit his preconceived image of the average high achieving, ball-busting, pretty on the outside, iceberg on the inside career woman he initially imagined her to be. But his gut feeling told him she wasn't that way at all. From the little time, he had spent with her she appeared to have more than a sufficient amount of smarts, style, sass, and sexiness, which said a lot.

He would be the first to admit that in the past it had primarily been a woman's body – particularly the curve of her hips, long, shapely legs, and nice, firm breasts – which piqued his interest, not her brain. With Trenay, he didn't think he would have to choose between the two. That is if he chose to go down that path.

Was she interested? Just thinking about how she had responded to his kiss put a smile on his face and sent a bolt of electricity straight to his groin. It wasn't just his imagination; there truly was a spark there. He'd bet money on it.

"Marshall, you've been pestering me about getting the appeal to you for the hospital bid and it's still sitting right where I left it."

Marshall snapped to attention as Zenobia blew into his office unannounced. He placed the newspaper on the desk and pretended to straighten a stack of papers.

"Please wipe that silly grin off your face. Nothing is that good in the newspaper." Dropping a stack of mail on his desk Zenobia stood poised, ready to berate him for wasting time, especially since he had been pushing her for the rebuttal from the moment they had received the rejected proposal, but she paused when she noticed the odd look on her boss' face. Picking up the newspaper and scanning the page her frown quickly changed into a wide smile. "Oh. So this is why you're not getting any work done today." She gently placed the newspaper back on Marshall's desk and made an exaggerated gesture to smooth out the pages.

"I don't know what you're talking about, Zen." Marshall grabbed the newspaper and threw it in the trash. He picked up the stack of mail and started leafing through it, hoping Zenobia would see he was busy or pretended to be, and go back to her desk.

She didn't buy the charade for a moment. Taking the seat across from his desk, she crossed her long legs and stared intently at Marshall.

"I think somebody's got a crush," she sang, with a look of amusement.

Returning the look with one more stern, Marshall stopped fumbling with the mail and replied, "I think somebody's got work to do and if she values her job, she'll leave my office and do it."

"But what fun would that be?" she asked, playfully, clearly unaffected by her boss' comment. "If you want my opinion, you could do worse - and we both know you have. This lady is different. I think I can say this with a bit of confidence, she's the complete package."

"Meaning?" he asked, with piqued curiosity, pretending to mask how much he cared about Zenobia's opinion of Trenay, but wanting to hear more.

"Meaning, she's nothing like those little tarts or ice queens you usually waste your time with. This one doesn't just have a job; she has a career. Appointed by the mayor, I heard, and shaking up things at City Hall, in a good way, if you ask me. Clearing out the riffraff and breaking up the good ol' boy's network. Plus, I like her style. She knows how to dress for a formal event without over or under-doing it. I will never forget the outfit your date wore to the fundraiser for Councilman Ryan. Talk about inappropriate."

Zenobia rolled her eyes upward. Marshall shifted uncomfortably.

"Also," Zenobia added, "she was nice to me when we

met. Not knowing that I'm your assistant, she could have immediately bared her claws and treated me like the competition, not unlike some of the trollops you've wasted precious time with in the past. Take note, boss, I think this lady has beauty, brains, and class. I like her. Don't mess up and scare her away."

Over the years and throughout many different circumstances Marshall had learned that amongst other things he could count on Zenobia to be a good judge of character. He not only valued her good judgment, he relied on it. She made no qualms about saying what was on her mind. As in this case, if she thought Trenay wasn't worth his time, she would have said so, in no uncertain terms.

Still pretending not to give too much weight to Zenobia's opinion, Marshall knew he needed to put a stop to this conversation while he was ahead. "Explain to me how this is relevant to anything we have going on in the office today."

Zenobia shrugged. "You never know. It might benefit us to have someone like her as a friend."

"I seriously doubt it. She seems pretty rigid and some of her environmental ideas are a little too 'flower child' for my taste." Actually, she didn't feel rigid at all when he held her in his arms and kissed her. Shaking his head to clear his thoughts, he continued. "The only reason I'm sending this rebuttal is to let her know that we aren't taking this denial lightly."

"If you ask me, I think you should tone down the ego a bit, listen to what she has to say about changing some of our construction practices and get to know her on a more personal level. There will be other projects."

Of course, Zenobia was right, but he wasn't about to admit it.

***

Trenay searched her desk for the notes from her meeting with the mayor. She could have sworn Cristina had placed them in her inbox. But since Cristina hadn't come in yet, she had to root through several file folders and a stack of papers by the printer to find what she needed, still coming up empty-handed.

Unable to sleep, Trenay had decided to get up and start her workday a little earlier than normal. She hoped coming into the office early would give her time to get a head start on an upcoming presentation. But so far, the only thing she'd managed to do was spill coffee on her blouse, lock her keys in the car, and snag her pantyhose on the corner of her desk.

Frustrated that her morning was quickly turning into a disastrous day, Trenay sat down with her second cup of coffee and made an effort to begin the presentation without the notes. Unfortunately, she soon realized most of her presentation centered on the key points she and the mayor had discussed, all of which were in the notes she couldn't seem to find. As she shuffled through yet another stack of papers, she tried to keep her frustration level at a minimum. It wasn't working.

Still unable to find the notes after searching through her briefcase one more time she gave up and leaned back in her chair, willing herself to calm down and refocus. This was not her typical Monday morning and she refused to let a few mishaps shape the remainder of her day.

Most people dreaded Mondays. In contrast, Trenay looked forward to them. She had a different approach to the beginning of the workweek. She rationalized that no matter what happened the week before, good, bad, or disastrous, Mondays were a clean slate. After a weekend of rest, she looked forward to starting the new week fresh, focused, and determined. It didn't matter if she had taken work home over the weekend or not. She loved her job, even though it occasionally included Mondays like this one. Yet, while she did feel determined, she didn't feel very fresh or focused. She struggled to remember even the most basic details from her meeting with the mayor which had only taken place just days before.

Determined, she picked up a pen and notepad and attempted to jot down what she could remember from the meeting. Unfortunately, as hard as she tried to focus on work she had other things on her mind, and after spending five minutes staring at the blank sheet on her notepad, she stopped struggling. Her pen rested idly in her hand and eventually ended up beside her notepad. Reaching for her coffee, Trenay took one long sip, then another. As she paused to let the effect of the caffeine kick in, her thoughts slowly turned from presentations and discussions about building code violations and faded into memories of last Friday night.

Not one single event she had attended since taking on her new role had been as interesting. She had planned her evening very carefully; from a perfectly timed arrival to the moment she could make a well-timed departure. She knew with whom she needed to meet and greet and exactly how much time she had to spend talking to each person. From the code inspector to the chairman of the hospital's board of directors everything had gone according to plan, that is, until she ran into Marshall, literally. Spending the better part of the evening talking to him and dancing had not been something she had expected, particularly after their initial meeting earlier that afternoon where she found him to be abrasive and his tone condescending. The man was not used to being told no. Despite his good looks and little hints of a decent human being peeking through, once he left her office she had written him off as someone she hoped to not see again. Then at the benefit, she saw a completely different side to him, a softer and more charming side, revealing a little more of the decent human being he'd been hiding earlier in the day.

Trenay picked up the pen and put it down again. Leaning back in her chair, she smiled to herself. Marshall had been amused when she questioned whether or not he had brought a date to the benefit. She wasn't even sure why she had brought up the question in the first place. Why did she care? He probably wondered the same thing. Something else she couldn't quite explain; why she felt relieved when she found out Marshall's date was his assistant and not a date after all.

Blame it on the wine, the casual but interesting conversation, or even being especially aware of how handsome and sexy Marshall looked in his tux. Or maybe it was the way he gazed into her eyes when they danced. Could all of those things have been responsible for her flirtatious and out of character behavior?

She inadvertently touched her lips with her fingertips. And then there was *the kiss*.

Trenay put her head in her hands and sighed. *What's wrong with me? Why did I let a stranger kiss me? And why did I kiss him back?* She wanted to regret her actions and pretend what she had done was wrong, and a little more than the tiniest bit crazy, but owning up to that wouldn't have been entirely truthful.

No matter how she tried to spin or rationalize what happened, she simply couldn't deny that the kiss was *hot*. She couldn't think of any other way to describe it. Marshall Oliver knew how to kiss a woman and leave her satisfied but at the same time wondering what other tricks he had up his sleeve.

To make matters even more complicated, Marshall had held her in a way that told her he meant business, not too forcefully but close enough to dispel any misunderstanding. And the gentle way his lips covered hers, his tongue dipping into her mouth. *Whew!* If he had her this twisted over a kiss, what more could this man be capable of?

"Good morning, boss. Hangover?"

Startled, Trenay's head shot up. She noticed the amusement on Cristina's face and groaned. How long had she been watching her daydream? She pretended to be annoyed by her assistance's suggestion that she could be hungover, while at the same time hoping to hide the fact that her thoughts of Marshall were way more intoxicating than any drink she could consume. "Of course not," she replied with a hint of attitude.

Switching gears Cristina placed the newspaper on Trenay's desk. "I don't know if you had a chance to see the newspaper this morning, but there was a fire that destroyed the main building at Fostoria Industries."

"A what? Where?"

Cristina pointed out the story on the front page of the Metro section. "A fire. Early this morning at Fostoria. I caught the story on Action Eight news while I was getting ready. According to that sexy reporter Leon DiSilva, the building is pretty much destroyed, a total loss. Investigators suspect arson."

Fostoria Industries had been one of the early projects Trenay's office spearheaded when their company was undergoing a major remodeling project. At the request of the company's president, Trenay had made several recommendations that were projected to save the company on its long-term energy consumption and bills. She counted the project as one of her office's early successes, thanks to Fostoria's president's willingness to make the recommended changes suggested by her office.

"Why would anyone want to burn their building down or cause problems for Fostoria?"

"Disgruntled employee, insurance fraud, somebody who doesn't like Mondays. Who knows?"

Trenay placed the newspaper on a stack of magazines and newsletters on one side of her desk and pushed aside thoughts of Marshall until later, deciding it would be best to immerse herself in more productive activities such as work. Her time would be better spent focusing on something other than hot kisses and an even hotter man. She picked up her pen and prepared to get back to work. "What's on tap for this morning, Cristina?"

Trenay waited patiently while Cristina recited a list of the activities for the day. As her assistant, Trenay relied on her to keep her on track, which she did exceptionally well.

"All right, now that we have the work stuff out of the way, let's move on to more important matters. I want to hear what happened at the benefit."

Trenay looked up from her notepad and frowned at Cristina. "Of course you do. I'm glad you brought it up. We need to talk."

"About?"

"Don't pretend like you didn't get my message about the dress."

Cristina smiled. "Oh, do you mean the voice mail about the mix up with the outfits? Hmm…still not sure what went wrong with the delivery. I could have sworn I gave strict instructions to the boutique to have your items delivered to your house once your suit was ready. Maybe they weren't able to complete the alterations in time. By the way, I thought it was nice of them to offer to rush the alterations in the first place. Guess some wires got crossed somewhere."

"You think?" Trenay remarked sarcastically.

"Well anyway, it all worked out in the end with the substitute dress. Oh yeah, about the *harsh* message you left, I'm pretty sure it came from the uptight, conservative Trenay. I'd be willing to bet hot, sexy Trenay had a good time and looked like a flamethrower in the black dress. I'm sure *she* would rather burn the ugly, old pantsuit instead of being seen in public wearing it."

Trenay rolled her eyes.

Undaunted, Cristina continued. "Admit it. The black dress was a much better choice. No matter how much you pretend you're mad about having to wear it, I'll bet you turned a lot of heads."

Well, she had caught one person's attention in particular, although she had no intention of divulging to Cristina anything about Marshall or the kiss they'd shared at the end of the evening. "That's not the point and I don't know anything about hot, sexy Trenay. The Trenay who has a sense of modesty and good taste felt uncomfortable all evening in that dress, which *I* was forced to wear because, well, you know what the rest of my wardrobe looks like."

Cristina dismissed her friend's pathetic complaint. "You were hot and you know it. The only reason you might have felt uncomfortable is that you're so used to being bound and gagged in buttoned-up blouses and conservative suits. It's time you stopped dressing and acting like an old grandma. You're thirty-six, not one hundred and six. Live a little. Wear a slinky black dress once in a while. Drink too much wine. Show some cleavage. Flirt with a handsome stranger. Throw caution to the wind. Allow yourself to be reckless for a change. You give so much to this job. What do you give to yourself? Very little! Before you know it life will have passed you by and all you'll have to show for your hard work is a house full of cats and neatly sorted recyclables."

Try as she might, Trenay couldn't argue against anything Cristina said – except for having a house full of cats. She needed to get out more and enjoy life, maybe not to the extent Cristina wanted, but she could at least consider doing more than going from work to home and back again. She pretty much had the same routine day in and day out. Yes, she enjoyed her work and her life in general, but shouldn't there be more? She had to admit, she did miss having a social life. Nothing wild or crazy, just spending time with someone, sharing good conversation, a meal, or a movie. It wasn't really a commitment that she missed, just companionship. Perhaps it wouldn't hurt to throw just a little caution to the wind and give in to being reckless at least a little bit. Thinking back to last Friday night…had she already started down that path?

Did kissing a stranger qualify as being reckless? What about flirting with a handsome man? It's certainly not something Cristina or anyone else she knew could imagine her doing. Well, no matter what Cristina thought or how routine/mundane her life appeared to be, she didn't think it likely that she'd be skydiving or dancing on top of a bar any time soon. However, where Marshall Oliver was concerned, she didn't know what she might be capable of.

"Once again, Cristina, you've shown how good you are at stretching the truth. A house full of cats? Really? Where exactly did that come from? Two cats do not equal a house full."

With a wave of her hand, Cristina dismissed her boss's comments. To signal the end of the matter she placed a stack of messages on the desk and mumbled something in

Spanish under her breath. Before heading out of Trenay's office, she turned and advised, "Just think about what I've said. There's more truth there than you care to admit. Life is short, Trenay. Time to start living for something other than work."

CHAPTER FIVE

Trenay pulled her notes up on the computer for the seminar she would be participating in that afternoon. The mayor had been called away on another matter and at the last minute asked her to fill in for him. She didn't mind saying yes. Representing the mayor's office wasn't anything she couldn't handle, she'd done it before. Today she would be sharing some basic information about his initiative to work with small businesses. She had heard him talk about his plan so many times she could practically recite the information in her sleep.

After printing her notes she left a list of tasks she wanted Cristina to complete when she returned from lunch. Gathering her purse, laptop, and briefcase she checked her watch. Frowning she realized she wouldn't have time to stop to pick up anything for lunch. The herbal tea and muffin she'd for breakfast had completely worn off. Unfortunately, lunch would be well after two o'clock or later and depended on whether or not the seminar's participants asked a lot of questions.

Hurrying from the underground parking garage to the stairway leading to the Milan Hotel she entered the lobby and followed the signs for the elevators. Once she reached the twelfth floor, she quickly found the grand ballroom. Trenay checked her watch to make sure she was okay on time. She wanted to set up her slideshow presentation and place the brochures and other materials she'd brought from the mayor's office on the information table before the participants arrived. The seminar was scheduled to begin in twenty minutes and more than a handful of attendees had already arrived and found their seats. Once she managed to get all of her materials organized and her presentation cued up, Trenay introduced herself to the other panelists, and found her place on stage, with a few minutes to spare.

Before long, the ballroom filled to capacity. She had no idea what the turnout would be but was pleased that so many small companies wanted to work with the city to provide materials and services and who were also interested in finding out what other business opportunities the city offered.

During the question and answer period, Trenay sat attentively listening to the variety of questions directed toward the city's zoning officer as he explained new code changes. The city's safety inspector discussed his office's procedures and policies, encouraging everyone to visit their website to obtain more information. Trenay did her best to stay focused but she was hungry and her stomach began to growl. She pulled a mint from her jacket pocket and hoped the small piece of candy and a few sips of water would be enough to stave off her hunger for just a little while longer.

Unfortunately, the tiny mint did nothing but make her wish for real food. Her stomach growled again, this time louder. The panelists on either side of her gave her polite looks. She could only smile back and eat another mint as she counted down the minutes until she would be able to get lunch.

After the moderator made her final remarks, thanked the panelists, and directed the seminar's attendees toward the information tables, Trenay quickly gathered her laptop, notebook, and the few business cards she had collected and made a beeline for the nearest exit. Her next meeting wouldn't be until three-thirty that afternoon, which would allow plenty of time to get lunch, and not just a salad and some fruit; she needed a real meal.

"Very nice presentation."

Facing the bank of elevators and ready to jump on the first available car, Trenay had been so occupied thinking about what she would order for lunch, she hadn't paid attention to anyone else waiting for the elevator.

She half-turned, ready to exchange brief pleasantries, but stopped short when the giver of the compliment turned out to be none other than Marshall Oliver.

"I would have expected nothing less," he commented.

Had he been in the ballroom? There were so many people in attendance she would have been hard-pressed to single him out in the crowd. However, after casually checking him out, she reconsidered. Clean-shaven, closely trimmed hair, eyes that sparkled mischievously, and wearing a dark blue suit, crisp white shirt, and "power" tie, had she paid attention to the sea of attendees she certainly would have noticed him.

While Marshall wore a suit like many of the other male attendees, she had to admit, he could definitely make the case of the man making the suit, and not the other way around. What was it about him that made her pay such close attention? Mocha hued, well dressed, tall, and distinguished, his very presence practically demanded she pay attention.

"I called your office and your assistant told me you would be here."

"Are you stalking me?" she asked, her thoughts no longer on food but the fine, good smelling brother standing too close for comfort.

"Why would I need to do that?" he asked, more amused than offended. "It's only stalking if the intent is to do harm or to annoy the other party. That is not my intention."

What was his intention?

Trenay punched the lighted elevator button again, knowing her repeated button pressing wouldn't do much to hurry things up but it did provide a needed distraction. Annoyed with the slowness of the elevators she wondered why out of three elevator cars, none had reached her floor yet.

"You left the benefit so abruptly Friday night that I didn't have a chance to tell you I had a good time." Leaning in, he added, "Couldn't seem to get your sexy lips and that kiss out of my head for the rest of the night. What about you?"

Trenay looked around to see if anyone had overheard him. She turned to him and frowned. "I thought the intent was to not annoy the other party."

"Well, I might be reading you wrong, but I'd have to say you don't look annoyed. In fact, I would probably say you have this sexy-smart vibe going for you right now. I like it," he added for effect.

Really? He thinks I'm sexy? Sure, she had been called smart before and once someone had even told her she was cute, but no one had ever called her sexy. *Don't get caught up,* her inner voice warned.

"Okay, Marshall, I see you like to play games. Well, I don't. I'm not sure what kind of women you're used to dealing with, but I can pretty much guarantee I'm not like any of them."

"You make an excellent point and I couldn't agree more, Trenay," he said thoughtfully. "I can still call you Trenay, can't I? Miss Bradley seems a little formal since we shared a kiss and all. I'm glad we moved past all of that formal stuff on Friday."

Is he serious?

Trenay contemplated taking the stairs, but the thought of lugging her briefcase, purse, and laptop case down twelve flights of stairs in heels didn't seem to be the smartest option. She punched the elevator button again.

Stuck waiting beside Marshall with his entire ultra-male attitude Trenay was at a loss for how to handle the situation and him. He knew she was flustered and he probably enjoyed every minute of her discomfort. He also knew he looked good, she thought. And he knew *she* thought he looked good, too. Standing just outside of her personal space but close enough for her to reach out and touch him caused images of being held and kissed by him to quickly spring to mind.

Redirecting her attention to the man and matter at

hand, she turned to face Marshall, searching for something to say that would put him in his place and force that smug look off of his face. Unfortunately, she couldn't think of anything fitting so she decided to cut right to the chase. First, she looked around to make sure no one was listening.

"Okay, Marshall, let me clear something up for you. Under normal circumstances, I'm not so *casual* with men I don't know. I won't make any excuses, but Friday night, I probably had a little too much to drink. Too much wine, coupled with too little food, a long day at work, and rushing to get to the benefit, well, I'm sure you get the picture. That whole scenario has poor judgment written all over it." *I won't even mention how nice it was to be in the company of someone interesting, handsome, and sexy.* "I don't want you to get the idea something happened between us when it didn't. We were both caught up in the moment or had too much to drink or both. Just so I'm clear and there is no misunderstanding, what I'm trying to say is that kissing strange men in public is completely out of character for me." *Even if your kiss set off all kinds of bells and whistles.*

Marshall paused before speaking and seemed to think about what Trenay had just said. "Wow. You called me strange. No one has called me strange since the seventh grade. I didn't take it too personally then because it just so happened to be weird Jenny Hunter who made the comment. Well, I've been called worse, so I guess I'll just let that go, for now."

Trenay looked at Marshall in total amazement. "Out of everything I just said the only thing you heard was that I referred to you being strange?"

Just then Trenay heard a ding and the elevator door in front of her opened.

Thank God. Could this man be any more aggravating...or fine?

Trenay hoisted her laptop case on her shoulder and stepped onto the elevator. She didn't waste a second pushing the elevator button to close the door. Hopefully, Marshall had other things to do that would take him wherever she wasn't.

Regrettably, it didn't look as if he did. Marshall stepped in the elevator car right after her.

"You know, I'm not sure what I did to you to end up on your radar," she began. "Are you punishing me because my office denied your bid? Is that it? Wait. I know what it is. You're trying to annoy me so I'll grant you an appeal or overlook my office's policies and grant you the bid based on, I don't know, good looks and charm. Sorry. That's not going to happen; I passed ethics class with flying colors. I have no intention of overlooking my office's policies or granting your company an appeal just because you're pestering me."

"How about lunch then?"

"Excuse me?"

"Lunch. That doesn't violate any of your high ethical standards does it?"

Lunch? Like a date? Nooo...

"Uh, no, thank you. I'm not hungry."

"Now that, Trenay Bradley, is a big, fat lie. I heard your stomach rumbling so loud a few minutes ago I thought we were having a thunderstorm."

During her exchange with Marshall, she had briefly forgotten about her hunger until the rumblings started again. She didn't know he had heard them, too. Yes, she was hungry, starving in fact, but sharing a meal with this man was a little more than she'd bargained for or had the mental strength to endure that afternoon.

Trenay didn't immediately respond and Marshall took her silence as rejection. "What? I can't buy you lunch?"

Trenay watched the numbers on the elevator's panel descend. This had to be the slowest elevator in the world!

Finally reaching the lobby Trenay stepped off and turned to face Marshall, determined to stop the cat and mouse game he had initiated and which she had no interest in continuing. "No, Marshall, you cannot buy me lunch, dinner, drinks, gifts, or anything else for that matter. And just in case you're wondering, you cannot persuade me to change my mind about your bid, and you will not make me second-guess my office's decision. Whatever it is you're trying to accomplish, it's just not going to work. I am not Councilman Ryan. I don't take bribes, I won't grant favors, and I don't play politics."

Trenay repositioned her purse and laptop bag on her shoulder and turned to leave, however, before she had a chance to take one-step, she felt a gentle but firm hand on her arm.

"Okay, now I'm offended. My invitation has nothing to do with my company's bid. Despite your assumption that I greased Chester Ryan's palms, you're wrong. I've accepted the fact that my company needs to make some changes and I'm willing to take whatever *legitimate* steps are necessary so we can be more competitive, not only because you suggested it, but because it's a good business decision. Furthermore, my lunch invitation was prompted by mutual attraction, at least I thought it was mutual. This crazy vibe we have going on between us – I don't even know what to call it – is something I wanted to explore and thought you did as well. Apparently, I couldn't be more wrong. For the record, you're not the only one who has high ethical standards, *Ms. Bradley*."

Marshall released her, strode across the lobby and out through the enormous, ornately adorned doors, shoulders squared, head held high. Trenay, resisting the urge to call after him and apologize, simply watched as he walked away. Without a doubt, she had struck a nerve.

CHAPTER SIX

The door to Marshall's office was slammed closed with such force the connecting walls shook. Gritting his teeth, it took every ounce of resolve to keep from putting his fist through the nearest wall. Pacing back and forth, he counted to ten, then twenty, forcing his anger down a few notches. Thankfully, Zenobia was out running an errand. He needed to be left alone as he was in no mood to explain what had just happened.

Trenay's accusation – he still couldn't believe it. She thought he was trying to buy her off? *With a twenty-dollar lunch? Really!* He only wanted to show her that there were no hard feelings. He knew he hadn't been on his best behavior when they first met and he had also taken a few liberties with her at the benefit. Lunch was meant to be a peace offering, an opportunity to show that despite his earlier condescending and somewhat demanding behavior and the subsequent unsolicited kiss, that not so deep down, he was a nice guy.

Okay, there might have been a little more to it than that. They shared an attraction. Obviously, *she* didn't seem interested, but he couldn't deny it. All he knew at this point was he felt something with Trenay and he wanted to explore it further. *That's all*, he thought, glumly. No ulterior motives or favors were being sought, just plain old, boy meets girl attraction. Period.

Remembering how much he had enjoyed dancing with her at the hospital's benefit Marshall's anger subsided a bit, allowing the good feelings from that night to resurface. After a somewhat shaky beginning, he had thoroughly enjoyed spending time with her throughout the evening. He had especially enjoyed it when they'd danced together. In their small, confined space Trenay had moved her body elegantly to the beat, hips swaying and flashing her long brown legs. He had taken her hand to lead and she followed, never missing a beat. He wished they could have slowed danced. It would have been exquisite. He smiled when he thought about the correlation between dancing and making love; and they had danced beautifully together, at least to the up-tempo songs.

Trenay may have blamed her response to his kiss and enjoying his company on too much wine, but Marshall knew she had felt something other than inebriation. She could have easily left him to mingle with the other guests or she could have lied and said she was with a date, but she didn't do either of those things. They spent time together talking and laughing, they danced…they kissed. For him, he could easily sum up their fledgling feelings in two words - *raw attraction*. She didn't want to admit that she felt it too.

Marshall had never had to fight this hard for someone's time and attention. Maybe when it came to Trenay Bradley it would be best to follow her cue. She apparently had dismissed the idea of anything happening between them. Why should he try to pursue something she didn't seem to give very much thought to or appear to care about taking further?

Marshall stared out of his office window, not looking at anything in particular. No longer angry, he resigned himself to cut his losses, which thankfully didn't amount to much. From this point on and as far as he was concerned, Trenay Bradley would be considered off-limits. From his experience, he knew she would likely be an all or nothing kind of woman; she would demand his all - and he would freely give it - and she would either return it in kind or she would take all the love he had to give and return nothing, leaving him brokenhearted and alone. Either way, he didn't need or want that type of drama now or ever again.

Thanks to his ex-wife Tiffany, he had learned all about the all or nothing kind of woman. He gave her his all and she freely took everything he had to give and then some, but gave nothing in return…nothing except heartache.

Loving Tiffany was one lesson he had learned the hard way. From the moment he met her he knew he had to have her. All of his friends had warned him that she was selfish and a user, but he couldn't and wouldn't hear it. As far as he was concerned, his friends were all just being haters. He had found a woman who had class, style, and was so hot she could melt butter. He smiled bitterly at the memory. Yeah, when his blinders finally came off he realized too late that Tiffany hadn't been any of those wonderful things he thought, but every bit of the picture his friends had painted, and then some.

Marshall had learned a lesson that would eventually toughen his heart: Some women simply don't know the meaning of love. They are only out for what they can get and then they move on. Those women are like locust;

consuming and leaving behind destruction and chaos in their wake.

Sadly, his marriage to Tiffany had left him skeptical and doubtful about love. Once the dust had settled after his divorce and after handing over half of everything he had to Tiffany, he decided that maybe he just wasn't cut out for the whole wife and kid's lifestyle, like his brother.

For a long time after his divorce, he had been able to keep his emotions in check, reminding himself about his failed marriage when it seemed as if his current companion was getting too close for comfort. Definitely not the ideal way to live but it kept him out of trouble and from getting hurt again. Besides, when he felt lonely he could always find someone willing to share his bed, no strings attached. For all intents and purposes, he had managed just fine. He didn't need love, commitment, or to be tied down. At least that's what his head believed even if his heart did not.

⁂

Trenay was startled when Cristina dropped a newspaper on her desk.

"Why are you so jumpy? Didn't you hear me come in?"

"I'm sorry. I'm a little distracted today."

Looking over at Trenay's monitor, Cristina replied, "I'll say. Didn't know you were in the market for male enhancement supplements."

Trenay looked up at her computer screen and saw the pop-up ad offering products and supplements to enlarge body parts she didn't even have. "Call tech services and let them know the spam filter isn't working again."

"By the way, it was arson," Cristina announced and pointed to the newspaper she'd just placed on Trenay's desk.

Picking it up, she scanned the story. "How did you get a copy of this already?"

Cristina winked. "I have a very dear *friend* who works at the paper."

"I can't believe someone would intentionally set fire to Fostoria. The company does so much good in the community. Who would want to destroy all of their hard work?" she asked, more to herself than to Cristina.

Suddenly, Trenay realized the fire at Fostoria was the third incident that involved a company linked to her office. First, there was the burglary and vandalism incident at the construction site for the new animal shelter. Trenay had worked with the private animal rescue group in building a facility that was not only cost-effective but eco-friendly and partially self-sustaining.

Next, was the chemical spill at a local dry cleaner. Gallons and gallons of toxic chemicals had spilled into a nearby stream, killing many fish and birds in the area. The owners of the dry cleaner had been fined by the Environmental Protection Agency for failure to properly dispose of its chemicals. Since she had personally worked with the construction company's project manager in supervising the design and remodeling of the building where the cleaners was located she felt a particular obligation to follow the investigation. But even after reading the investigative report, it all seemed very suspect to Trenay. Although the EPA issued the owners a citation,

Trenay still had a hard time understanding how the spill could have happened in the first place.

Now, the fire at Fostoria. She didn't know if she was being paranoid or if something else was going on. She wondered if anyone else had made the same connection whether on purpose or unintentionally.

Folding the paper neatly she placed it in her lap drawer. Paranoid or not, she felt a nagging urge to pay closer attention to everything going on around her, and more importantly, to those whom she called "friend".

CHAPTER SEVEN

It had been a long week and Trenay only had three things on her mind to bring it to a proper ending: a hot bath, a pizza from Antonucci's with everything on it except onions, and a work-free weekend. For the first time in a long time, she had decided against bringing homework from the office. Cristina would be so proud, she thought.

After picking up her pizza and chitchatting with the shop's owner for a few minutes she began the drive home. After making all the necessary stops and turns, Trenay moved on autopilot. The work issues of the week started to fade into her subconscious as other thoughts rose to the surface, the most prevalent one involved Marshall Oliver.

It had been several days since she had last seen or heard from him. While she tried to convince herself that not hearing from him was a good thing, she couldn't completely get him out of her head. At one point she had thought about sending him an email to apologize for accusing him of dishonest behavior, but she thought better of it. She figured after he got over being angry, he probably never gave her or their last conversation another thought.

Let sleeping dogs lie.

Balancing a bag of groceries, her purse, the pizza, and her dry cleaning, Trenay successfully made her way out of the garage and into the kitchen without dropping a thing.

Plunking everything on the kitchen table she thought it odd her two cats, Felix and Oscar, weren't at the door to greet her. Typically one or both of them would meet her at the door mewing and circling her legs, clamoring for attention, often causing her to stumble as she walked through her kitchen.

"Oscar. Felix," she called thinking they must be napping upstairs on her bed and hadn't heard the garage door open. She took out the toothpaste and mascara she bought from the drugstore and a few other things that needed to go in the upstairs bathroom and started up the stairs to her bedroom to change clothes and put away her dry cleaning when she noticed something odd. The door to her office was closed. She always kept that door open.

She tried to remember the last time she was in there and wondered if maybe she could have accidentally closed it. But no matter how many different scenarios she came up within her head, none of them included her closing that door.

Still holding the dry cleaning and other items, she placed them on the stairs, being careful not to make any noise. Backing down slowly off the step she looked around to see if anything was out of place and wondered if she should call the police or investigate for herself. Debating the wisdom of calling the police without proof something was actually wrong, she decided to investigate for herself. With trembling hands and unsure steps, she cautiously approached the office door, but not without the feeling that something was very wrong. Her heart hammered against her chest and she silently prayed that nothing crazy was about to happen once the door was opened. Holding her breath she carefully placed one hand flat against the door and made a fist with the other. Gently, pushing the door open wide enough she peered inside. A small amount of light coming from a window on the other side of the room allowed her to see inside without turning on the overhead light. She pushed the door a little harder to open it fully. It hit the wall with a dull thud causing her to jump.

Taking a second to regain her composure she quickly surveyed the room. Books, papers, furniture, artwork, all seemed to be in order. All of her papers were stacked neatly on the desk. A small pile of books was on the floor beside the desk, just as she'd left them. None of the desk drawers were open. Her chair still had her old black sweater resting across the arm. Everything seemed to be in place.

Trenay stepped fully inside her office. Crossing the room she checked the windows to make sure they were still locked, but stopped suddenly and turned when she heard movement. Something was behind the loveseat. Startled, she backed into the side of the desk, knocking a stack of papers to the floor.

"Oscar," she said with a sigh of relief when she saw her black and white tabby run from behind the loveseat and out of the room. Felix soon followed.

Why were they hiding behind the loveseat?

Clutching her hand to her chest she took several deep breaths as her heart raced and pounded so loudly it was all she could hear. Willing herself to calm down, she made sure the windows were locked and closed the blinds before going upstairs. Gathering the things she had left on the steps Trenay tried to dismiss the uneasy feeling that now replaced the fear she'd felt before. Looking back over her shoulder and in through the open door of her office, she couldn't shake the feeling that while it appeared nothing was wrong, someone had been in there and in her house. Although nothing appeared to be missing and she couldn't say for certain what was different, something just wasn't right. Oscar and Felix were not afraid of anything, but something or someone had spooked her cats.

***

Bricks. *Check*. Shovel. *Check*. Paving sand. *Check*. Spacers. *Hardware store*. Wheelbarrow. *Time to get a new one.*

Before beginning any job Marshall liked to have everything laid out and within easy reach. He detested getting halfway through a job only to have to run back to the store because he forgot something. Today he needed to go to the hardware store to get a few more things but for the most part, his project was a go.

Marshall had decided today would be the day to fix the stone walkway that led to the back of his house, something he'd put off longer than he should have. For the most part, he had picked a good day – sunny, mild temperatures, and not too windy. Everything seemed good, except for his mood. He hoped a little manual labor would be the therapeutic key to a better frame of mind.

It had been more than a week since he had seen or heard from Trenay. He told himself over and over again that he could and should forget her, except he couldn't. He still wanted to be angry with her for accusing him of being shady, but it wasn't that easy. Once he thought about what she'd said, he couldn't completely blame her for the jaded opinion she formed about him.

Marshall had been in the construction business since before he could legally drive a car and certainly long enough to know that some contractors, along with unscrupulous public servants, didn't always keep their business dealings on the up and up.

In trusting Chester Ryan, Marshall may have made a misstep that he hoped hadn't tarnished his business' reputation. By no means could Councilman Ryan be considered a saint nor was he the scum of the earth, but he wasn't exactly the type of person with whom Marshall typically conducted business. However, Marshall had seen an opportunity to gain a lucrative contract and Ryan was the person he had to go through to get it. Despite the circumstances and no matter what anyone thought, not once had Marshall or anyone from his office done anything that could be considered underhanded or unethical.

The fact that Trenay thought otherwise didn't sit well with him. He wanted to explain his side to her, to let her know that he knew better than to shortcut or scheme his way into a favorable bid. In all honesty, his company and everyone who worked for him was better than that.

Then again, why should he be the one doing the explaining? He had done nothing wrong. Maybe she should explain why she had been so quick to assume that he was involved in questionable dealings with Chester Ryan.

Why am I spending so much time thinking about this woman? Why do I even care what she thinks?

Backing his truck out of the driveway Marshall forced himself to focus on making plans for his next home project once the walkway was completed. He didn't quite know what it would be, but as long as it required manual labor and lots of it, he would do it. At the moment his plan for the weekend was to keep his hands and his mind as busy as possible. Hopefully keeping busy digging up and replacing the stones along his walkway would prove to be a much needed and welcome distraction. Unfortunately, he knew he would need another project to move on to quickly or his mood would continue to grow worse. A good place to spark ideas just happened to be his first stop of the day, the hardware store. With his current mood and his plan to remain distracted by projects at home, he just might manage to have everything on his to-do list crossed off by the end of summer.

Walking up and down the aisles of his favorite hardware store, Marshall couldn't help smiling to himself as he watched the "weekend warriors" all around him with their shopping carts filled with tools, plants, paint, and construction materials. It amused him that the same guys who sat behind a desk all week sought to regain their sense of manhood by swinging a hammer and dusting off their seldom-used power tools on the weekends. Often the result would be the need to call in a professional to fix the job that the overly ambitious but under skilled weekend craftsman had botched. Over the past several years Marshall had noticed many weekend warriors were now women. In his opinion, there was something sexy about a woman who knew her way around power tools.

Like the honey standing in the home security section. Wearing a baseball cap, tight-fitting t-shirt, and jeans that seemed to hug every curve, for a brief second Marshall forgot all about why he had come into the store in the first place. He might have just found his next distraction.

Marshall stepped into the aisle, ready to offer his assistance until something familiar about the woman caught his attention.

"Trenay," he said under his breath but louder than he intended.

Trenay turned toward the sound of her name.

"Marshall? What are you doing here?" she asked, looking as surprised to see him as he was to see her.

"The same as you," he replied. "I didn't mean to sneak up on you. I was walking by this aisle and I thought I saw someone I knew and…I mean you looked familiar…I didn't recognize you with the cap on." He knew he sounded scattered but he didn't know what else to say.

Looking past Marshall, Trenay sighed. "I had the customer service desk page someone ten minutes ago and no one has shown up yet. What do I have to do to get some help in this place?"

The store was pretty busy, especially for a Saturday. There wasn't a clerk in sight and the chances of one showing up any time soon seemed slim to none.

"You might be waiting for a while."

Trenay seemed agitated but he wasn't sure if it was due to the lack of available help or him. He wondered if he should walk away and go about his business or offer to help. It didn't take long for him to decide on the latter.

"What do you need?" he asked, deciding to temporarily put off getting the materials for his walkway, which ironically was supposed to be the project to keep him busy so he wouldn't think about Trenay.

She held up two boxes. "Which one is better?" she asked, giving up trying to decide for herself after studying the vague descriptions printed on the boxes for security latches.

"I don't know. Are you trying to keep something out or in?"

Before she could answer, Marshall took one of the boxes and placed it back on the shelf. "That one is flimsy and cheap. You might as well put duct tape on the window. My little nephew could dismantle that thing with his toy screwdriver."

"What about this one? Do you think it's any good?" she asked, wondering if what she really needed was a professional security system and not something she could buy off a store shelf and install herself.

Marshall noticed a strange expression on Trenay's face, different from the look of agitation she had earlier and she seemed nervous. Choosing window locks should not be this serious. He wondered again if her reaction to him had anything to do with the disagreement they previously had. The last time they'd spoken things had gotten a little heated. Then again, maybe her behavior had nothing to do with him. After all, she probably hadn't given him or their last conversation another thought. Since he wasn't sure, he decided to play it cool.

"I guess it all depends on what you're trying to keep in or out. Which is it?" he asked again.

Trenay wondered if she should tell him exactly what she needed. For a minute, she hesitated, not because she didn't know him well enough to confide in him or because she didn't want to appear neurotic, she simply felt a little silly. What details could she share with him that wouldn't sound crazy or paranoid? She needed to improve her home security, which at the moment consisted of simple locks on her windows and the standard locks on her external doors, apparently, not much of a deterrent to crime or even keeping someone from snooping around her home. While she didn't have any real evidence of anyone being inside her house, her gut feeling told her someone had been. At the very least, she wanted to protect herself as best as she could to prevent any more intrusions.

"Well? Are you going to give me any more information so I can help you pick the right device or not?"

"I just want to make sure my house is secure," she blurted out. "You know, windows are reportedly one of the best ways to enter a home. For break-ins, I mean, not just getting in. I saw something on the evening news about it. It's a good idea to be proactive, don't you think?"

Marshall noticed the look again. For some strange reason, Trenay seemed nervous and he was pretty sure she wasn't being completely honest with him.

"Okay, let's go over to the next aisle. I think we'll find what you need over there."

Trenay followed Marshall until they stopped in front of shelves filled with contraptions and gadgets that were as foreign to her as surgical tools. She shook her head. "I have no idea what all of this stuff is."

Marshall turned to her and smiled reassuringly. "That's why I'm here. I do. First, you'll need this." He placed several metal gadgets in her basket. "Is your house one or two stories?"

"Two."

"When was your house built?"

"Why?"

"Standard window sizes have varied over the years."

"Late nineties."

"How many windows are on the first floor?"

Closing her eyes Trenay mentally went through each room on the first floor of her house counting windows. "Seven. No, eight. I forgot the little window over the kitchen sink."

Marshall placed several more items into her basket. "Do you have any tools at home?"

She frowned. "Of course I have tools. What do you think? I'm the kind of woman who doesn't know better than to use a butter knife for a screwdriver and the heel of her shoe for a hammer?"

Marshall raised his hands in defense. "Sorry! I didn't mean to offend you. I figured you had tools but I wanted to be sure before you left the store."

Trenay lowered her eyes and took a deep breath. "No, I'm sorry. I overreacted. I didn't sleep well last night and I guess I'm a little on edge." Truthfully, she hadn't slept at all, not until the first rays of daylight crept into her room, and then she had only fallen asleep for about an hour or so.

Again, the look. This time Marshall reached out and touched Trenay's arm. "Okay. I know we don't know each other that well but I can tell something's wrong. Do you want to tell me what it is?"

She raised her eyes. The look of concern she saw on his face gave her enough courage to let her guard down, just a little. Maybe he wouldn't think she was crazy. She hoped.

"When I came home last night I noticed something didn't seem right."

"What do you mean?"

"Well, I always came in from the garage and put my purse and groceries down in the kitchen. Usually, my cats are waiting for me at the door when I come in. Most of the time if I'm not careful I practically trip over them, except this time I didn't see or hear them. I didn't think much about it at first so I started to go upstairs to my bedroom to change clothes and that's when I noticed it. I went past my office and I noticed the door had been closed. Not all the way, but almost."

She studied Marshall's reaction before continuing. He was still listening and didn't seem to have dismissed her as being irrational so she went on. "I never close my office door. Ever. At first, I listened outside of the door to see if I could hear any sounds coming from inside, and when I didn't I somehow mustered up enough nerve to go inside and look around." Trenay paused before continuing. "I know you're probably going to think this doesn't make any sense at all but I looked around and nothing seemed out of place, but I noticed some of my things weren't exactly how I left them. It seemed like a few things had been moved and then put back, but not exactly. They were kind of slightly off. While I was standing there trying not to freak out I heard something. I think I nearly passed out not knowing what was moving and making noise until I saw a flash of fur run by. My cats were hiding behind the loveseat in my office. They never hide unless they're afraid and even then it's because of a storm or fireworks during the fourth of July that scares them. We didn't have any thunderstorms yesterday and it's definitely not the fourth. Something else had to have spooked them."

"Wait, you're saying someone broke into your house?" Marshall asked in a voice that sounded slightly strained. Now he knew why she had been acting so strangely. She must be terrified.

Trenay hesitated and took a deep breath. "Well, I don't have any real proof but I'm pretty sure someone was in my house."

"What did the police say? Was anything stolen? Did they take a report? Dust for fingerprints?"

Trenay shook her head. Confiding in Marshall made her feel a little better, but listening to him now question her about actions she should have taken when she first suspected a break-in made her feel even more foolish. She should have called the police. They could have checked everything out and would have been able to say for sure if someone had broken in. Or they could have thought she was nuts and dismissed her suspicions as unfounded, making her feel like an idiot. She sighed. This whole ordeal was turning her into an emotional wreck. One-minute anger dominated her emotions, the next fear. Right now, she just wanted this whole thing to be over and she wanted to feel safe in her home again. "I didn't call the police," she answered in a small voice.

"What? Trenay, why didn't you call the police?" he asked as calmly as he could.

The look on her face spoke volumes. Fear, uncertainty, apprehension, and doubt and a look in her eyes that let Marshall know that no matter how tough and in control she normally was, right now she was afraid. A sudden overwhelming need to pull Trenay into his arms and comfort her surprised Marshall, while at the same time quick, intense anger made him want to find the person who had invaded her privacy and stolen her sense of security. God only knew what he would do if he ever found them.

"I told you. I don't have any real proof."

"You still should have called them. They are trained professionals who could have checked things out for you. At the very least they might have checked for fingerprints or found out if your doors or windows had been jimmied."

"Maybe, but like I said, *thinking* someone had been in my house was only a feeling, not a fact. For one, none of the windows or doors were unlocked. Secondly, I checked the files I had on the desk in my office and they were all there. My jewelry, TVs, and all of my electronic gadgets are still there, but something just didn't feel right. It's like I said, it seemed like some of the things in my office had been moved. They were all there, but not where I remembered putting them."

Marshall reached out and touched her arm. He wanted so badly to hold her and let her know everything would be all right and assure her that she would be safe. But realistically, he couldn't make that promise. He hardly knew Trenay and he certainly didn't know who or what was behind the situation at her house. He had no idea what she had going on in her life or who she was involved with. Even if he did have more information he couldn't stand guard at her house or follow her around to make sure she was okay. Charging headfirst into a situation that he knew very little about or which might be too hot to handle was something he needed to avoid at all costs.

"To answer your question, I didn't call the police because I didn't want to look like an idiot. Do you know how silly I would have sounded and felt saying that I think I've been robbed but nothing was taken, all the windows and doors were secure, but my cats were hiding and I think my files and books were in a different place than where I remembered leaving them?"

Marshall paused for a moment. He understood, but still thought she should have called the police and had them make an assessment. Unfortunately, there was nothing he could do about that now. Instead, he concentrated on how to help Trenay while at the same time not overstepping any boundaries. Then he had an idea. "Come on," he said and took the basket of items from Trenay and they walked toward the checkout counter in silence. "Do you need anything else?" he asked before stepping in line.

She shook her head.

Trenay waited patiently as the cashier rang up and bagged her purchases. Just talking to Marshall about how she felt did make her feel better. Now all she had to do was figure out how to keep another *ghost* intruder away using the gadgets she had just purchased.

The entire time Marshall had been examining items and placing things in her cart Trenay had done little more than barely glance at one or two of the devices. Now looking more closely at one of the packages she pulled out of the bag, she noticed it only included basic installation instructions. She wondered if all of the devices had the same cryptic and vague directions. It didn't matter. She would have to figure out how to install the devices or spend another sleepless night feeling afraid and insecure. Besides, how difficult could it be? Whatever she couldn't figure out she was sure someone else had already mastered and posted a video of the process online. It would probably take her the entire weekend to figure everything out and get it all installed, but in the end, it would be something she prayed would help her to feel safe again.

"Where did you park?"

Marshall had been kind enough to help her and even walk her out to the parking lot, but she had taken up enough of his time. "Oh, I don't need any more help. I can carry this stuff to the car. You've done more than enough already. I'll be fine. Really. I guess my cats weren't the only ones spooked." She tried to sound lighthearted but she didn't actually pull it off, although still a little on edge, she did feel better.

"Where did you park, Trenay?" Marshall asked again, enunciating each word.

"Why?" *What was he up to?*

"I'm going to help you load all of this stuff into your car and I'm coming over to install the locks and reinforcement material on your windows."

Is he asking me or telling me? "Uh, you don't have to do that. I can call the handyman service I use and see if I can get someone to do the work, I mean if I can't figure it out myself."

Marshall tried very hard not to lose patience with Trenay but she didn't make it easy. "Trenay, it's a Saturday. The likelihood of you getting someone to come out today is pretty slim. Besides, if you don't install the devices correctly it's the same as not having them at all. I can have this work done in no time flat. And," he added with a wink, "My rates are pretty reasonable." Although he also tried to keep the mood light, he wouldn't rest until he knew she would be safe in her home.

Marshall was offering to do something for her that she wasn't sure she could do herself. He seemed to know exactly what she needed whereas she would have still been standing in the same aisle trying to figure it all out if it hadn't been for his help. Maybe he was right, she reasoned. Call it a weak moment, lack of sleep, or plain fear, she simply did not have the will to fight Marshall on this.

With that, Trenay nodded and led Marshall to her car. Somehow she didn't think he would take no for an answer anyway.

CHAPTER EIGHT

Trenay occasionally checked her rearview mirror to make sure Marshall still followed behind her. She sort of wanted to be annoyed with him for being so insistent, almost bullying, about helping her out, but deep down she knew that she didn't want to spend another sleepless night worrying about her safety.

Marshall's huge truck made her little compact look like a toy car in comparison. *Of course, he would drive a huge gas-guzzler*, she thought as she tried to think of reasons to not like him so much, but he made it pretty hard. From the first day he came into her office to the night they kissed at the benefit and even now, Trenay had a feeling that Marshall Oliver wasn't the type of man she could easily forget, even when she tried. She had tried to tell herself that he wasn't her type, as if tall, dark, broad-shouldered, and insanely masculine didn't appeal to any woman with a pulse.

However, Marshall didn't just have the kind of good looks that made a woman's imagination run wild, he seemed to possess a kind of toughness that made her wonder just how close he would allow her to get – if she wanted to get close.

Yes, admittedly he teased her and awakened a certain degree of sexual tension that she instinctively knew he could satisfy, but was Marshall the kind of man who wanted more than a sexual conquest? What exactly would a man like him want? What did *she* want?

"Irrelevant," Trenay said aloud in the privacy of her car. The kind of man she wanted in her life would not have a quick temper like Marshall. He would be gentle, respectful of her feelings, and above all, cool, calm, and collected. Not only that, but he would also share the same values and ideals as hers. And he definitely wouldn't be driving a huge, gas-guzzling road hog.

Of course, she drives a hybrid, he thought wryly. *Probably prefers riding a bike to driving, too.*

Marshall followed Trenay the short distance to her house and tried to focus on the only reason he was going home with her - installing window security devices.

He had already convinced himself that he was doing the right thing, for the right reason. She needed help, except she didn't want to admit it.

Helping Trenay is *the right thing to do, regardless of how difficult she makes it to even offer.*

If his father hadn't raised him to be such a gentleman, he would have left her standing in the parking lot literally holding the bag. Well, maybe not exactly. He would have liked to, but he knew he couldn't have left her to fend for herself, considering he had very little tolerance for stubborn women. And Trenay Bradley personified stubborn.

She had practically thrown his offer to help right back in his face. Clearly, she had no idea what to do with all the hardware and other devices he'd selected. Why couldn't she have admitted she needed help?

He should have left well enough alone. Let her figure things out for herself. She wanted to be tough and independent, then let her!

Marshall shifted uncomfortably in his seat. Who was he kidding? He could no more leave Trenay to fend for herself than he could anyone who he knew truly needed his help, although Trenay wasn't just anyone.

Who would want to frighten or hurt her, he wondered. *An ex-boyfriend, ex-husband, or worse, a current one?* She never said if she was married or attached. She didn't wear a ring, but that didn't mean she wasn't married. Truthfully, he had assumed she was single. Zenobia seemed to know a lot about her. She would have made it her business to know if she was married or not. It didn't matter. If he had anything to do with it, no one would get to her, and no one would dare try to hurt her.

Marshall continued to follow Trenay as they turned off the busy street into a more quiet residential area. The next street Trenay turned down featured modest homes lined up neatly on both sides. Groomed lawns, trimmed hedges, and everything looked neat and tidy.

As Marshall pulled into the driveway of a small but quaint two-story brick house with late spring and early summer flowers blooming in the front yard and neatly trimmed hedges lining the driveway, he smiled. Yes, this is the type of house he imagined she would live in. He could picture her puttering around in her yard, tending to her flowers, trees, and shrubs, making sure to compost grass clippings and dead leaves. While her house looked pretty much like the rest of the houses on the street, Marshall felt it was Trenay who made this house a home. Now someone was threatening her sense of home. Still unsure of the situation and mindful that there was still a lot he did not know about Trenay, once more he cautioned himself against getting in too deep. For now, his only directive would be to help her and to leave well enough alone.

Marshall helped Trenay unload the bags from her car. She led him through the garage where neatly stacked bundles of newspapers and bins containing bottles, cans, and plastic jugs lined one wall.

Of course, she recycles.

Walking behind her into the kitchen Marshall practically rear-ended Trenay when she came to an abrupt stop.

Posted like guards at the door, Trenay stepped around her two cats to avoid stumbling or stepping on them. She leaned down to pet them as they each vied for her attention, completely ignoring him.

"Marshall, I'd like for you to meet Felix and Oscar."

"Which one is which?" he asked as he stepped around her and the cats, placing the bags on the counter.

"Felix is the handsome guy with the grey coat and Oscar is the equally handsome fella with the black and white coat."

Marshall, not much of a cat person, felt ignored as the two cats purred and soaked up all the attention Trenay showered on them. They had barely acknowledged his presence, preferring Trenay's attention instead.

"Give me a few minutes to put some food in their

bowls and I'll show you where everything is. By the way, if you need tools mine are in the garage. You'll find them on the work table near the green storage bins."

Marshall went to where Trenay told him to go in the garage but he didn't see the tools. He looked around, above, and behind the green storage bins but came up empty-handed. After a few minutes, Trenay joined him.

"I don't see them."

"Right here, silly," she said pulling a case from the small table near the green bins.

Marshall stared at the case then looked at Trenay. "Okay, not quite what I expected. The case is pink."

"I know! The tools are pink, too," she exclaimed, opening the case to reveal a pastel-colored hammer, a set of screwdrivers, and a socket set. "Don't you just love them? My dad got them for me when I bought this house. They are specially designed for women." She picked up the hammer. "See."

Marshall looked at the hammer and tried to maintain his composure. He didn't know whether to laugh or be annoyed. Not only were the tools pink, but the grips also looked too small for his large hands. He would end up either breaking the tools or his hand in the process of trying to use them. Fortunately, he'd left his toolbox in his truck, grateful he wouldn't have to fight with the pink tools.

Trenay let Marshall back inside and gave him a quick tour of the house. After shooing her curious cats away she left him alone to begin installing the reinforcement materials and locking devices. By most accounts fitting the devices on the windows did not require that he delve too deeply into his cache of handyman skills. Moving from room to room Marshall made light work of his task.

Once he finished the last window he called Trenay.

"Wow," she said, inspecting one of the windows. "I can't believe you're finished already. You know, I could have helped."

"Don't take it personally. I work best alone." Moving aside, he said, "Now, let me show you how these work."

Trenay moved in closer so she could see Marshall demonstrate how to properly disable the new window devices. Standing close to him she listened intently as he explained how to set the lock when the window was completely closed and how to adjust it when she wanted to leave it partially opened. She liked that she could open her windows to let air in but keep them locked in a partially opened position at the same time. She tried to listen as he told her about other features she could use, but she couldn't help noticing how good he smelled.

"There's something else," he said.

"What?" she asked, forcing herself to focus on the important matter at hand.

No longer focusing on the windows or demonstrating how the devices worked, he said, "Do me a favor. The next time you *think* someone has been in your house or if you feel uneasy about anything and you don't want to call the police, call me. You don't have to be Super Woman, Trenay. I won't mind occasionally investigating things that go bump in the night. It might also be a good idea to have a security system installed, or at the very least get a big mean dog. Your cats are awfully cute but I don't think they offer much in the way of protection."

Trenay smiled. In just a matter of a few hours and with very little effort Marshall had managed to restore her sense of security and had put her at ease. *Score one for the big guy.*

"I'll consider your offer," she said, "that is if you'll do one more thing for me."

Marshall stopped repacking his tools. He looked uncomfortable. Uh oh. She wanted a favor. *What if she asked him to do something, which would violate his promise to leave well enough alone?* He thought about it for a second. Did it matter? Whatever she needed, he didn't think he would be able to say no to her.

"Stay for lunch."

Lunch? That's all? Phew! Lunch was safe, right?

At least she hadn't asked him to do something crazy like diffuse a situation with an ex or current boyfriend or husband. He could stay for lunch. That should be harmless enough considering he had pretty much abandoned his plans for finishing the walkway anyway. That project would just have to wait. By any stretch of the imagination spending a little more time with Trenay was way more appealing than replacing paver stones.

A harmless lunch, with a friend, he thought, trying way too hard to convince himself that Trenay's invitation and his eagerness to accept was nothing more, nothing less. "Where can I get cleaned up?"

After putting the rest of his tools away and gathering the extra materials Marshall joined Trenay in the kitchen.

"My carpentry skills far outweigh my cooking skills, but is there anything I can do to help?"

"Nope. You've done more than I expected. Sit back and relax. Like you, I do my best work alone, in the kitchen, that is."

Marshall watched Trenay move about the kitchen and listened while she told him about her neighborhood and the plans to start a neighborhood watch program. She seemed more at ease now than when he first ran into her at the hardware store. That made him feel better.

"You mentioned your father gave you tools when you moved into your house. Do your parents live nearby?"

"No." She placed a glass of iced tea in front of Marshall. "My parents live in Washington. The state. Redmond to be exact."

"Beautiful part of the country."

Trenay began chopping vegetables, wondering momentarily if Marshall would prefer something more substantial. "Salad?"

Marshall nodded. "That's fine."

She decided to add roast beef sandwiches and potato chips to go with their salad. Even though he didn't say otherwise, she knew he would need more than leafy greens.

"Yes, Redmond is beautiful, but there's not enough sunshine for me in that part of the country. It's a nice place to visit, but I don't think I could live there."

"So," Marshall began cautiously, hoping he wouldn't upset Trenay with his next question but hoping to answer a few unasked questions, "if your parents live over two thousand miles away, and you're not married or in a meaningful relationship, who takes care of you?"

Trenay plated their food and joined Marshall at her small kitchen table. After sitting down she hesitated. Instead of eating, she looked down pensively at her plate. The silence was a little awkward as she sat thinking of the best and most honest way to answer Marshall's question. "Before last night if you, or anyone else for that matter, had asked me that question I would have been offended and said, without hesitation, that I'm more than capable of taking care of myself."

"And now?"

Trenay reached to grab her fork but hesitated again. She looked up at Marshall and replied honestly. "Now, I would have to say that I've never felt more afraid, vulnerable, or alone than I did last night. Your house is the one place you're supposed to feel safe and I've always felt safe here. My parents used to worry about me being single and living alone and I would constantly reassure them there was nothing to worry about. Now I need to reassure myself. But," she added quickly, willing herself to sound strong, "I'm a big girl. This is just something I'm going to have to work through. And I will."

Exactly the answer he expected. "I know you will but I also want you to remember what I said. You don't have to be Super Woman, Trenay. It's perfectly okay to ask for help if you need it."

Trenay took a sip from her glass and smiled. "All kidding aside, the truth is even though I was afraid last night, I will *not* be afraid in my own house. This is the place where I'm going to feel safe again. I'm just going to have to toughen up," she said, not sure who she was trying to convince.

Marshall changed the subject and for the remainder of the meal, he purposely kept the conversation lighthearted and as far away from anything he thought might upset Trenay.

At this time his primary goal was to help restore her sense of security as much as he could and to assure her he would be there if she needed him.

When Marshall finished eating and once he had helped Trenay cleanup he promised himself one thing: No matter what it took he would do his best to make sure that no one hurt her. However, the one question he couldn't answer: Exactly what would it take to keep that promise?

CHAPTER NINE

Trenay rose early to bright sunshine streaming through her bedroom windows. Quickly assessing her surroundings, she relaxed once seeing everything was in order and nothing had been disturbed.

Felix slept soundly at the foot of her bed and Oscar had found a comforting sunbeam cutting a bright swath across the floor near her dresser, perfect for early morning basking. After everything that had gone on over the past few days at least her cats were no worse for the wear.

Trenay turned over and gripped her pillow feeling deliciously lazy and not at all rushed to get out of bed and having no real reason that would require her to do so. She had slept peacefully the night before and had begun to feel safe in her home again. For that, she had Marshall to thank.

Her opinion of him had taken a few twists and turns since their first meeting, particularly after yesterday. Not only had he completed the work securing all of her windows, but he had also checked the locks on her front and back doors and the door leading from her garage, even fixing a few loose hinges. After his inspection, he strongly suggested she get sturdier deadbolts for all of her external doors.

By the time he left she not only felt safer but had a few other things on her mind to contend with, one being a nagging and growing attraction to Marshall.

No matter how she tried to resist, Trenay had a natural tendency to examine things and situations closely, sometimes to a fault, especially if her emotions were involved. True to form her attraction to Marshall would undergo the same scrutiny, particularly since he was so different from anyone she'd ever been attracted to. So there was no avoiding it. Good, bad, or indifferent, that's how she did things. Giving in, she mentally kicked off the process.

She started with Marshall's physical appearance. While focusing first on looks might seem a little shallow she decided to quickly note his most favorable physical features and move on to more of his substantial characteristics. Since this assessment was only taking place in her mind, this seemed like a reasonable compromise.

By most accounts, Marshall was very attractive. If only to herself Trenay had to admit pointing out Marshall's attractiveness was more than citing a case for the obvious. She didn't necessarily want to focus solely on his looks, but there were some features she simply could not ignore: rich chocolate skin with the occasional nick or scar mysteriously hinting at a past sports or work injury; a solid body and no stranger to pushing physical boundaries; the confidence in his stride, a tilt of his head, and curve of his jaw complete with slight stubble on his chin like yesterday; beautiful dark brown eyes set off by long curly eyelashes; square shoulders, and strong hands that seemed capable enough to wield a hammer yet gentle enough to caress her cheek.

Rarely did her attraction to a man have much to do with looks alone. The qualities she routinely sought were social and economic consciousness, gentleness, trustworthiness, strong character, spiritually centered, and career-focused. With the men she'd dated in the past she had gotten all of that, at least in bits and pieces, in one form or another. Unfortunately, those attributes had also been paired with a heaping helping of dullness. Yes, overwhelming dullness had been the one element that could be attributed to the demise of almost every one of her past relationships. If she had to be completely honest a big contributor to her failed relationships might also be attributed to her. She needed someone who challenged her socially and intellectually, could make her laugh, cared deeply about her, and aroused her sexuality. Until a few days ago she didn't know there was something else she needed – a sense of protection. Marshall offered every single one of those attributes and then some.

He had a take-charge-I'm-the-man type of manner, which she found both likable and irritating. However, looking at it from one point of view, she knew, even without him saying it or having any real evidence of whether she was right or wrong, Marshall would fiercely protect those he cared about. That quality she liked. Then again, looking at it from an entirely different angle, he could be quite stubborn and a little too take-charge for her taste. That quality she didn't necessarily care for. She needed the freedom to be able to figure out and handle things for herself, notwithstanding putting the hardware on her windows. Admittedly, carpentry wasn't one of her top skill sets.

Continuing her examination she began to evaluate the things she knew for sure about Marshall, apart from his good looks, nice body, and ego. He liked her. If she had to explain it to someone how she knew he liked her she didn't think she would be able to put it into words. It was something she sensed more than anything else.

Truth be told, she liked him, too. She didn't feel as if she had to justify or analyze the reasons why. There was no need to right now anyway. Maybe if or when she decided to pursue a relationship with Marshall she would give it a little more thought. But right now it was way too early in the game to do anything about her feelings. She didn't even know if she wanted to. Relationships were hard work and she wasn't sure if she had the time, patience, or stamina to have a man in her life, particularly Marshall.

Well, for the time being, she would be keeping her assessment of Marshall all to herself. Armed with what little she knew about him and everything she knew about herself, she didn't quite trust herself with him just yet. There was still a lot to learn about Marshall Oliver. Although, the little she did know beckoned her to dig a little deeper – for better or worse.

***

Marshall lay in bed, arms resting behind his head, staring up at the rotating blades of the ceiling fan. He had been awake for a while but hadn't felt a real need to get out of bed yet. Every once in a while he allowed himself a lazy morning. Today would be that day. He thought about getting ready for church but decided instead to go to the evening service.

On a lazy morning like this, he would typically mull over small details concerning his business – contracts, current, and future projects, whether he had enough workers at his sites, or even small projects he needed to complete at home. This morning, his thoughts shifted instead to Trenay. Actually, since the first time they'd met she had frequently been on his mind. This morning was no exception.

Spending the afternoon with her yesterday had been an unexpected, yet pleasant turn of events. What were the odds of running into her at the hardware store? Whatever the odds, he was pleased they had shifted in his favor.

Despite the busy day spent with Trenay, he hadn't managed to get much sleep last night. Every time he closed his eyes sultry images of her in tight jeans and a t-shirt or a long black evening gown filled his dreams. Unexpectedly, those dreams caused him to wake more than a time or two in a state of longing for something, and someone he felt was quite possibly off-limits.

He blamed his dreams on the fact that Trenay had been on his mind before he fell asleep. As a little boy, his grandmother once told him that to avoid bad dreams he only needed to think about fun and happy things before falling asleep. He had put his grandmother's advice in practice more than a few times over the years, not so much to avoid bad dreams but typically to keep the day's worries out of his nocturnal thoughts. Last night his grandmother's advice had worked like a charm.

Marshall had fallen asleep wondering what it would

feel like to kiss Trenay again. Would it be better than the last time? More exciting? More passionate? He thought so. She had beautiful lips, the bottom one slightly fuller than the top, soft, sweet, and both very kissable. The one kiss they'd shared had made him want more, and he didn't necessarily mean more kisses. He felt no shame in admitting that on the night of the benefit when they had kissed he hadn't wanted to just stop at her lips. He had wanted to kiss and touch her all over, feeling her soft, silky skin beneath his fingers, her body stretched beneath him, writhing in ecstasy.

She not only looked beautiful that night, she felt it, too. He remembered taking every opportunity to touch her – handing her a drink and touching her hand, brushing an imaginary piece of lint from her shoulder, placing his hand on the small of her back while leading her off the dance floor.

And then there was the dance. *Ah, the dance.* Vivid memories of the dance they shared quickly brought a smile to his lips and warmth to his loins. Sharing the dance floor with Trenay and watching her body move had been enough to make his heart skip every time he thought about it. They had been so in tune with each other that night, physically and for a brief moment, emotionally. To put it simply, they fit, rhythmically, and literally. During one part of the dance she had allowed him to spin her around then bring her body back to his, her curvaceous body had practically melted into his. A perfect fit.

In synch on the dance floor, in synch in bed? Try as he might, he couldn't stop himself from wondering, what kind of lover would she be?

Marshall shifted onto his side and flipped his pillow to the cool side. For those who knew him well and who knew the kind of man he was would suspect he had a strong attraction to Trenay. Although, if he wanted to keep his true feelings under wrap and protect himself from disappointment, he might pretend as if the attraction was purely physical and his main goal was to get her into bed. Hell, who wouldn't want to get Trenay between the sheets? The woman had a body that taxed his self-control *and* common sense and he didn't even need to be near her, just thinking about her did it! But in reality, pretending the attraction was just about lust might be too hard of a charade to keep up.

Enough with the physical stuff, he thought. He could be accused of a lot of things, but being a dog wasn't one of them. Admittedly, Trenay had a lot more going for her than a hot body. He genuinely liked and admired her, particularly her spunk, ambition, drive, and character. Until yesterday those characteristics and the little he'd picked up about her from their brief encounters were the only clues he had to go on to figure out exactly what made this woman grab and hold his attention.

Something else about Trenay had also unexpectedly grabbed his attention. He couldn't quite figure out why but he could not shake the feeling that she needed protection. Maybe she didn't necessarily need his protection, but he felt she needed someone's.

By her own admission, Trenay had let it slip that she sometimes overlooked things going on around her, not unlike most people, especially when she was in familiar surroundings. Had someone been in her house before and she had been too tired or distracted to notice? Was she being watched? Stalked? Could there be someone close to Trenay that she needed to beware of?

Marshall stirred. Once again, the same thought nagged at him. He couldn't ignore what he felt in his gut. He needed to keep Trenay safe. He didn't exactly know how he would do it, but somehow he would have to figure it out.

CHAPTER TEN

Brilliant slivers of light pierced the early morning sky as the sun peaked over the horizon, appearing pale in comparison to the even more brilliant flames from the warehouse fire, on the verge of burning out of control. In the distance sounds of the warehouse's combustible materials crackled and sizzled as the fire rapidly consumed the building.

As planned no one was around this time of the morning. It was too early. The warehouse only ran two shifts, first and second. By the time someone showed up for the first shift, probably around seven-thirty, the building would be fully engulfed and a total loss. The absence of workers at Stark Warehousing provided the perfect opportunity for the fire to catch quickly and rapidly burn out of control. Even if the fire department did manage to get here soon, they'd be helpless to battle the raging blaze.

Too bad no one else was around to enjoy the show. It was most impressive.

At some point, someone would begin to connect the dots. The plan had been designed that way. Once the dots were connected everyone would begin to blame her, and rightly so. Sooner rather than later each clue would lead to a connection and each connection would lead straight to Trenay Bradley.

***

Monday morning and Cristina was running late. Again. Trenay didn't mind since experience taught her she could expect a colorful story – most likely involving a dark, handsome stranger, too much wine, and some other foolishness that was sure to make Trenay wonder how her friend ended up in so many *interesting* situations.

They were supposed to both be in early this morning. Trenay needed to file answers on several bid requests by noon that day, thanks to Councilman Ryan. The sooner she got those done the better since she expected to have to cover for him a little while longer. She'd heard from the mayor that Ryan's recovery wasn't going very well. She couldn't say she was surprised. Cigar smoking, bourbon guzzling, overweight, and an outright nasty disposition couldn't be good for anyone, sick or well.

Trenay liked being in the office early before the normal hustle and bustle began. No phone interruptions, emails, or people unexpectedly dropping by her office. In her opinion, this was the best time of day to get work done.

After settling in at her desk with a cup of tea and a muffin Trenay spotted a plain manila envelope sticking out from under her keyboard. She wondered why Cristina had placed it there and not in her in-basket. While she waited for her computer to boot up she cut through the envelope's seal. Pulling out the contents of the envelope Trenay stiffened as a cold chill washed over her body.

Fear gripped her as icy fingers revealed the contents. Inside the envelope were pictures, each one of her going about her daily tasks, completely oblivious to anyone watching her. Some showed her at the grocery store, others at the dry cleaners, pizza shop, and getting her mail at her house. *Her home.*

She went through each picture with rapid succession, wanting to see something that told her this was all a joke and she shouldn't be afraid. But that assurance didn't seem likely. She reached the last picture in the stack. Unlike the others, she wasn't the subject. It was something else. A place that was familiar to her. The building in the picture was on fire.

The image of the burning building was chilling but the words scrawled across the top in bold, red letters terrified her even more – *You will know what it's like to lose everything, Trenay Bradley.*

Trenay dropped the stack of pictures on her desk, afraid to touch them any longer.

What did this mean?

Who sent the pictures?

What did they want?

She couldn't form the questions fast enough in her mind, especially since there were no ready answers. But one question weighed more heavily than the others and brought tears to her eyes. *Who was watching her?*

Suddenly, feeling vulnerable and frightened beyond anything she'd ever felt, Trenay realized that someone other than Cristina had put those pictures in her office. Cristina hadn't arrived yet to sort through the weekend mail, and she would have noticed the envelope before she left Friday. No one had been in the office when she left for the weekend.

She needed to leave. She didn't feel safe all alone in her office. Panicked, Trenay grabbed her purse and keys. Just then, she heard the door to the outer office open. Gripped with fear she stood motionless hoping – praying – that it was Cristina, but too afraid to call out.

She waited to hear something familiar, anything to let her know that whoever stood outside her office meant her no harm.

The carpeting in the outer office only slightly muffled the sound of footsteps. Even so, she knew the steps were too heavy to be Cristina's. Straining to hear the sound of her assistant's keys, deep down she knew she wouldn't hear them. Afraid to breathe for fear that she would be heard, she willed herself to be still and not cry out.

The footsteps came closer to her office door. With each step, her heart beat faster and louder, she could barely hear anything else. Standing deathly still, her eyes darted around her office. She had nowhere to go. Taking a shallow breath, she waited, poised, and ready to face whoever was outside her office. The footsteps stopped. Her breath caught in her throat, she closed her eyes and prayed.

CHAPTER ELEVEN

"Trenay. Trenay"

What? She tried to answer but no sound came out.

"Trenay!"

The voice calling her sounded muffled but seemed too far away for her to recognize who it was. Why were they calling out to her? she wondered. Was something wrong? She tried again to answer but still couldn't make a sound. Maybe she was dreaming. *Yes, a dream.*

"Trenay!"

This time the voice seemed closer, more urgent, and slightly familiar. Still unable to recognize the voice, she allowed herself to be drawn in and moved closer to the sound. The voice became stronger and clearer. Her eyes fluttered open.

"She's coming to!"

Trenay opened her eyes fully, blinking to clear her vision. From an awkward angle, she looked up and saw Cristina standing over her. Her assistant was crying.

"What's wrong?" she asked, confused and disoriented. As her vision became clearer Trenay looked around, seeing and hearing a flurry of activity in her office. Just seconds before she thought she had been in the midst of a dream. But none of what she was hearing or seeing now felt much like a dream especially since she wasn't at home in her bed.

Strong hands grabbed her by the waist and lifted her

to a seated position. "Here, drink this," someone ordered and then pushed a cup into her hand.

Sitting on the floor with her back leaning against the desk, she tried to understand why so much activity seemed to be centered inside her office. It felt as if someone had plopped her in the middle of a scene in a movie but forgot to tell her what role she was supposed to be playing.

"What's going on?" Someone else asked the same question she wanted an answer to.

As she struggled to make sense out of this odd scene Trenay looked past Cristina and saw someone she recognized from the security station. Several security guards, police officers, Mayor Hanover – and Marshall – were all speaking in hushed tones.

Slowly, she started to remember. She had come in early to work that morning. Cristina was supposed to meet her there but she was late. Then something happened. Sitting at her desk drinking a cup of tea and waiting for her computer to boot up had been when she saw it. The envelope. The pictures. The message. But there was something else, something that had frightened her more than seeing herself in the pictures. She'd heard someone outside her office, someone she felt might have meant her harm. *What happened after that?* She honestly couldn't remember. The only thing she could recall was the feeling of fear, griping her like a vice, squeezing the very breath out of her body. Then…everything went dark.

Panicked, Trenay attempted to stand up. Marshall stepped away from the small group and rushed over to her.

"Hey, take it easy," he said in a voice that he willed to

sound calm. "You fainted. Give yourself a minute or so to regain your bearings."

"I did?" Trenay asked more to herself than anyone else. She paused for a second, wondering if she had been hurt, but she felt all right except for…she looked up at Marshall with fear in her eyes. She needed to tell him. "The pictures! Look at the pictures on my desk. Did you see them? Someone left them in my office, under my keyboard."

"I know. Don't worry about that right now. The police are here. Whoever it was must have gotten scared off. You're safe now." Hearing the fear in her voice Marshall knew he had to act quickly to reassure her that she needn't be afraid, at least for the time being. Although he didn't feel very confident about assuring her of something he knew very little about.

Standing with the help of Marshall, Trenay glanced at her desk.

"The police have them," he said, answering the question before she asked it. "They're evidence. There seems to be a link between whoever left the pictures and yesterday's warehouse fire."

After the detectives took her statement and the mayor practically ordered her to go on administrative leave until everything could be sorted out, Trenay sat very still in the chair across from her desk typically reserved for guests. She didn't know what to say or do, so she waited…waited to wake up or for someone to hit the rewind button so she could start her day all over again, this time without the frightening events that left her feeling alone, confused, and more frightened than she had ever felt in her life.

Trenay looked around at the various people poking around her office. Uniformed and plain-clothed officers wearing serious expressions continued to file in and out. Over in a corner in the outer office, she noticed Marshall talking to the mayor. She couldn't make out what they were saying but judging by their body language and the worried expression on the mayor's face, it didn't look good.

With all of the crazy thoughts swirling around in her head and the flurry of activity going on around her, something struck her as odd. She didn't remember having an appointment with Marshall. *What was he doing here?*

Before she could figure out that one small detail, a detective approached her.

"Ms. Bradley, if you have somewhere other than your house to stay, that would be advisable."

"What?" Trenay looked at the detective and blinked, dumbfounded.

"Is there someone you can stay with for a while? It's probably not a good idea for you to go home."

"I can't go home?"

"Only to get your things, but I don't recommend you stay there, not until we can apprehend whoever is threatening you or at the very least figure out who this person is."

"But I don't have anywhere else to go. My parents are out of the country and I don't have – there's no one else. I can't go home?" she repeated, her voice quivering. "But I have to."

"You can stay with me," Cristina spoke up quickly as she tried to be brave for her friend.

"I don't think that would be a very good idea," the detective advised. "You're directly linked to Ms. Bradley and it would be too easy to find her through you, putting both of you in danger."

Danger?

Trenay looked at her friend with tears in her eyes. She was in danger. What was she going to do?

Cristina and Trenay talked for a moment, both women trying to be strong through their tears. Since no one seemed to know who they were dealing with Trenay would not put her friend in danger.

"She can stay with me."

Trenay, Cristina, and the detective looked up as Marshall rejoined them inside Trenay's office.

"I-I can't do that," she started.

"Why not?" he asked. "It's not safe at your house. You can't go to your parents'. Where else are you going to go?"

The detective looked from Marshall to Trenay as each debated the next course of action. Trenay mentioned going to a hotel but that idea was quickly nixed. Marshall mentioned the possibility of endangering every guest staying at the hotel, not to mention the isolation she'd feel sitting in a hotel room for several days. Then the detective stepped in.

"Ms. Bradley, those are good points. Staying at a hotel may not be in the best interest of you or the other guests. Also, keep in mind we don't know who this person is, if they are working alone, or any such details. The person watching you could check into the hotel to be even closer to you. We just don't want to take any chances. We don't know when the pictures were taken, but your boyfriend is not in any of them. That could be because the person or persons who took them doesn't know about him."

"He's not my boyfriend," she said absently. Trenay could hardly think straight. This was all too much to absorb at one time.

"Look," Marshall pleaded with her. "I have a place where you can stay that's away from all of this, it's secluded and safe. No strings attached. No one will find you there unless you want them to." Marshall looked to the detective for support. "No one can connect us."

Trenay looked at the faces in her office – Cristina's, the detective's, and Marshall's. Everyone seemed to agree on what was best for her. They just needed her to agree, too. She wished she had more time to think but knew time was of the essence and getting out of harm's way sooner rather than later left her with very few options. Ultimately, the decision was hers. She had to make the right decision for her safety and her sanity.

However, seeing no other option and feeling too weary from everything that had happened to argue, she reluctantly agreed to stay with Marshall for a few days until all of this blew over. She didn't know where he was taking her or what lie ahead. The one thing she did know, after today, her life would never be the same.

CHAPTER TWELVE

Sitting motionless and staring out the passenger side window, Trenay watched as the scenery become less familiar with each passing mile. She tried over and over again to process the last several hours in her mind but only managed to create more questions than answers.

Why would someone want to hurt her? She had certainly never intentionally hurt anyone in her life, just the opposite. In both her personal and professional life, she tried to treat people fairly, with kindness and compassion, the way she wanted to be treated. But where had it gotten her? The fires, the vandalism, and the pictures had all led up to this: Going into hiding and running away from everything and everyone, she cared about. The acts of fear and intimidation directed towards her had affected her in a way that would surely leave a lasting impression.

Was that the intent, to hurt her? Frighten and intimidate her? *Mission accomplished*, she thought bitterly.

Her whole life had been turned upside down in a matter of hours and for the first time in her life, she had no control over anything. The control she once had and took for granted now belonged to someone else, someone she couldn't even put a name or face to, confront, or ask why.

Trenay looked over at Marshall, who had been silent for most of the trip, as he stared straight ahead, lost in his thoughts. She wondered what he thought about all of this. He, too, was deeply affected, in more ways than one. She saw the tension in his tightly set jaw. He looked as troubled about this whole nightmarish situation as she did.

How would she make this right? What did she need to do to make everything normal again? Turning back to stare out the window and at the now completely unfamiliar scenery Trenay felt an overwhelming sense of sadness in addition to the helplessness, anger, frustration, and confusion she was already feeling…so many questions and emotions, so few answers.

Slowly one lone tear ran down her cheek. Then another, and another. Soon the first of many tears began to stream down her face.

Turning when he heard Trenay's sobs, Marshall took his attention off the road long enough to see the last ounce of her resolve dissipate before his eyes. "Hey, hey," he said, not sure if he should pull the car over or continue on their journey to get her as far out of harm's way as possible.

Hearing her sobs and seeing the look on her face, he had his answer. She needed him. Maneuvering the truck over to the side of the highway and onto a small service road, Marshall was careful not to draw unnecessary attention toward them.

Shutting off the engine, he got out of the truck and went around to the passenger's side. As soon as he opened her door, Trenay shot out of the truck and into his arms, sobbing uncontrollably.

He didn't speak but simply held her until he felt her

body sag from fatigue and what he imagined to be despair.

As the tears subsided Trenay's sobs quieted. Feeling drained and a little embarrassed from the onslaught of emotion, she offered a halfhearted apology. "I'm sorry," she said, her voice hoarse. "I didn't mean to lose it like that. I just…I needed to-I mean, I felt-"

"You don't have to explain or apologize."

She pulled away from Marshall, needing to draw from his strength but at the same time angry that she had to. "I have been replaying everything in my head and trying to make sense out of this-this craziness, but I can't. The vandalism, fire, and threats…none of this makes any sense. I don't have money, power, or anything else that someone would want. And I certainly don't pose a threat to anyone."

As she paced back and forth Marshall listened while she talked. She needed to get her emotions in check, but right now she needed to vent. And he allowed her to do just that.

After a few minutes she stopped pacing and stood in front of Marshall, looking off in the distance, she asked the one question that taunted him, too. "Why?"

Just like her, he had no answers.

"Let's get back in the truck. It's just a little further. Once we get settled in and you're able to get some rest, we can think about this in more detail. Maybe we'll be able to come up with a little more information for the detectives."

Marshall led Trenay back to the truck. Circling back to the driver's side he took a cautionary look over his shoulder before getting inside.

On the outside, he appeared strong, protective, and calm, but on the inside, it tore him up to see Trenay so afraid. He wished he could do more to help, if nothing else he wanted to restore her sense of security and independence. But for now his immediate and number one concern was to get her as far away as possible from the person who wanted to hurt her.

They continued to drive along the highway in silence. The closer they came to Benton Lake the better and more in control Marshall began to feel. His hometown was familiar territory and he could protect Trenay there until the detectives caught the person trying to hurt her.

The secluded property Marshall had purchased several years earlier was located about a mile from the main road and sat back in a heavily wooded area off the lake. He loved his sanctuary, as he and his family had dubbed the isolated property. Surrounded by dense trees he had easy access to a remote area of the lake that most townsfolk avoided because of its seclusion and tourists knew nothing about. His home away from home served as a place where he could be alone without feeling lonely.

The house that sat on his property had at one time been nothing more than a hunting cabin. Marshall had since gutted it, put in a new kitchen, an additional half bath, and a room addition that he used as an office/guest room, even though he rarely had guests. Nevertheless, for him, the house offered comfort, tranquility, and refuge when he needed to recharge or put life's situations into perspective. Now his home would serve a different purpose; a safe house.

As he took their bags from the car, Marshall watched Trenay out of the corner of his eye. She looked tired and completely defeated. Pulling the last bag from behind the seat, he slammed the door to his truck, causing Trenay to jump.

He put the bags down and reached out for her. Holding her at arm's length, he faced her and said, "No one outside of my family can link me to this place. You're safe here. Do you understand? I am not going to let anything or anyone hurt you."

She nodded, wanting and needing so very badly to believe him.

Marshall gave Trenay the largest bedroom and left her alone sitting on the bed, staring off into space. He suggested she lie down and get some rest.

Trenay sat on the spacious bed and looked down at her unopened suitcase. She barely remembered packing her things. Had she gotten the suitcase from the basement or had Marshall? Had she even remembered to bring her toothbrush? A nightgown? Her laptop?

What did it matter?

She thought about the pictures that had been left in her office. Someone had been watching her and she hadn't even noticed. They had seen her at her home and several other places around town while she remained oblivious to being watched. Now she was pretty sure the same person had also been inside her house.

Just thinking about it made her want to cry, get angry, and lash out, but she didn't have enough strength to do any of those things. Her body weary and worn out and her mind spinning with details and events she couldn't make sense of, made her want to shut herself off from the world.

Not even bothering to remove her shoes, she pulled her legs onto the bed and laid down on her side. She felt so tired. Maybe if she laid down and closed her eyes she could turn off her troubled thoughts and fall into a deep sleep. Sleep until this all went away, like a bad dream.

***

Trenay woke from a fitful sleep to bright sunlight streaming through a small opening in the heavy curtains that covered the window. It was morning. She had slept all night.

Sitting up she surveyed her strange surroundings. It only took a few seconds to recognize where she was.

Almost immediately, everything came rushing back to her – the pictures, leaving her home, staying with Marshall. She pushed off the blanket she didn't remember covering herself with and sat for a minute on the side of the bed. Her shoes had been removed and placed neatly beside the bed along with her slippers. Still wearing the same clothes she'd had on the day before, she scanned the room for her suitcase. The room was small but had been furnished with the essentials – bed, dresser, chair, and nightstand. Walking over to the closet door to see if Marshall had placed her suitcase inside, she was surprised to see some of her clothes hanging neatly inside. Checking inside the dresser drawers, she found more of her things. Too numb to be embarrassed about Marshall handling her most intimate garments, she grabbed a change of clothing.

Her bedroom door was slightly ajar allowing the aroma of coffee to waft in. She made her way to the small bathroom adjoining her room. Marshall had laid out towels. On the sink, she saw a brand new toothbrush still in the wrapper, toothpaste, shower gel, deodorant, and lotion. Most of the toiletries had come from her house and the rest she assumed Marshall had purchased or had already.

After a quick shower, Trenay felt slightly better. She went through the motion of washing her face, brushing her teeth, and combing her hair while trying to make herself and her circumstances feel normal. It wasn't working very well. Before leaving the bathroom she paused long enough to look at her reflection in the mirror. Eyes puffy and red she fought back tears and quickly turned away. She looked as tired and defeated as she felt.

Turning from the stove when he heard movement, Marshall greeted Trenay with a smile as she entered the kitchen. She looked only a little better than she had the day before, he noticed.

"Coffee?"

"Please," she responded quietly.

Marshall placed a steaming cup of coffee on the table and motioned for her to sit. "Cream and sugar?"

She nodded. "What time is it?"

"Almost ten."

"I can't believe I slept all night. Why didn't you wake me?"

"For what? You needed your sleep."

Trenay took a sip of the strong coffee and winced.

"Too strong?" Marshall asked, concerned. He liked his coffee strong and black. If he wasn't buying a cup or two from the local coffee shop, or drinking the coffee Zenobia made at the office, he tended to be a little heavy-handed when he made his own.

"A little, but that's okay."

"Hungry?"

She shook her head and took another sip of the strong coffee.

Marshall sat a plate in front of her with a small portion of scrambled eggs and sausage and a piece of toast. "You can't survive on coffee. Just try to eat a little."

Sitting down across from her Marshall uttered a quick prayer of thanks and began to eat the same breakfast he had served Trenay but in much larger portions.

"Your place seems pretty remote. How close is your nearest neighbor?"

Trenay sat stiffly in her chair, taking small sips of coffee. She had glanced at the front door at least three times. She hadn't touched her food.

"I don't have neighbors. I own all of the land as far as the eye can see," he replied, smiling reassuringly.

"How far is it to town? I wasn't paying attention when we came in yesterday."

"We didn't come through town. I brought us in the back way."

She nodded; placing her cup down on the table and picking it back up but not drinking.

Marshall put down his fork. "You're not eating."

Pushing her plate away, she placed her cup beside her

plate and crossed her arms protectively. "I'm sorry. I wish I had known you were going through all of the trouble of cooking breakfast. I'm just not very hungry right now."

"Cooking breakfast was no trouble. You need to eat."

Trenay fidgeted with her napkin.

"Aside from your appetite, what's actually bothering you?" He'd hoped that getting her out of the city would make her feel better, safe.

"Everything," she said sadly. "I just can't shake the feeling that someone is watching me and no matter where I go, I won't be safe."

Marshall reached across the table and took her hand. "Trenay, I told you before I brought you here that you'd be safe. If that weren't true and the fact that I could protect you here, then I would never have brought you to my cabin."

"I want to believe you, Marshall. Really, I do."

"Look, I know I'm asking a lot from you right now. I understand that. But the one thing I'm asking you to do above everything else is to trust me. I'll do the rest."

Marshall's sincerity was obvious, but hopefully not as obvious as the fear, which had thrown her into a tailspin over the past twenty-four hours.

Needing a distraction, she looked away. Right now her feelings were raw and she felt so exposed and vulnerable that she couldn't even trust her instincts, let alone anything or anyone else. Marshall offered safety and security and she needed those things just as much as she needed air right now, but at what price? What would she be giving up to take advantage of what he offered?

Again taking small sips from her coffee, she tried to relax. So far, Marshall had been true to his word. He offered her a safe place to stay with no strings attached.

"You have a nice place," she said, changing the subject.

She looked around at the brightly lit kitchen. There wasn't a lot there – a small stove, refrigerator, no dishwasher, a few gadgets, and canisters on the counter. Simple, functional, quaint, and very masculine.

Trenay finished her coffee, leaving Marshall sitting at the table, and walked out from the kitchen into the open living room. Just like the kitchen, she noticed all of the necessary things, but very few extras or special touches. Also, like her bedroom, this room wasn't overly furnished, however, the pieces that had been chosen to fill the space were functional, comfortable, and fit nicely into the spacious area.

Hardwood floors covered with colorful rugs, two accent tables, a few floor lamps, and fluffy pillows scattered over the sofa and loveseat gave the room a cozy and welcoming feel, which was not entirely wasted on her.

Trenay took a seat at the end of the large sofa and hugged one of the throw pillows. "I like this place," she said sincerely. Under different circumstances, she imagined it being a nice place to spend the weekend, a quaint home away from home.

"I'm glad," Marshall replied, secretly pleased. He took a seat on the sofa beside Trenay. "I want you to feel comfortable here, and safe."

Trenay leaned back against the couch's cool leather

upholstery and sighed. "I will, eventually."

He nodded, knowing he couldn't ask for anything more this soon.

"I want to thank you for everything, Marshall. You didn't have to do all of this, you know, especially for someone you hardly know."

Marshall thought carefully before responding. "Look, I don't want you to think I have an ulterior motive for helping you. I'm doing it because you needed help and I want to and am in a position to help you. No strings attached. Okay?"

She thought about what he said and reluctantly nodded in agreement. Sadly, she had no other choice but to trust him.

"By the way, how was it that you ended up at my office when, uh, everything happened?"

"I was filing some permits, which Zenobia typically does, but she was out of the office."

Trenay's mother was fond of saying that everything happened for a reason. This time she was inclined to believe her.

"Can I say something to you without you taking it the wrong way?"

"Can I stop you?" she asked, smiling weakly.

"You're going to make it through this," he stated.

"How can you be so sure?"

"Because you're a lot stronger than you think you are. I know you feel the exact opposite right now but that's to be expected. The way I see it anyone else would have folded under the stress. Not you."

Trenay shook her head and blinked back tears. "Funny, I don't feel very strong. Honestly, what I feel most right now is fear, anger, defeat, and confusion. And the worst part is that I don't know how to even begin to process all of this."

"Okay. Then let's talk about it. I know you might not feel like it right now, but let's talk about everything you can think of that may or may not have anything to do with what lead up to yesterday."

"Like what?"

"People you've met who may have said or done something odd. Places you've gone where something may have happened that seemed a little out of the ordinary."

"Don't you think I've been thinking about that already? I've tried to think of anything out of the ordinary, weird, strange, or different. People. Places. Phone calls. Situations. Meetings. Nothing is jumping out at me. My life is so routine it's practically boring. I travel in the same circles, same grocery store, same church, same dry cleaners, the same branch of the library, same pizza place. I don't cheat on my taxes, steal cable, date married men, or break any other rules. I don't bother anyone," she said, trying to hold in her anger. "Everything I do is to help people, not hurt them, which seems pretty ironic about now."

Marshall touched her shoulder. He needed her to stay focused, so he asked more specific questions.

"You said there were pictures of you at random places and times. Did you notice anything out of the ordinary when you were at any of those places? Maybe at the dry cleaners or grocery store?"

She shook her head.

"Come on, Trenay, think."

"I told you, nothing out of the ordinary happened. I bought my groceries, paid the cashier, and I left. I couldn't tell you if the cashier was a man or woman. I don't remember if people were standing in line with me or not. I can barely remember what I bought. My trips to the drycleaners were even more uneventful and just as unmemorable. Do you want to know what I did there? I dropped off dirty clothes, picked up clean ones, paid the cashier, and left."

Marshall pressed her. "Could there have been someone lingering near your car or that you saw more than a few times while you were shopping?"

"I don't think so…maybe…I don't know…I don't pay attention to who's watching me and who isn't." Agitated she stood and walked over to the window. "Marshall, I know you're trying to help, but I don't pay attention to the people around me when I run errands, get my mail, buy groceries, or when I'm anywhere for that matter. I just do what I have to do and I go on about my business. Do you pay attention?" she snapped, her voice rising. "How many different people do you run across at the grocery store, on your way to work, or at any of the other places you go?"

Marshall could hear the strain in her voice and decided not to push her further, at least not now.

"Okay. Let's take a break. We can talk about this later."

"I'm sorry," she said, a little more calmly. "I know

you're trying to help. You hear stories all the time about people who were hurt by someone who had been stalking them and women are always cautioned to pay attention to their surroundings. Well, as you can see, I never really paid attention to the warnings. I should have known someone was watching me and taking pictures of me, but I didn't." Trenay's shoulders slumped and she sighed. "At work I pay attention to every detail of a project, trying to figure out the best way to meet the needs of the customer and the environmental requirements. I look at cost, EPA reports, building standards, best practices; you name it, all with a fine-toothed comb, whatever it takes. My personal life," she laughed bitterly, "not so much. Seems as if the only thing I have managed to do is to make myself an easy target."

CHAPTER THIRTEEN

There was too much activity in and around Trenay's house to risk going inside. Just one good look around would be enough. One simple clue like an address, name, or phone number to a friend or family member would be enough, enough to track her down.

Somehow she had slipped away. Amidst all of the confusion with the cops and security guards and even with His Honor the Mayor, she had slipped through his grasp. He wasn't sure if the cops had whisked her away but she wasn't at her house. He'd checked. Now the police were there. One reason he couldn't risk hanging around too much longer.

He would have to employ other methods to track down Trenay, having exhausted the easier ones. The annoying secretary at Trenay's office refused to give out any information. At least he managed to find out Trenay wasn't staying with her. He had followed her home from work and staked out her house. He smiled. These women made it so easy. He could slip in and out of their lives with ease, never raising an eyebrow or the slightest suspicion, except now. His smile faded into a scowl.

Talk about rotten luck.

Everything had been going according to plan until he was almost caught.

He had followed her from her house that day. It was

trash day and she had taken out two small bags of garbage – she rarely had more than two – and some recyclables. She got in her car, stopped by the coffee shop for a cup of herbal tea with lemon and honey, and a poppy seed muffin. Sometimes she got blueberry, sometimes banana.

He had followed her all the way to work and not once did she see him, not at the traffic lights or when turning from one street to another. She was preoccupied. Still, he was careful. No need to be cocky after all of his planning and care. Why tempt fate?

She had been all alone in her office just like a lot of other mornings. Standing outside of the door he could hear her puttering around in her office preparing for the day, booting up computers, turning on printers without a thought or care in the world.

No one was around that time of the morning. It was too early for most of the city workers.

He had listened and waited for just the right time. She had found the pictures just like he'd planned. He had more, but it would have been overkill to have shown her all of them at once. He'd picked out the best ones. They served the purpose beautifully.

He laughed. The gravelly sound echoed in the car. He had been able to sense her fear even though he couldn't see her face. She had been in her office, ready to flee. Her keys had jingled then made a muffled sound as they hit the floor. He knew her heart pounded with fear. His pounded with excitement, anticipation.

Taking his own sweet time to walk into her office was done on purpose, to set her on edge. She had no way out except to come past him. They would have met that day, officially, face to face, under circumstances he created and on his terms. Beads of perspiration dotted his forehead and his palms became clammy as the memory played over in his mind.

Everything was going beautifully! Subduing her would have been like taking down a child. Too afraid to fight back, he could have had her away from the office and moved to a more secure and intimate location in no time flat. But his plan hit a kink. He never expected activity outside of her office. How could he have missed the union meeting planned for that morning? All of a sudden people were milling around in the hallway. Too many potential witnesses. He had to abort the plan.

Once he realized he would have to carry out his plan another day, he quickly retreated and made himself inconspicuous amongst the crowd of people attending the early morning meeting.

Another day. Another opportunity. His time would come. And so would Trenay's.

All he had to do now was to find her. How hard could it be? *Follow the breadcrumbs,* he thought with a smile on his face. It was all just a matter of time.

***

The detective working Trenay's case sat at his desk well past quitting time. He had been examining the pictures left in her office. Looking at them from every possible angle, under different types of light, and even with a magnifying glass, he still couldn't garner anything more than the myriad of unanswered questions nagging him.

"Okay, Sam, quitting time was two and a half hours ago. I'm sure your wife won't appreciate you getting home this late."

Detective Sam Prosser gathered up the pictures, placed them in an envelope, and locked them securely in his desk.

"You're right, Linda. I think I need to look at this case with fresh eyes tomorrow." Taking off his reading glasses, he rubbed his tired eyes. "None of this is making sense to me right now, but I know there's something, some tiny clue, I'm missing."

"Is that the stalking case?"

Sam nodded. "Stalking, arson, and breaking and entering are all linked to this woman in a way that hints she may not be a victim but the perpetrator, but my gut tells me she didn't have anything to do with these other crimes. Do you want to hear the craziest part about all of this?"

"Sure. I'll bite," Sam's co-worker responded.

"I don't even think the intent here is to make us believe she committed the crimes but to make us think she is responsible in some secondary way."

"She's being framed?"

"Not exactly but she has a connection with two fires and a case of vandalism. Well, maybe connection is too strong a word. Her office, part of some new initiative the mayor established, is linked to each business that's either been burned out or vandalized."

"Linked how?"

"Her office played a major part in helping all of the

businesses with some aspect of building, remodeling, or getting their business up to code."

"Okay, so you're thinking…"

"I'm thinking I need to look beyond the obvious clues and see why someone has gone from trying to ruin this woman's reputation to causing her serious harm."

CHAPTER FOURTEEN

"Who was on the phone?"

Lee Oliver hung up the phone and smiled when he heard his wife come into the room. He didn't want to worry her so he pretended to be unconcerned by his brother's phone call.

"Marshall. He's in town. He told me to tell you and the kid's hello."

Katrice eyed her husband suspiciously. "Really? Just hello? He didn't say anything else? He didn't want to come by?"

"Uh, he'll probably stop by later. You know Marshall; he operates on his own schedule."

"Later, huh? Yes, I know Marshall but I also know my husband quite well. So what's going on that you're trying to hide from me?"

Lee knew better than to try to hide things from his wife, especially where their family was concerned. She was right, she knew him too well. "I don't know. The only thing he told me was that he's staying out at the lake and wanted to know if he could come by the office to talk."

"He didn't want to come by here? That seems odd. Did he say anything else?"

Lee shook his head and sighed. "I'm not so concerned about what he said. It's what he didn't say that has me worried."

***

It had been less than a week since they arrived in Benton Lake but Marshall knew he needed to do something to snap Trenay out of her funk. They had spoken very little about the stalking case, the pictures, or anything else. Trenay mainly spent her days in her room with the door closed, sitting on the porch staring out into the woods, or sleeping.

Marshall had left early that morning to go into town to pick up groceries and his mail he'd had Zenobia forward to the local post office. Asking Trenay to go with him into town would have been a waste of time so he didn't even bother.

After retrieving his mail from the post office and checking in with Zenobia, he drove to his brother's office.

Marshall pulled into a parking space directly in front of Lee's office. An attorney, Lee had opened his practice when he moved from Columbus to Benton Lake several years earlier. Lee's clients kept him pretty busy considering he was one of the few attorneys to service Benton Lake and several surrounding rural counties.

Marshall considered his brother to be one of the lucky ones – lucky in life and love, that is.

Lee enjoyed living and working in a small town. By most accounts, he was happily married to a woman whom he adored and who equally adored him. They had three beautiful children and a life most people would envy.

Marshall wasn't jealous of his younger brother, he simply wondered why finding someone to love seemed particularly elusive to him.

Lee stepped out into the outer office to greet his brother when he heard the exterior door open. After exchanging "bro hugs" and a few playful punches, the two men sat down in Lee's office.

"You've done a pretty nice job of fixing this place up," Marshall commented. "It's hard to tell it was once a paint store."

"Yeah, a lot of blood, sweat, and tears went into getting this place in shape. Dad did almost all of the carpentry work and Katrice and Kyra were the interior decorators," he chuckled. "Seriously, if it were left up to me there would have been nothing more than primer and paint over the drywall, no artwork or pictures on the walls, a few folding chairs and maybe a card table with old sports magazines for my clients to read while they waited for their appointments."

"So, how are my favorite sister-in-law and the little rug rats?"

"Katrice and the kids are good. You're going to have to stop by and see them. You know Katrice would never forgive you if you didn't come by for dinner at least once."

"Yeah, I'll come by. Are Dad and Miss Vonda okay?"

"Yup. Still acting like two teenagers in love. I still think it's a little weird to see Dad all googly-eyed whenever he's around Miss Vonda, but Katrice thinks it's cute. You know they're helping to take care of Miss Vonda's uncle in Nashville and won't be back until the end of summer."

"I know. I talked to Dad last week. I think he's found a new fishing buddy with Miss Vonda's uncle."

Lee nodded.

"How's Kyra? Is she adjusting and doing all right at Central State?"

"She seems to like it. I just hope she remembers the reason she's there is to get an education and not to be a social butterfly."

Marshall shifted in his seat. "You don't have to worry about her. She's got a good head on her shoulders. She'll be fine. Before you know it she'll graduate and be off on her own."

After a few more minutes of small talk, Lee folded his arms and leaned back in his seat. "Okay, Marshall, you know I can talk about Katrice and the kids all day long, but I'm pretty sure if I do I'll continue to get that same blank look you've been giving me for the past five minutes. Are you ready to tell me what's going on?"

Marshall closed his eyes and rubbed his forehead. He needed to talk to someone and he knew he could trust Lee to listen without too much bias or unsolicited advice. Marshall exhaled slowly. "I honestly don't even know where to start."

Concerned, Lee gently prodded his brother. "How about at the beginning?"

"I think I may have gotten myself into a situation and I don't quite know how to handle it." Marshall paused, thinking carefully about what to say next, realizing that no matter where he started or finished, he'd feel better after talking to Lee.

"Okay. Go on."

"Do you remember me telling you about a bid my company was making for a construction project at the hospital?"

"Yes, but I thought that bid was denied."

"It was, but the person I had been working with suddenly went on medical leave. I had to not only deal with another person but someone in an entirely different department."

Lee listened patiently, allowing his brother to lay the groundwork for whatever he was ultimately trying to get off his chest.

"The woman who heads the department and who was also responsible for handling the bid appeal proved to be a little more difficult to work with than I had expected."

"In what way?"

"Well, there were a bunch of new regulations that had been put in place that we weren't aware of. Environmental stuff – green building practices." Marshall answered his brother's unasked question. "Properly handling post-consumer waste, using environmentally safe products, and a whole bunch of other rules I won't bore you with. Anyway, most of the regulations are things we probably should have been doing all along. I just didn't need it thrown up in my face all at once, especially at the cost of a lucrative project."

Lee struggled to follow Marshall. So far he managed to learn Marshall's company had missed out on a prime project because they didn't adhere to certain new practices the city had put in place. He also caught something about a woman heading an office who seemed difficult to work with. But he couldn't tell if what bothered Marshall had to do with the denial of the bid or his company having to make changes, possibly costly ones, to be more competitive with other companies. "So, you're upset about something with the bid process and you came to Benton Lake to…? I'm sorry but I'm not following you."

"No, no…" Marshall stood and began pacing. "I know I'm not making a lot of sense right now. This doesn't have anything to do with the bid or my company, well, not exactly. I said all of that other stuff to tell you about the woman I've been dealing with at the mayor's office – Trenay Bradley. I guess I should have cut to the chase from the beginning. Someone is stalking her, Lee. They've been following her for God knows how long and now they are threatening her."

Lee saw the anguished look on his brother's face and he tried to put all of the disjointed pieces of information together so he could help him, but he still didn't know what he was talking about. "Marshall, you've completely lost me. What do this woman and everything else you just told me have to do with you being here?"

Marshall stopped pacing and turned to face his brother. "What I'm trying to say is…Trenay is here."

"Here as in Benton Lake? At your place out at the lake?"

"Yes, in Benton Lake at the cabin."

Lee shook his head, still confused. "Because?"

"I told you, someone is stalking her. They broke into her house and her office. I had to bring her here. Her parents live out west and they're out of the country right now."

"Do you even know this woman?"

"In a sense. I've gotten to know her a little – outside of work – and what I do know about her made me feel this is the right thing to do." Marshall looked to his brother for understanding. "She didn't have anyone else, Lee, and this is the safest place I know."

Lee stepped from behind his desk and leaned against the front, facing Marshall. "Okay, man, I know we could get into a long, drawn-out discussion about what you're doing and the real reason why I think you're doing it, but we'll save that for another time. I'm sure – no, I hope – you know what you're doing. My only advice to you right now is to be careful. You don't know who or what you're dealing with. I'm sure I don't have to tell you stalking situations can be pretty tricky and very dangerous."

Marshall nodded his understanding and acknowledged his brother's concern. "I'll be careful. Just trust me on this. I wanted you to know what's going on in case we need your help. At least I feel better knowing whoever is stalking Trenay can't trace her back to me."

Lee nodded, still struggling to digest everything his brother told him.

"I feel better getting that off my chest. Thanks for listening and for not thinking I'm crazy, or at least not saying it out loud."

Long after Marshall left, Lee continued to replay the details of their conversation, trying to make sense of everything he'd heard. Lee loved his big brother and he had a tremendous amount of respect for him. Over the years, he had seen him face many situations and watched as Marshall escaped more than a few tight spots, emerging no worse for the wear. Sometimes Lee and their other brother Shaun were there to help him out of jams and sometimes Marshall handled things on his own. This time seemed a little different. Lee was worried, not so much because of what Marshall had explained to him, but because of what had yet to be revealed.

CHAPTER FIFTEEN

It was early afternoon when Marshall returned from town. He knew more than likely Trenay hadn't eaten anything since breakfast so he had stopped by his sister-in-law's bookstore/coffee shop and picked up some brownies and cookies and a few sandwiches from the diner at the edge of town. He had also gotten a few magazines he hoped Trenay would like.

When Marshall pulled up to the cabin he noticed all of the curtains had been closed, not the way he'd left them that morning. His heart sank. While he had hoped Trenay would begin to feel more comfortable and safe at his place, she had become more and more withdrawn with each passing day.

"Trenay," he called when he walked into the living room.

No answer.

"Trenay!" he called again with a little more urgency.

"I'm here," came the muffled response.

Trenay unlocked her bedroom door and came out to join Marshall. She was still wearing her bathrobe.

At a loss for yet another way to assure Trenay of her safety, Marshall continued to rack his brain for new ideas. He couldn't allow her present state of fear to shape how she would live the rest of her life. He had to do something and he had to do it quickly.

"Have you eaten?"

Trenay shrugged. "I had some coffee a little earlier. There's still some left if you want a cup."

Marshall looked at Trenay in her robe, shoulders slumped, hair mussed, wearing a look of utter defeat. He sat the bags down on the table and went around opening up the curtains to brighten up the room. He didn't like the idea of her being cooped up inside on such a beautiful summer day. Maybe if she got dressed and went outside in the sunshine she'd feel better. Warm, sunny days always put him in a good mood. Then Marshall had an idea. He grabbed a large tote from the pantry and began packing bottles of water, fruit, and few other items into the bag. When he finished he turned to Trenay and said, "Get dressed."

"No thanks. I don't feel like going anywhere right now."

Marshall placed the bag by the front door. "That wasn't a suggestion."

Trenay was sitting at the table staring into a cup of coffee. Hearing the change in Marshall's voice, she looked up. "What?"

"That wasn't a suggestion, Trenay," he repeated firmly. "I want you to get dressed. A pair of jeans, a t-shirt, and some comfortable shoes should be sufficient."

"Really, Marshall, I don't feel like being around people today. I just want to go back to bed for a little while."

Trenay got up from the table and placed her cup in the sink. She turned to go back to her room, avoiding looking at Marshall. She didn't know if he was upset or what, but she didn't have the energy to argue. As she brushed past him she felt a hand on her shoulder. Marshall turned her around to face him. Trenay closed her eyes and exhaled. She simply did not have the strength to persuade him to leave her in peace. All she wanted to do was sleep. Couldn't he leave her alone to do that?

"I'm sure you have something better to do," she said quietly.

"Look at me, Trenay."

Slowly, she opened her eyes. Expecting to see anger, instead, she saw concern.

"No, I don't have anything better to do. I'm needed right here. I'm worried about you. I'm worried about this," he said, motioning to the robe and her mussed hair. "Over the past week, I've watched you transform into someone I don't even know."

"At least you got that right. You *don't* know me, Marshall. You never did," she said harshly.

Refusing to back down, he continued, "That's not true and you know it. The first time we met you let me know in no uncertain terms that you were in charge and you knew what you were doing. You refused to let me intimidate you. When you thought someone had broken into your home, you did everything you could to make sure that would never happen again. And when I kissed you the night of the benefit I foolishly thought I was in control, but I couldn't have been more wrong. You nearly brought me to my knees that night, Trenay, and it wasn't just because of the kiss or how beautiful you looked, it was because of your confidence and the way you commanded my attention. That's when I knew that you were a force to be reckoned with."

"I'm not that person anymore."

"That couldn't be further from the truth."

"What do you want from me, Marshall?" she asked wearily.

"I want you to fight."

"How do I fight a ghost?" she asked as she let her shoulders slump as angry tears burned her eyes. "I have no idea who or what I'm fighting, and no matter how hard I try to figure it out I keep coming up with nothing. Nothing! I haven't hurt anyone but clearly, someone wants to hurt me. Tell me, how do I fight against that?"

"You fight by not becoming a victim. Don't let this defeat you. You have to push forward even when you don't feel like it. Look, I know this is hard to process right now but remember when I told you the first day we came here that I admired your strength? My opinion has not changed one bit." Marshall softened his voice and wiped Trenay's tears. "You're not powerless, so stop acting as if you are. Get angry and fight back."

"I told you, I don't know how," she said in a shaky voice.

"Get dressed. I'll show you."

CHAPTER SIXTEEN

Trenay followed Marshall down a path that lead into the wooded area surrounding his cabin. They continued along in silence walking away from the lake until the trail became narrower and the foliage denser. While the weather was warm and the sun strong the more heavily wooded area was cooler and the shade more inviting. She hoped they stayed out of the open where the sun shone bright and unyielding.

Swatting at flies and mosquitoes she trudged on. Resisting the temptation to complain, it seemed they were walking so far into the woods it might have been a good idea to leave a trail of breadcrumbs.

"How much farther?" she finally asked after what seemed like an eternity.

"We're almost there."

After walking a few more minutes they finally came to a clearing. Marshall stopped and began unpacking the tote, ignoring the puzzled look on Trenay's face. He proceeded to unpack bottles of water, a blanket, and a black bandana.

Trenay looked on not sure if she should offer to help or just go with the flow. Either way, she felt she could trust Marshall.

While he busied himself with the contents of the tote, Trenay looked around at her surroundings. Tall trees, dense shrubs, short trees, and more shrubs. Except for the clearing where they were standing, there wasn't much else to see.

"Okay," Marshall announced, "let's get started."

"Doing what?" she asked as she swatted a fly.

"Self-defense."

"Excuse me?"

Marshall ignored Trenay's obvious confusion. He walked over and handed her a can of insect repellent he had retrieved from the bag. "Self-defense, Trenay. I think part of the reason you've been so withdrawn is because you feel helpless. I want to help you gain your confidence back."

"With bottles of water, bug spray, and a scarf?" she asked sarcastically, wishing she was back at Marshall's, safe in her bedroom, cocooned in her robe and under a comforter.

Refusing to be discouraged, he continued, "We won't need a lot of equipment. I'm going to show you how to work with what you have available. By the way, you might want to go ahead and use that insect repellent. The mosquitoes get pretty bad in this part of the woods."

Trenay looked doubtful about Marshall's plan but applied the insect repellent to at least keep from being eaten up by mosquitoes.

"Whether you know it or not, you already have the instincts and the physical build of a fighter. You just need to tap into what you have inside and remember how to fight."

She raised her eyebrow. "Physical build, huh?"

"I don't mean like a heavyweight. More like a

flyweight," he said with a wink.

Over the next hour, Marshall showed Trenay how to use common things as weapons – keys, her shoe, fingernails. She practiced a series of punches and kicks he'd shown her, sometimes hitting a pillow and sometimes Marshall's open palm.

He taught her how to be in tune with her surroundings by blindfolding her and prompting her to recall seemingly insignificant items around her. He asked her about the things she noticed on the walk to the clearing. At first, she could only remember seeing tall trees, weeds, and shorter trees. Then, with some prodding, he was able to get her to remember the fallen tree that partially blocked the path and a secondary trail that he told her led back to the lake.

Sitting on a fallen log in the clearing, he also had her close her eyes and tune into specific sounds she heard in the woods.

When she did as he asked she was able to make out the sounds of crickets chirping, birds singing and calling out, and something scurrying into the woods that Marshall told her was probably a rabbit or a squirrel. They repeated this exercise until Marshall seemed satisfied Trenay had grasped the concept, the beginning stages at least. She needed more practice but a lot of progress had been made in a short period.

"Let's take a break," Marshall suggested when he noticed Trenay getting tired. He handed her a bottle of water and walked over to retrieve his bag of supplies. After spreading a blanket in the grassy area of the clearing, he motioned for her to sit down.

Without hesitation, Trenay took a seat on the blanket, enjoying the period of rest.

"You're strong. I like how you use your height to your advantage and you don't try to shrink into your body like I see some tall women doing. By the way, how tall are you?"

"Five-eight."

Trenay noticed Marshall rubbing a spot on his arm.

"What's wrong?"

"Whoever said girls don't hit hard, lied." He grimaced, pretending to be more hurt than he was.

"I'm sorry. I guess I got carried away. But in my defense, you told me to hit harder. I guess that'll teach you to be careful what you ask for," she said smiling mischievously.

He smiled too.

"Now what?" she asked, allowing herself to relax a little. She pretended she didn't find his smile absolutely charming. It wasn't easy. His easy manner and reassurance helped her to feel at ease, which in turn opened the door for her to experience the full effect of his charm.

"It's good to see light back in your eyes." Watching her as narrow streams of sunlight shone on her face she appeared to be in better spirits than when they left the cabin earlier. She seemed more like her old self, or at least as much of her old self as he knew about. He hoped she might be emerging out of her funk.

This was the Trenay he'd first met. The one whose smile made him readily smile in return. Whose beautiful eyes shone full of light. The woman who didn't back down and who made him want to kiss her for no other reason other than to taste her and feel her soft lips against his. *This* Trenay made his heart skip a beat.

But he knew he couldn't kiss her now or pull her into his arms the way he longed to. He had to resist the urge. Still very vulnerable, he never wanted it to seem like he was taking advantage of her. *But if things were different...*

Trenay smiled in spite of herself. If she dared admit it to Marshall and risk an "I told you so", she would say she felt better than she had in days. Maybe her mood shift did have something to do with the warm summer day, the physical exercise, and getting out of the house. Then again, maybe her lighthearted and playful mood also had more than a little to do with Marshall.

While Marshall had been busy searching for something in his bag, she wanted to go over and hug him. Of course, she didn't but she wanted to show her gratitude to him for giving her back a little piece of her old self. If he hadn't forced her to leave the cabin that afternoon she would have continued doing what she'd been doing for the past several days – sleeping for hours on end and allowing herself to sink deeper and deeper into despair.

At almost every turn, Marshall did something to surprise her, from their very first encounter right up to this afternoon. When she first met him the one word she would *not* have used to describe him was *gentleman*. Although, over time and on more than one occasion he had proven himself to be that and a whole lot more. Aside from his gruff and almost overpowering demeanor, he treated her with the kind of care and attention that she had never experienced before. *But why?* What did he have to gain?

Despite everything going on it surprised her that she had begun to notice a slight shift in her interactions with him. At first, she didn't want to think about it, but eventually, she started to pay a little more attention. She couldn't quite figure it out, but what had once been somewhat casual and unintentional now felt more personal - a lingering touch, a warm smile, a hand on her shoulder. Just yesterday, she had noticed a small vase with wildflowers on the table. These things were all small gestures but they somehow had become more intimate. Perhaps it could be her imagination toying with her or maybe her desperate need to feel something normal or to feel anything that didn't resemble fear. Tucking the observations away for another time she decided to enjoy the day and the time spent with Marshall, expecting nothing more and nothing less.

"Here." Marshall handed Trenay a sandwich wrapped in white deli paper and a bag of chips. "You need to eat. I haven't seen you eat much of anything these past few days. I was beginning to think you didn't like my cooking."

This time Trenay didn't refuse the offering of food. She ate the sandwich, chips, and even an apple that she found while rummaging through Marshall's bag. An afternoon of physical exertion had made her ravenous.

While he finished eating his sandwich, Marshall made small talk. He told Trenay stories about growing up in Benton Lake, the ups and downs of living in a small town, and the different places he'd lived over the past several years. He surprised her when he admitted no other place felt as comfortable or more like home than Benton Lake. She had pegged him as more of a city boy who liked to be surrounded by every modern convenience. Well, it wasn't the first time she had been wrong about Marshall and it probably wouldn't be the last.

He talked about a lot of other things, too, keeping the conversation light and fun, purposely avoiding the subject of the chaos that hovered over them like an ominous storm cloud.

"How long have you lived in Columbus?" she asked, wanting to prolong the feeling of peace and contentment and needing desperately to think about something normal.

"I lived in Cincinnati before moving to Columbus last year. What about you? Are you a native Buckeye?"

"Yep. Born and raised. I grew up near Cleveland. Before I was born, my parents lived in southern Florida. My dad's job transferred him to Cleveland and my parents stayed there until they both retired a few years ago."

"Siblings?"

"Nope, I'm an only child. You mentioned that you have family here. Do your parents live nearby?"

"My dad and one of my brothers and his family live in town. I have another brother who just moved to North Carolina. My mother passed away several years ago."

"I'm sorry."

"Thank you. She was a real lady which couldn't have been easy with a house full of men."

After they finished their picnic meal, Marshall stood up and pulled Trenay to her feet.

"Ugh, more work," she complained. "Can't a girl get a break?"

"You just had one!"

"Can you at least pick some easier things for me to try that are little less Bruce Lee inspired? I have a feeling I'm going to be sore tomorrow."

"All right, how about I show you a few more moves that I think you'll find simple and effective, and then we'll call it a day?"

She nodded.

"There are several maneuvers you can use when someone grabs you from behind. I'm going to show you one of the simple ones."

Trenay stood with her back to Marshall, listening closely as he gave her explicit instructions.

"I'm going to pretend to grab you. For the sake of demonstrating this move, I'm not going to use a lot of force. Plus, I don't want to end up with a black eye or broken jaw, or worse." He put his arm around her neck applying just enough pressure to make it seem somewhat realistic. "Take my arm and do this," he instructed, demonstrating a defensive move.

"Like this?" Trenay reached over her shoulder; using both hands she grabbed Marshall's hand.

"Yes. Now stomp on my foot with your heel and twist my arm. Get a good hold on my arm. Remember, if I'm an attacker, I'm not going to stay still until you get your technique down. You've got to act and you have to do it quickly."

Trenay attempted to do as she was instructed but

somehow made an awkward move and took a misstep. Instead of twisting, the way Marshall had instructed her to she turned the wrong way and ended up facing him. She remembered to stomp his foot but missed and found that she was quickly losing her balance. As she tried to regain her balance, it was obvious she was failing in her attempt and she held on to Marshall's arm as she felt herself falling. Marshall reached for Trenay's free arm caught her and made a slight turn with his body, but he too lost his footing and in what seemed like slow motion but in actuality was mere seconds, they both fell.

"*Oomph...*" Marshall grunted when he hit the ground. Thankfully, he had landed on a softer grassy patch instead of on the harder ground. Regaining his equilibrium Marshall smiled when he realized Trenay landed squarely on top of him, albeit with her eyes tightly shut.

"Are you all right?" he asked relishing how good she felt in his arms as a surge of desire instantly coursed through his body.

Slowly opening her eyes she realized what had just happened. She had landed safely in Marshall's arms and on top of his broad chest and tone body. Breathing heavily she felt her breast pressed against his chest, her legs tangled in his, and an unmistakable bulge that she knew wasn't house keys or a wallet. Scrambling to get up, she apologized. "Sorry about that. I guess I made a wrong move."

Slowly rising to his feet Marshall brushed off his clothes. "Not necessarily," he remarked, his voice husky with desire. He cleared his throat and took a deep breath.

"Do you want to try again?"

Trenay nodded. "I'll be more careful this time."

If the result was the same, he wouldn't mind if she never learned the move.

However, after they practiced the maneuver a few more times, he seemed satisfied with Trenay's effort, and eventually, she was able to successfully escape his grasp. At that point, he kept his promise. He could tell she was getting tired. So was he, not so much from the physical exertion, but more from trying to keep his desire for her in check. She didn't make it easy. Every time he approached her from the back, she pressed her body into his before grabbing his arm. The technique was correct but it had some serious side effects. *Sheer torture.*

For the record, he considered today a good day, a really good day to be exact. He had managed to get Trenay out of her bedroom and out of the cabin for a few hours. In the process, she successfully ran through the series of drills he had designed for her with much more determination than he had expected. She wasn't quite ready for the mixed martial arts arena, but soon she'd be able to have a few solid self-defense techniques under her belt. He hoped that she would never need them.

Marshall was also pleased that he had gotten Trenay to relax, that is, until the awkward fall. He couldn't tell if she had been more embarrassed or he more aroused. Damn if she didn't feel good in his arms.

Gathering their lunch trash and other items, they started the walk back to the cabin. Marshall was in good spirits. He had made progress with Trenay today. Slowly she was regaining her confidence and he could see an inkling of her old self-returning.

Walking along the trail back to the cabin Marshall shared points of interest from his childhood years – the tree his brother dared him to climb, resulting in a nasty fall and broken arm; the spot where he ran into a skunk when night hiking with his buddies; the tree where he carved his and Janette McClure's initials, declaring his undying love for her at twelve years old.

"First crushes," Trenay said. "I don't know about you, but I'm glad those kinds of crushes are only temporary. I can remember doing some crazy things to get Miles Lawson to notice me."

Marshall laughed. "Tell me about it. The twelve-year-old me who was madly in love with Janette was more than a little crazy. I couldn't eat, sleep, or do anything besides think about her. I saved up my allowance for a whole month to buy her a present for her thirteenth birthday. And guess what."

Stopping just at the edge of the clearing in front of the cabin, Marshall heard Trenay inhale sharply. Icy fingers gripped his arm as she stopped cold. Following her gaze, he, too, saw the car parked in his driveway.

CHAPTER SEVENTEEN

"Trenay, I'd like you to meet my brother, Lee."

Still shaking, Trenay fought to pull herself together as she extended her hand. But she was too shaken up to do anything more than that. After exchanging forced pleasantries, she excused herself and left Marshall alone with his brother.

"Why didn't you tell me you were coming out today?"

"Calm down. I didn't think it was a big deal. I'm sorry I didn't call."

"Yeah, I'm sorry, too."

"Look, I said I was sorry. Really. I didn't realize until I saw the look on Trenay's face that I messed up. Man, she looked like she saw a ghost and her hands were as cold as ice."

Marshall motioned for his brother to join him on the couch. Offering him a bottle of water, Marshall leaned back against the plush cushion and sighed. "It has taken everything I could think of to get her to trust me and feel safe here. She's been through a lot. "

"Like what?"

"I told you already – the pictures, the stalker. Remember?"

"Yeah, I know what you told me, but I can't help thinking there's more. I don't think I've ever seen you like this."

Marshall shrugged off his brother's comment. "I don't know what you're talking about."

"I think you do. I thought you were going to hit me when you walked in the door. You acted as if I was the one threatening Trenay. I don't think I've ever seen you this protective of anyone. Are you sure there's not something else going on here?"

"Change the subject, Lee."

Judging by the sharp change in his brother's demeanor, Lee knew he had hit a nerve and a raw one at that. Knowing his brother the way that he did, choosing to continue down this path would prove to be counterproductive. He decided to steer the conversation in a slightly different direction or risk alienating him.

"Get a grip on your feelings, big brother. You're not going to be any good to Trenay like this."

Marshall gave his brother a warning look. He didn't know what Lee *thought* he knew, but he'd had enough of his prying. "Like what?"

"Getting emotionally involved with her."

Lee walked over to the kitchen table and retrieved a manila envelope from his bag. Tossing it on the kitchen table, he turned and took one last glance at his brother before leaving.

***

Marshall sat at the kitchen table with his head in his hands. He wanted to be angry with Lee for forcing him to confront his feelings for Trenay. But if he was totally honest with himself, something he had not been up to this point, he could only be angry with himself. Against his

Alicia Wiggins

better judgment, he had let his feelings for Trenay get the best of him.

He prayed those same feelings wouldn't cause harm to the one person he needed to protect.

***

"I'm sorry. Your brother must think I'm a basket case."

Marshall turned away from the stove when he heard Trenay enter the kitchen. He motioned for her to sit down at the table. "No, he doesn't think that. He understands the situation you're in."

Trenay sat down heavily in the chair. "He does? *I* don't even understand it."

Marshall sat a plate of food in front of Trenay and placed one across from her for himself. His heart grew heavy when he noticed how much she had retreated into her shell.

"Remember what I asked you to do earlier?"

Staring off into the distance, she shook her head. "You've asked me to do a lot of things today."

Marshall reached across the table and took Trenay's hand in his. He needed her to focus, to resist falling back into victim mode.

"Trenay, what did I say you had to do above everything else?"

"Fight," she said quietly.

"Yes, sweetheart, fight. You made a lot of progress today. You'll make even more progress tomorrow, and the next day, and so on."

Trenay pulled her hand away. Marshall was strong. She

wasn't. She couldn't so easily replace her fear with his strength. She sighed heavily. "How long do we keep this up? You have a life. You have people who love you and depend on you. No one is trying to scare you into hiding or is stalking you. Be honest with yourself, Marshall, you can't babysit me forever."

"You're right. I'm not the victim here, but neither are you. I know you're afraid but you don't have to face this mess alone. I'm here for as long as you need me, period. How long? Well, that's for me to decide and not for you to worry about. I'm going to make sure you get your life back. I promise."

"How can you make that kind of promise? You don't even know who or what we're dealing with."

"That's not entirely true. My brother dropped off some information from the investigator." Marshall got up and retrieved the envelope from the counter where he had placed it after his brother left. He hadn't looked at the contents yet but thought now would be a good time.

Taking a seat at the table, he pulled out the documents and handed them over to Trenay.

She gingerly took the papers from Marshall, wanting to see what was inside but at the same time afraid to come face to face with the situation that drove her from her home and her life.

Marshall watched as Trenay scanned the papers, trying to gauge her reaction.

After a couple of minutes, she straightened the stack of papers and placed them back in the envelope.

"This didn't help at all," she said sadly. "I know the

police are doing everything they can to get to the bottom of this, but I didn't see anything other than some reports from my neighbors and colleagues which basically stated that they didn't notice anything out of the ordinary. Pretty much the same thing I told the police."

"Let's be optimistic. Something will break soon. My brother knows the investigator assigned to this case. He said he's really good and extremely thorough. Let's trust the police to do their job. In the meantime, try not to get discouraged."

Trenay wanted to share in Marshall's optimism but it was too hard. No matter how she approached her situation the only thing she came up with were more unanswered questions.

"Easier said than done," she replied.

Marshall sighed as he watched her walk back to her room and heard the door close behind her.

CHAPTER EIGHTEEN

The day after Lee's unannounced visit Marshall had to practically drag Trenay out of the cabin. But after getting her to understand that her strength was her biggest weapon and the more strength and confidence she gained the less power her adversary had over her, she reluctantly agreed to continue with the lessons. Unfortunately, it rained nearly all-day and early into the evening. That morning they had barely made it halfway along the trail before the sky turned dark and opened up, sending them running back to the cabin amidst a huge downpour. The weather forecast predicted rain for most of the day. So since they weren't able to practice outdoors Marshall and Trenay did what they could inside.

"I hate that it rained all day and we couldn't be outside."

Marshall handed Trenay another plate to dry. He didn't mind the rain. In fact, he had enjoyed their day inside, talking, listening to the rain, and watching movies.

"At least it cooled off. I don't know if I could stand another ninety-degree day with above ninety percent humidity."

Trenay finished putting away the last of the dinner dishes. "So what do you want to do this evening?" she asked.

"Hmm…good question. We could watch another

movie."

"Nah."

"Want to sit outside on the porch for a while?"

Trenay shrugged, not committing one way or another. Having gotten a taste of being outside in the woods the day before had felt good. Today she felt cooped up because of the rain and didn't necessarily want to be confined indoors if she didn't have to, but the options were limited. She wanted to take a walk but since it had gotten dark that no longer seemed an option.

Just then Marshall had an idea. He left the room and after a few minutes returned with a flashlight, a bag, and a blanket.

"Are we going camping?" Trenay asked jokingly.

"Nope, something better." Marshall plunked everything down on the table and went to the cupboard. He seemed to be searching for something. Finally, locating what he needed he pulled out a package of graham crackers and a plastic container with something white inside.

"Let's go down to the lake," he announced.

"It's dark."

Marshall held up the flashlight. "We'll use this. Besides, the moon is bright enough that we'll have plenty of light once we get out into the open."

"You don't think it's going to be too cool or too wet?" she asked already warming up to the idea.

Marshall stopped packing the bag long enough to chide Trenay. "Come on. Where's your sense of adventure?"

Trenay smiled. Marshall probably was tired of being cooped up inside, too. She gave in without too much arm-twisting and helped him finish packing the bag.

Walking along the trail Trenay carried the blanket, a tarp, and the bag of goodies. Marshall carried a bundle of wood and a few other things to make a fire.

When they reached a clearing, Marshall found a reasonably dry area for which to lay out the blanket. However, to be on the safe side, he put down the waterproof tarp first. After that, it didn't take long for him to build a fire.

"Comfortable?" he asked taking a seat close to Trenay on the blanket and looking out over the lake.

She nodded.

For a while, the two of them sat quietly listening to the fire crackling and the night sounds while enjoying the magic of perfect summer night.

"This is nice," Trenay remarked.

Marshall nodded.

"I love how peaceful the lake looks with the moon shimmering over the surface. It almost looks almost like a painting."

"I guess I never really paid much attention before. My brothers and I used to come here a lot with our dad to go camping. We only paid attention to the lake when we were fishing, swimming, or out in our boat."

"Sounds like all the typical things little boys like to do."

"And girls. Some of my girl cousins were better than my brothers and me at fishing. When we were younger we'd spend all day fishing and pretending we were explorers. One time my brother Shaun decided he was going to hunt rabbits and squirrels. So he made a slingshot out of some rubber bands and a stick."

"Did it work?"

Marshall chuckled at the memory. "No. He only managed to tick my dad off when he accidentally shot out the window of his truck."

"Funny. Despite that little mishap, the rest of it sounded like fun. My parents took me camping once. I don't remember much about it except when I asked them why we had to sleep outside."

"What? You don't like sleeping outside under the stars? Catching your dinner and cooking over an open fire?" he asked reading the expression on Trenay's face and already knowing the answer.

"Sorry. City girl here. To be honest I've been wondering this whole time what you're going to do with the graham crackers and the other stuff in the container you brought. Seems like an odd snack."

Marshall turned to face Trenay with an exaggerated look of disbelief. "You're kidding, right?"

She shook her head.

"Are you telling me you've never made s'mores?"

"You got me," she admitted sheepishly.

"Well, we need to correct that right now!"

Marshall dug into the bag and pulled out the graham crackers and container of marshmallows. He broke a graham cracker in half and handed one piece to Trenay. "Here," he said, handing her two fat marshmallows and a stick. "Roast those over the fire until they are golden brown. The trick is to get them gooey and melty until they're almost ready to fall off the stick."

"Is *melty* a word?" she asked walking over to the fire.

"It is today."

"Now what?" she asked after a few minutes of meticulously turning her marshmallow over the flames to get it gooey and brown the way Marshall had instructed.

Marshall motioned for her to sit on the blanket. He broke off a piece of a chocolate bar, placed it on her graham cracker, told her to place her hot marshmallows on top and he sandwiched the whole thing with the other graham cracker.

"Go ahead. You get the first bite," he announced, presenting the gooey treat to Trenay.

Leaning forward she tried to take a bite without getting chocolate and marshmallow on her mouth. She failed.

Marshall took the s'more and devoured the rest of it in two bites.

"You like?" he asked, licking melted chocolate from his fingers.

Trenay nodded enthusiastically. "That was sinfully delicious. Can we make another one?"

"See, you want *some more*? S'mores. That's where the name comes from."

After making and eating two more s'mores Trenay fell back on the blanket with a huge smile on her face. "So that's what I've been missing by not going camping?"

Marshall looked down at Trenay. She looked happy,

content, and extremely kissable. He was pretty sure she had no idea how beautiful she looked in the silvery moonlight with the glow from the fire illuminating her face.

Leaning up on her elbows, she looked at Marshall with concern. "What's wrong? Do I have chocolate and marshmallow on my face?" she asked, licking her lips.

Marshall reached out and wiped a little smudge of chocolate from her chin, just below her lip. His finger only grazed her skin for a fraction of a moment but it was enough contact to cause butterflies to flutter in his stomach.

Once again this woman had reduced him to being a flustered twelve-year-old boy. He wanted to say something but the words wouldn't come out.

"Thank you," Trenay said.

"For what?" he asked huskily, wishing Trenay didn't look so beautiful and that he wasn't so attracted to her.

"For this evening. I had fun. And thanks to you I'll also have a life-long addiction to s'mores."

After a few minutes more of sitting by the fire and enjoying their solitude, Marshall checked his watch. As much as he wanted to stay with Trenay by the lake, it was getting late and they needed to head back home. There was still a lot he wanted to teach Trenay to help her feel safe, and he liked that they had developed a bit of a routine. He had learned that she was a creature of habit and it seemed to make her feel better to have an established schedule.

After they gathered and packed their things Marshall poured water and dirt over the fire. As the embers were extinguished he wondered how he would ever douse the flame Trenay had ignited in him.

CHAPTER NINETEEN

For more than a week, Marshall and Trenay followed the same routine – pack a lunch, have a light breakfast, and then walk through the woods to the spot where they practiced more self-defense techniques.

The one thing Marshall harped on with Trenay was paying attention to her surroundings. She struggled at first, only noticing the obvious – a fallen tree, a patch of wildflowers, or birds singing. Eventually, with some coaxing, she began to pay closer attention; partly because she knew Marshall would quiz her about it and because she felt it would prove to be essential to her overall feeling of safety, not just in Benton Lake, but where ever she happened to be.

After their sessions, they would typically come back to the cabin, have an early dinner, watch a movie, or sit out on the porch and talk until it was time for bed.

Today, Marshall had something different planned.

Trenay stepped into the kitchen dressed and ready for breakfast. Wearing jeans, a t-shirt, and tennis shoes, she was prepared to embark on another lesson.

"No coffee?" she asked looking over at the counter. "If we're out I can make tea."

"No, we're not out. I wanted to do something different today."

"Are we foraging through the woods for our food this

morning?" she asked, only half-joking since she didn't see or smell anything cooking on the stove.

"No, I thought we might go out. There's a diner I'd like to take you to for breakfast. They have the best-"

"In town?" she asked before he could finish. He had to be kidding, she hoped.

Prepared for the opposition, Marshall walked over to Trenay and stood looking down at her, wanting to pull her into his arms, letting her feel his strength, but hesitating because he didn't know if he would ever be able to let her go.

"It's going to be all right. No one in town knows you. It will be a chance to get out for a little while. Aren't you sick of my cooking by now?" he asked smiling, hoping she would return the smile.

"We go out every day when we go into the woods to practice."

"True. But this is one more step to regaining your sense of security, being around other people."

Trenay chewed her lower lip. She wanted to say no, and she knew Marshall would honor her feelings, but she also knew she couldn't hide from the world forever. She had to start living again and that meant venturing outside of her comfort zone, which is what Marshall's cabin had become.

"I like your cooking," she said quietly. "And I like being here. It feels safe. But I also understand why you want me to do this. I won't be a victim." She closed her eyes and took a deep breath. "Let's get breakfast."

This time Marshall didn't hold back. He pulled Trenay

gently into his arms. He felt her body melt into his and she clung to him in a way that made it difficult for him to let go, but he had to, although not completely. Holding her at arm's length he said, "You, *we*, can do this. It's a big step, I know, but I won't let you out of my sight. Okay?"

Reluctantly, she nodded and allowed Marshall to lead the way.

***

The town of Benton Lake had a few more amenities than Trenay had imagined, making it a little less like the small farm town she had pictured in her mind. Looking down a few of the side streets they passed she noticed well-manicured lawns, tree-lined streets, and older, well-kept homes. Down the main drag, she spotted a salon and day spa, a vintage clothing boutique, a sprawling grocery/department store, and a quaint bookstore and coffee shop. She had seen very little of the town when they first arrived in Benton Lake, although she doubted she would have remembered any of it even if she had seen it.

Pointing to a building on his right, Marshall said, "That's my sister-in-law's bookstore. I can't say that I'm much of a reader, but her coffee shop has the best variety of coffee and teas and hands down the best cookies in the tri-county area. When you're up to it, I'd like for you to meet my brother's family."

Trenay nodded and continued looking at the people walking to and fro going about their business. They all looked completely and utterly harmless – a mother pushing a stroller, two men dressed in suits going into the bank, and a group of teenagers skateboarding on the sidewalk – could she trust her judgment the way she used to? Was everyone as harmless as they appeared?

They continued to drive a little further until Marshall pulled his truck into a semi-crowded parking lot. The building sitting in front of them looked pretty nondescript except for the large plain lettering spelling out the name of the restaurant and featuring a picture of a dancing hamburger and what looked like a singing hot dog. Describing the picture as "cheesy" would have been an understatement. A message underneath the hamburger and hot dog read, "Hungry? EOM!"

"This is it. The best diner in town," he announced. Sensing Trenay's hesitation he turned off the engine and waited until she was ready before he made a move to get out of the truck.

"The best in town, huh? Doesn't seem very busy. Uh…since when do hamburgers and hotdogs have arms and legs?" she asked nodding toward the musical sandwiches. "And what does that message mean? Why would they ask if you're hungry then end it with EOM? Doesn't that stand for *end of message*? I don't get it."

Marshall smiled. Used to the cartoonish pictures on the front of the diner he didn't consider it odd until someone not familiar with them pointed it out. "It's all part of the charm," he assured her. "EOM doesn't stand for *end of message*. In this case, it's supposed to mean *eat out more*, preferable right here. Anyway, I'm glad they're not very busy right now. I think we managed to miss the breakfast rush. The only people left are the retirees and the folks who are playing hooky from work."

Trenay still hadn't made a move to get out of the truck so Marshall got out and came around to her side. He opened the door and held out his hand.

She sat in the truck willing herself to get out. *Unbuckle the seat belt and swing your legs around.* That's all she had to do. There was nothing to be nervous about. Marshall wouldn't have brought her anywhere that wasn't safe.

She felt her heart racing. All she had to do was to make a move. Somehow, it proved to be a much bigger effort than she imagined.

"Come on, Trenay. I told you, there is nothing to be afraid of. I won't let you out of my sight. You're in good hands."

Trenay looked around the parking lot, at the building, and then back at Marshall. Searching for reassurance, she managed to smile despite her fear, because what she saw on Marshall's face was more than enough to give her the courage she needed. As she unbuckled her seat belt, swung her legs around, and reached out to take his hand, she realized for now that was all she needed.

***

Marshall had not exaggerated one bit. After nursing a cup of coffee and assuring herself that everyone from the elderly couple sitting a few tables over to the gruff sounding cook who occasionally popped out of the kitchen to greet the regulars to the waitress with the beehive hairdo was all pretty harmless, Trenay finally began to relax. Soon after, she had no choice but to give in to the sumptuous smells circling all around her, which were causing some serious hunger pangs. After briefly glancing at the menu she couldn't decide what she wanted to eat. At the advice of the waitress, she ordered the weekday special, which consisted of three banana, apple pecan, or blueberry pancakes, ham, bacon, or sausage, and a side of seasonal fruit. On a whim, Trenay ordered banana pancakes, deciding to try something she'd never had before. Curious about the seasonal fruit, the waitress told her it was a mixed array of berries and melons from local farms. She promised Trenay she wouldn't be disappointed.

She wasn't. The side bowl of fruit, which accompanied the rest of her breakfast, contained the juiciest and most tasty strawberries, raspberries, honeydew, and blackberries she'd ever eaten.

"Good?" Marshall asked as he watched Trenay devour her food.

"Uh-hum," she responded between bites. "These pancakes are really good. I think they may be my new favorite thing."

"I won't say I told you so."

To which Trenay answered by making a face and swiping one of his sausage links. "Then don't."

After the waitress cleared their plates Marshall settled back in his seat while he enjoyed another cup of coffee. He noticed Trenay still looked up every time someone entered or exited the diner, noted by the dinging bell over the door.

Marshall had purposely selected a booth at the back of the restaurant and placed Trenay facing the door. He didn't want her to feel boxed in or have her back to the door.

"Do you want anything else?" he asked. What he really wanted to know, he didn't ask.

"Not really," she responded with a sigh.

"Are you sighing because you're content or is there another reason?"

"Both, I guess."

"Care to explain?"

Trenay looked up when the bell over the door clanged. It was a middle-aged couple exiting who had been sitting at the counter. The woman had ordered the same meal as Trenay but she had ordered her eggs scrambled instead of over easy. The woman hadn't finished her fruit, the man with her had. Before Marshall's training, she would never have noticed or cared about people sitting in a diner eating breakfast. She wasn't sure if she liked being this aware of her surroundings, but she knew she would never be able to be as unaware as she had once been. So much had changed in such a short time, she thought wearily. In this case, change wasn't necessarily a good thing.

"It's not just one or two things. It seems as if I have a thousand thoughts going through my head and I am struggling to sort them all out."

"Who said you had to?"

"Me. I'm struggling to balance this," she said, looking around the diner and waving her hand. "This, here today with you, is nice. But it's not real. Being with you at your cabin is nice, too. But again, it's not real. Being away from my job feels strange. I'm not used to doing nothing. I need to be busy. I need for my life to have some structure. I like working and I miss it. I feel like, like…I don't even know how to describe exactly what I'm feeling."

"Disconnected?"

Trenay shrugged. "I guess that's as good a word as any to describe my situation and jumbled up feelings."

"I understand. Really, I do. I don't know what I can do about your job situation but all of this right now – staying at my place and something as simple as enjoying a meal together – *is* real."

"Maybe I shouldn't have said it wasn't real. It just feels strange, that's all. If I was back home, I would be preparing for a meeting or presentation or reading emails. I'd be doing something productive. I wouldn't be kicked back in a diner sipping coffee and checking out every single person who steps through the door."

Marshall did understand, but he didn't know what else to say. He decided to simply listen; hoping Trenay would feel better once she got some things off her chest.

"Look, I don't mean to sound ungrateful. I am very grateful for everything you've done and for everything you have sacrificed to help me. If I haven't told you lately, thank you. When this is all over, I know I'm going to owe you big time –"

"What?" Marshall interrupted her.

"I'm going to owe you. Trust me; I don't have a problem with that. I understand that you've put everything on hold for me. Not many people would do that. I fully intend to make it up to you, once I figure out how."

Trenay looked up again, when the bell over the door chimed, completely missing the expression that suddenly and completely darkened Marshall's face.

"Are you ready to go?" he asked tersely.

She nodded and followed Marshall out to his truck.

On the ride home, neither of them spoke very much, both lost in their thoughts. When they reached the cabin, Trenay went to her room and closed the door. Marshall sat on the steps of the porch for a while wondering how and why he felt the way he did. It was as if he'd been kicked in the gut. Clearly, Trenay didn't understand how what she said in the diner had affected him. He didn't know if he felt more angry or hurt.

Going inside to retrieve his keys he quickly scribbled a note and drove off, putting some much-needed distance between him and Trenay.

CHAPTER TWENTY

Perfect. Anyone who knew Trenay Bradley would likely describe her in that manner. Perfect job. Perfect life.

Not for much longer. Not when he was finished with her.

Sitting on the bed in the dismal motel room, he wondered if she was enjoying her perfect life right now. How could she? Thanks to him, her life had been turned inside out.

Sometimes you don't miss what you have until it's gone.

He knew she was in hiding. Unfortunately, he didn't know where. He couldn't be sure but he'd be willing to bet Trenay's life wasn't the same in hiding as it had been when she went freely about her daily activities oblivious to everything and everyone around her.

What must that be like? So safe and secure nothing harmful would ever touch you.

No worries though. It was simply a matter of time before he would find her. A little slip up by someone would be all he needed. She couldn't stay away forever. Sooner or later she would have to come back home, get back to work, and be right where he needed her to be.

Then it would be time for little Miss Perfect to see what life is like when everything isn't handed to you on a silver platter or comes neatly wrapped up in a secure little bundle.

The cold, hard truths of the world had proven over

and over that life isn't always perfect or neatly packaged.

At least it wasn't for me.

There are disappointments and times when you have to fend for yourself because there's no one there to help you. For some people, life isn't always fair or beautiful or filled with wonderful memories.

Unlike Trenay, my life would never be described as golden. I didn't have the charmed life she had.

Looking at the various newspaper clippers chronicling Trenay's graduation from college, articles from her school newspapers regarding her induction into various academic honor societies and clubs, and highlighting her outstanding community service, it was enough to make a grown man ill.

Trenay had been a child of privilege. Her path had been cleared of all hurdles, allowing her to be the successful woman people saw today.

How would she have turned out if she'd had my life?

If everyone had the kind of life she had, the world would be a wonderful place.

The sound of hollow laughter echoed throughout the sparsely furnished room.

Enough!

Let Trenay see the world as it was, without privilege, without people paving a smooth pathway ensuring success, and without parents who doted on you and gave in to your every whim.

Watching as the stack of clippings fell to the floor signaled the need for a break. He was getting worked up about this and needed to keep his hatred in check. There was too much at stake to lose control now. Ultimately staying focused would prove to be the key to success. And success was the ultimate goal. But this time the measure of success would not be weighed against anything Trenay Bradley had done, but ironically what would be done to her.

***

"Is that your complete list of suspects?"

Detective Prosser nodded.

"Anyone standing out from the pack?"

"Sorry to say, the one person who has the most to gain by destroying Trenay Bradley's reputation is recovering from heart surgery. I seriously doubt that he had the wherewithal or strength to pull off the fire or would have been able to place himself in the strategic places around her house or follow her for the length of time it took to take all of these pictures."

"But you still have him on your list."

Detective Prosser rubbed the stubble on his chin and looked at his colleague with concern and frustration. "I'm just having a hard time ruling him out. I have discovered some pretty shady activity that he's involved in and who's to say he didn't pay someone to do what he couldn't?"

"True. What about the other suspects on your list?"

"Not actual suspects but there's an ex-boyfriend who turned out to be squeaky clean, a few civil servants who were less than thrilled with the mayor's appointment of Miss Bradley, and a couple of nut jobs who have confessed to practically every case we've opened in the past five years. So basically I don't have any suspects that look good enough to be more than a person of interest."

"So where does this odd list of non-suspects and the evidence lead you?"

"Sadly, down a road to nowhere."

CHAPTER TWENTY-ONE

"I cannot believe her!" Marshall paced back and forth, pausing only when he needed to articulate yet another point. "She acts as if I'm running some kind of *service*. What kind of price tag does she think I'm putting on my *services*? Am I supposed to be keeping a tab?"

Lee had seen his brother upset before, but not quite like this. He didn't even try to get a word in edgewise.

"Room and board, seventy-five dollars a day. Laundry, ten dollars a load?"

"Seems kind of low on the laundry. Women are picky about how they want their things washed. You know, separating colors, the special way to handle delicates, and making sure to put fabric softener in at the right time. I would bump that figure up by at least five bucks."

Marshall stopped pacing and turned toward his brother, who was doing everything within his power to keep from saying "I told you so".

"What's with the smug look and the jokes?"

Finally, unable to contain himself any longer, Lee gave in to his need to smile, which irritated his brother to no end. After a moment, Lee pulled himself together and tried to take things more seriously.

"I'm sorry," Lee said, still smiling.

"Yes, Lee, you are pretty *sorry*. I don't know how you find any of this funny."

"Come on, man. Under a completely different set of circumstances, this would be kind of comical. Believe me, I know this is serious business, but this woman has you all tied up in knots simply because she feels as if she owes you a debt of gratitude and you don't like it. She wants to repay your kindness. Hmm, imagine that. How many uncaring, ungrateful, gold-digging women have you dated over the years? Let's look at this from my point of view for just a minute."

"I would but I don't think I could get my head that far up my a-"

"Uncle Marshall!" exclaimed a small-excited voice.

Marshall turned his attention away from his brother and toward the patio door. His sour mood changed immediately the moment he saw his young nephew running toward him. Scooping him up in one swift motion and lifting him over his head, Marshall spun him around, kissed him on the forehead, gave him a *noogie*, and placed the giggling child back down to the ground.

"Uh, where are your clothes, champ?"

Marshall's nephew looked around nervously and then back at the patio door before answering.

"He's supposed to be on his way to take a bath," remarked Katrice.

"I'm coming, Mom, but Uncle Marshall is here and I just wanted to say hi."

Marshall couldn't help smiling at his young nephew clad only his tidy *whities*.

"Inside, mister," his mother ordered.

Looking as if he was heading to the gallows, Taj

reluctantly headed inside for his bath. He didn't see why he had to take a bath *every* day but knew better than to argue with his mother.

"Hey, champ, if your mom says it's okay, stop back out and give me a hug before you go to bed."

"Okay!" he exclaimed excitedly. "Will you tell me a story, too?" Stealing a sideways glance at his mother, he added, "I mean, if Mom says it's all right."

"Will do," Marshall promised, winking in Katrice's direction. Sometimes when he visited around bedtime Marshall liked to make up stories of adventure for his nephew. There were times when, at Taj's urging, the stories would get a little wild.

"Nothing too crazy or scary, Uncle Marshall. We want to make sure all little boys sleep in their beds tonight."

"No scary stories tonight, Mom," Marshall assured his sister-in-law.

Marshall sat down on the chaise lounge beside his brother. "I can't believe how much he's grown."

"Yeah, he's a little scamp. Don't let the cute face and dimples fool you though. He gives us a run for our money."

"After I read Taj a story I'll stop in and see the baby. You don't think I'll wake her, do you? I don't want to imagine what Katrice will do to me if that happens."

"Are you kidding? Lily sleeps like a rock."

Marshall leaned back and stretched on the lounger. He remained silent for a while, mulling the conversation he'd had with Trenay over and over in his head, only breaking the silence with an occasional sigh.

"What am I going to do about Trenay?" he said finally.

"What do you want to do?"

"It's not about what I want to do. I need to know what I *should* do."

"Care to hear what I think?"

"I asked you, didn't I?"

"I just want to make sure you *really* want to hear what I have to say."

Marshall took a swig from his bottle of beer. It had grown warm but he didn't care. He had more pressing things on his mind. All kidding aside, at least from Lee's perspective, he braced himself for what he knew would be a frank assessment from his brother.

"From the outside looking in and from what you've told me about Trenay including everything that's going on with her, I would say things are pretty complicated."

Marshall turned to his brother and gave him a blank stare. "That's your assessment? Are you serious? Please tell me you've got something besides that. Somebody sure wasted a lot of money on law school."

"You didn't ask for legal advice, Marshall. When you came over here tonight ranting and raving about Trenay feeling as though she owed you a debt of gratitude because you're hiding her at your cabin, I thought you were going to hit the roof."

"First of all, I'm not *hiding* her. I'm just allowing the smoke to clear and giving time for the police to do their job so she can go back home and back to a normal life."

"And out of your life?"

This time when Marshall spoke it was with anger

instead of sarcasm. "You think I'm taking advantage of this situation because of how I feel about Trenay? You think I want her to feel obligated to me and that I'm afraid for her to leave?"

"I don't know. Are you?"

"No!"

"Are you sure?"

"I said no, Lee! Yes, I'll admit it. I have feelings for Trenay."

"Strong feelings," interjected Lee.

"Okay, strong feelings," Marshall conceded. "But I don't want her to think I have some hidden motive for trying to protect her."

"I'm going to tell you what a wise man once told me: Lay it all out for her. Tell her how you feel and see what happens."

"I can't do that."

"Why not?"

"Under normal circumstances, I would. These aren't normal circumstances."

"Well, I'd say you have your work cut out for you. Somehow, someway you're going to have to help Trenay regain her bearings. Once she does the two of you are going to have to figure out how to deal with the feelings you have for each other, and not necessarily in that order. You're falling in love with her, Marshall. You know it, I know it, and Trenay probably knows it, too. You'd better face it and deal with it, regardless of the circumstances or prepare to be pissed off every time she relegates you to being   her   bodyguard."

CHAPTER TWENTY-TWO

What am I doing? Why am I pushing away the one person who has stuck his neck out for me?

Trenay leaned against the kitchen counter and stared out the window into the darkness. She knew her comment about paying Marshall back had struck a nerve. But how else could she gain control of the situation? She had to make it all seem businesslike and far less personal than where it was heading.

Spending time with Marshall had started to become way too comfortable. Yes, she missed her life and her work, but she had also begun to grow accustomed to their modified life. She liked Benton Lake, the little she'd seen of it. She felt comfortable at Marshall's cabin and she adored the quiet serenity of the lake and woods surrounding the cabin. She particularly liked how safe, protected, and cared for she felt, all thanks to him.

The way Marshall looked after her was something she had never experienced before. Attentive, kind, funny, tender, and considerate were just some of his nicer qualities. Stubborn, opinionated, and bossy were a few of his not so nice ones. But even when he exhibited those qualities she didn't particularly care for, she knew it was all for her wellbeing.

She had more than an inclination that the attraction she felt for him would cause complications once the police caught her stalker and she resumed her normal life.

Normal. What exactly would that mean?

Her feelings for Marshall aside, Trenay knew her life would never be the same again. Knowing she would eventually have to define a new normal had been difficult to wrap her head around at first, but now, realizing life inside of Benton Lake's haven couldn't go on forever, forced her to look at her life from a different perspective.

Never again would she take her safety and security for granted. Until now she had pretty much moved through life relatively easily, unaware of anything except for what directly affected her. She didn't exactly walk around with her head in the clouds; a normal amount of attention was paid to obvious everyday perils, but Trenay had always enjoyed, and taken for granted, a certain measure of safety no matter where she lived, went to school, or worked. Now, thanks to whoever had taken it upon themselves to turn her world upside down, she could no longer look at her world so innocently.

Marshall was teaching her to pay attention to her surroundings, being aware of the clearly visible and not so visible threats. He had repeated over and over again that self-defense started long before any physical contact ever took place. Now she understood what he meant. Once back home she would be mindful to not only park in well-lit areas but also remember something as simple as having her keys out before reaching her car instead of fumbling through her purse, leaving herself vulnerable to an attack. Marshall taught her to trust her sixth sense, her "gut". If something didn't feel right, get away. She hadn't trusted her gut feelings the first time she thought someone had been in her house. What if she had called the police that night? Would things have ended up differently?

It wasn't just that night either. Maybe if she had paid closer attention sooner, she might have noticed someone following her. She could have reported her suspicions to the police and maybe everything wouldn't have spiraled to the crazy situation she found herself in now.

Marshall was good to her and more than patient. He taught her things without making her feel naïve or stupid. He took his time, making sure she understood but at the same time not scaring her to the point she would never want to leave the house again. He did it all because he cared about her and wanted her to feel safe with and without him. He wasn't trying to make her dependent on him, but independent with and without him.

She still struggled with the *why* of all of this. He had practically dropped everything and brought her to the one place he felt would be safe, a place where she could collect her thoughts and where she could do so in private. There weren't many people in her circle of friends who would or could have done the same thing. Yes, Marshall was a nice person, but is this the kind of thing he would do for anybody? What made her so special? Could all of this be more than just the care and concern one human being has for another?

Trenay wasn't sure. She certainly didn't want to misread his feelings for her.

One thing she didn't have any doubts about was the sexual tension between them. Marshall had taught her to be more aware, and she was very aware of him. Call it a basic physical need or attribute it to their close quarters or maybe their growing feelings for each other, she didn't know exactly what to blame, she just knew those feelings existed. In fact, to some degree, she had felt the sexual attraction as far back as the night of the hospital's benefit. Back then she didn't dare act on it, but now…

Trenay poured herself a cup of tea and sat down at the small table, confused and conflicted. While she waited for the tea to cool, she pondered the psychology of relationships hoping to make sense out of her feelings for Marshall.

Under normal circumstances most people get together, feel each other out, and if there's a real connection, they eventually face the inevitable ups and downs that are part of a regular relationship, along the way strengthening the bond as their feelings develop into something more meaningful. On the other hand, if at some stage the process gets too far off track and it doesn't seem feasible to continue, there might be a mutual agreement to cut their losses and end the relationship. At some point afterward, often sooner rather than later, if there hasn't been too much emotional damage, the individuals move on to start the process all over again with someone else. Trenay's relationship experience had often followed a similar path and unfortunately had not been very exciting, fulfilling, or memorable.

With Marshall, the normal relationship series of events seemed irrelevant and as far from customary as anything she could have ever imagined.

Where exactly did she stand with him? What did they expect to happen when all of this craziness ended and they returned to their respective lives? Did they even have a basis for a relationship? Was a relationship with Marshall something she actually wanted or needed?

What did *he* want? *What did Marshall need?*

Trenay shook her head and sighed. What a mess. With everything else going on it seemed foolish to even think about a relationship with Marshall or anyone else for that matter. She couldn't go back home and pick up where she left off. How could she? Her life as she knew it had come to a grinding halt. Getting her life back on track should be her main focus. But she knew her life without Marshall in it would seem…empty.

She had heard stories of women falling in love with the person who had rescued them from a tragic situation. Hero worship, it was the stuff chick flicks were made of. Women falling madly in love with men with whom they had nothing in common except he was their knight in shining armor and them, the classic damsel in distress.

She took a sip from her cup and burned her tongue on the still too hot tea. She grimaced and pushed the cup away.

Is that what I've become? Had she allowed herself to become a damsel in distress, someone who needed to be rescued and taken care of? *No!* She thought defiantly. *I may have to fight tooth and nail but I refuse to lose that one piece of myself. I've lost enough already.*

CHAPTER TWENTY-THREE

Marshall awoke from a fitful night's sleep to the inviting aroma of freshly made coffee. He swung his legs around to the side of the bed and stared at his partially closed door. *What kind of day would today be?*

Trenay had been asleep when he returned from his brother's last night. He was glad about that. His mood when he returned home hadn't improved very much from when he'd first left. So it served them both that he had taken a shower and gone straight to bed, avoiding any additional contact or conversation with Trenay.

The coffee's aroma taunted him and the need for caffeine forced him to get out of bed. Sooner or later he would have to face Trenay. Their living quarters were too close to have tension between them. He needed to clear the air, to set the expectation that he didn't want Trenay to feel obligated to him for anything. He did what he did, and would continue to do whatever needed to be done because he cared about her. That's all she needed to know...and all he could share with her right now.

Following the beckoning aroma to the kitchen, he surprised Trenay.

"You're up early. What's the occasion?" he asked, looking in the cabinet for his favorite mug.

Silence.

Trenay had already retrieved his mug from the

cupboard. Recognizing his need for coffee, she poured him a cup and placed it on the table. "Can you sit down? We need to talk."

Marshall sat down but avoided looking at Trenay, still a little ticked off at her.

Trenay poured herself a cup of coffee and took a seat across from him. Summoning the courage to say what was on her mind she took her time adding cream, then sugar. Taking extra care to stir her coffee as she prepared to say what she had been thinking about all night.

After taking several sips from her cup and stalling as long as she could, she set her cup down on the table, squared her shoulders, and took a deep breath.

"I owe you an apology," she began, sounding more rehearsed than sincere.

Marshall took a sip of coffee and paused before asking, "For what?"

Oh, so he's going to make me grovel?

"I said something to you yesterday that I probably shouldn't have said. In an attempt to take control of a situation that feels – at least to me – completely out of control, I tried to level the playing field by putting a value on everything you've done for me."

Marshall could have stopped her at any time, but decided he would let her get everything out in the open. Her words had felt like a kick in the gut yesterday and he wasn't about to let her off with a simple "I'm sorry". Plus, he had some things he needed to say, too.

He continued to calmly sip his coffee.

Say something already! Trenay wanted to scream. He

wasn't making it easy for her to apologize.

"I know you may not like it, but I do feel as if I owe you something for helping me," she continued. "I don't know how I'm going to repay you for everything you've done and given me, but I have to think of something."

She noticed Marshall's jaw clench, a sure sign he was angry, but she continued, "I have never been the kind of person who takes without giving something in return. Of course, something like this has never happened to me, but for me to feel better about everything you're doing, I feel like I need to do something for you."

"Why?" he asked, trying to hide his anger and hurt. "Why did you feel like you have to minimize what I consider to be basic goodwill into something you can put a price tag on?"

Trenay avoided looking at him and shrugged her shoulders, struggling to find the right words and feeling awful for the way she had made him feel yesterday and continued to make him feel right now.

He pushed his coffee cup away and fell heavily against the back of his chair. "Help me to understand, Trenay, because I am struggling with this."

"You don't think I'm struggling with this, too?"

"Are you? You seem to have it all figured out. One reason. Just give me one reason why."

"Well, I guess I don't have just one reason, but several."

Marshall crossed his arms and looked at her point-blank. "Go ahead. I've got nothing but time. Explain it to me. Please."

Marshall practically stared her down while he waited for an explanation but she refused to shy away. She had to tell him how she felt. What else could she do at this point?

"I guess the best way to start is to get you to understand that I have always been able to take care of myself. When you came along to 'rescue' me I didn't know how to handle it. At first, I was fine letting you take control of everything because frankly, I couldn't. Mentally and emotionally, I was a giant mess."

Trenay paused, still searching for the right words.

"Keep going," Marshall urged, uncrossing his arms and softening his gaze.

"Okay, but I don't know how to say this."

"Whatever it is you can tell me."

"I don't want to lose my sense of who I am or my independence. I knew if I said those things about paying you back it might hurt you, but I took that chance. Saying it seemed like the best way to give me some control over the situation. Even though I meant what I said, I didn't mean to hurt you by saying it."

Yes, you did hurt me. Marshall thought about what Trenay had just said and it made him think about how he had handled everything. Maybe initially he had been overprotective and too eager to take charge, but he did what he felt what was needed at the time. Why should he apologize for that?

"I'm not trying to take away your independence," he said quietly. He looked at Trenay as she folded and unfolded her napkin. There was something else, something she wasn't saying but wanted to. For reasons he didn't understand she still felt she couldn't be totally honest with him. He needed to remove that barrier between them once and for all. "What else, Trenay? What are you not telling me?"

"That's all," she said, clearly lying.

"Be honest. Please."

She sipped her coffee trying to think of a delicate way to say what she was thinking and needed to say out loud.

"Trenay?"

"Okay," she said sounding completely exasperated, "I don't want to fall in love with you based on some crazy hero worship." There, she said it.

Wow. She was afraid of falling in love. Letting Trenay's confession sink in, this time Marshall had to pause and search for the right words. She didn't want to fall in love with him period or under these circumstances? Is that what was happening? Was she falling in love with him? Would that be so terrible?

"Can I ask you something?"

"No, I'm not this crazy all the time," she said, hoping to infuse a little humor into what had turned into more of an emotional conversation than she had expected.

"Are you afraid to fall in love with me?"

"I'm afraid to fall in love with you while I'm in this protected, unreal environment we've created."

"Trenay, this is as real as it gets," Marshall remarked honestly.

She shook her head and looked at him earnestly. "I don't think so. What's going to happen when this is all over and we go back to our normal lives?"

"Then we continue where we left off and we see what happens from there. I don't have a crystal ball to show you what our lives are going to be like when we get back home. I wish I did, but I don't. Look, there's no denying we have strong feelings for each other. If we're being completely honest, we had feelings for each other before all of this craziness began. This," he said, looking around the room, "us, this environment, and everything else in our lives are as real as it gets. Good, bad, or indifferent, we just need to deal with each situation as it comes up. We can't do anything more than that."

Trenay nodded solemnly. She agreed with Marshall up to a point. This whole thing with her stalker was certainly at the far end of real and something she knew most people would never have to deal with in their lifetime. But Marshall was right about one thing: It had to be dealt with just like anything else.

"Let me put your mind at ease about one thing. I'm not here to take away your independence or change who you are. You know what you want out of life and up to this point, it seems like you haven't let anyone or anything stand in your way, including me. That kind of confidence is one of the many reasons I think you're pretty special. Your independence – and your stubbornness – amongst other things, is what makes you so damn sexy."

Why did I just say sexy? I was thinking it. I didn't mean to say it!

Sexy? He thinks I'm sexy?

As Marshall watched her take in everything he just said, he figured he might as well continue and get a few more things off his chest.

"Trenay, I don't doubt that we can build on the feelings we have for each other. Maybe it's just me but I'm looking forward to it. I want to see where our feelings lead." Marshall stood and walked over to the counter, his back to Trenay. He knew he was throwing a lot at her but he felt as if he needed to lay it all out on the line. He also knew he would have to choose his next words carefully before revealing too much too soon of what was in his heart and on his mind.

He turned to face Trenay and leaned with his back against the counter, partially for support.

"Trenay, before I asked you to be honest with me, now I'm going to be honest with you. The whole time we've been here in Benton Lake, staying here at the cabin, I have struggled with how I feel about you." Marshall looked up to the ceiling and sighed. "Okay, that sounded rehearsed. Let me try again. I'm just going to have to say what I feel. I'm crazy about you. I haven't met anyone like you...ever! There are times when you make me mad as hell but at the same time, there is no one else I would move heaven and earth for, except you. I know I probably sound pretty corny right now but I don't know any other way to tell you how I feel."

Marshall tried to gauge Trenay's reaction, wondering if he should keep going. *Why not? What did he have to lose?*

"This isn't just a physical attraction. I love the intense passion you have for your work and the way you're committed to the things you believe in. I don't know very many people who live their lives that way. On top of everything else you're smart, funny, ambitious, and so damn sexy I sometimes get all bent out of shape just being around you. You make me feel like a twelve-year-old with a serious crush."

Trenay stared at Marshall wide-eyed and at a loss for words.

He continued, not wanting to lose his nerve particularly since he'd been granted a window of opportunity to lay out his feelings for her. "If I actually thought about the feelings I have for you I could truthfully say that they didn't just start when we got here. But I can say they've grown stronger with each passing day."

Marshall walked back to the table and sat down across from Trenay. Again he tried to read her reaction beyond the obvious surprise he saw but aside from that, he couldn't register what else she was feeling. *Was she happy...sad...shocked?* It was killing him that he didn't know what she was thinking.

"Wow," she said quietly after a few minutes. "What do I say?"

"You don't have to say anything. All I'm asking is that you keep an open mind where we're concerned. Can you do that?" He hoped she would agree.

It seemed like an eternity while he waited for her to answer. Something as serious as this, she would need time, not pressure from him. Realistically, he didn't have any other choice than to give her all the time she needed.

He had just laid it all on the line and he knew she had to digest it all. It had been a lot for him to come to terms with, too. Not since his ex-wife had he been this honest and open with a woman. But Trenay was different than any other woman he'd known. He felt he could safely open up to her without reservations or repercussions.

Slowly Trenay got up from the table. She knew Marshall was expecting a response and she had one.

She turned to face him and replied, "I think it's time for me to go home."

CHAPTER TWENTY-FOUR

"Oh my goodness!" Cristina quickly stepped from behind her desk and wrapped Marshall in a bear hug.

"Thank you so much for calling. How are you? How is Trenay? Is she all right? Did she have anything to tell me? Is she going crazy not being able to work? I know she's worried about everything here at work and especially those two spoiled cats of hers, but tell her I have everything under control. I miss her so much."

Marshall waited patiently for Cristina to take a breath as she fired off questions and comments in rapid succession.

Finally taking a moment to breathe she looked around the office and nodded. "As you can see, everything is just fine here but kind of lonely without her. I hate to admit it but I'm going crazy trying to dole out her work to people who don't have the same passion or eye for detail as she does, but what're you gonna do? Don't tell her I said that though. Oh, but make sure you do tell her Felix and Oscar are fine. And tell her I miss her very much."

Cristina smiled awkwardly when she realized how she must sound. "I said that already, didn't I? You'll have to excuse me," she apologized. "I didn't mean to overwhelm you. When I'm excited or nervous I tend to get carried away. I was more than a little excited when I saw you 'cause you're my only connection to Trenay right now.

She's more than a boss to me. She's my friend, too."

"No need to apologize. I completely understand." He understood how Cristina felt. Trenay meant a lot to him, too.

"I hear the police think they may have a lead."

"Right now they're just trying to connect the dots which seem to all lead back to Trenay. The hard part is finding out where the dots began and who they should lead to."

"So is she all right? Does she need anything? Is she going crazy not being able to come to work? Most days she was the first one in and the last one out. That woman is a workaholic if there ever was one. Taking files home, pouring over bid proposals on the weekends, writing up recommendations," Cristina paused. "Sorry, I'm doing it again."

Marshall smiled. "Don't apologize. Yes, she's getting a little antsy at my place. She's used to being busy; you know that better than anybody. There's not a whole lot for her to do right now and life as she knew it has pretty much stopped."

Cristina retrieved an accordion file from her desk stuffed with several manila folders. She then pulled a small box from beneath her desk and handed it to Marshall. "Well, this should keep her busy for a while. I don't know how she'll be able to reach me if she needs anything. I don't suppose she can remote in from where ever she's staying," she remarked wondering if Marshall would reveal their exact location.

He didn't. Only Detective Prosser knew where he had

taken her.

Marshall shook his head. "I'm afraid not."

Cristina nodded. She hated that her friend had to go into hiding. Coming into the office just wasn't the same without her, in fact, it was downright depressing. "Do you have any idea how soon she'll be able to come home? I don't want her to be in danger or anything. I was just wondering, that's all."

Marshall placed the folder on top of the box. He tried to smile hoping to mask his feelings. "Soon." But not too soon, he prayed.

***

Patiently watching from various locations over the past few weeks had proven futile, although there was no hurry to give up. Eagerly waiting to catch a glimpse of Trenay or someone who could lead him to her would ultimately be worth all of the watching and waiting.

That secretary of hers hadn't been much help. He'd called trying to set up an appointment with Trenay only to be told she would be out of the office for the next several weeks. He tried to chat up the secretary in an attempt to worm a little information out of her, hoping to get just enough to maybe pick up her trail, but she had been tight-lipped.

The mayor's office hadn't been much help either. He had pretended to be a disgruntled business owner who had submitted a contract bid and wanted to file a complaint because his bid was rejected. He had specifically mentioned the Office of Green Building Practices thinking that would get him some information. He had even chided the mayor's admin for having incompetent staff members who left their offices unattended. Nothing came of that either.

"Where, oh where, could Trenay be?" he sang in a quiet childlike voice.

Repositioning himself in the driver's seat to get more comfortable, he nervously tapped his fingers on the steering wheel. Even with the tinted windows rolled halfway down it was getting hot in the car. Reaching over to turn on the little portable fan he kept handy for surveillance jobs, he rummaged under a pile of junk, looking for something to snack on. The front and back seats were littered with fast food containers, candy bar wrappers, plastic sports drink bottles and empty coffee cups. He was practically living out of his car, only going back to the fleabag motel where he had a room long enough to shower and put on a change of clothes. Even though it was a dive, he had chosen the motel because it was the kind of place where one could be anonymous and where nobody asked questions as long as you paid for your room and didn't cause trouble, which suited him just fine.

While the motel was seedy enough to offer him the anonymity he needed, he spent as little time there as possible. He didn't want anyone identifying him or remembering some little detail in case he'd left a loose end and the cops came snooping around later. The fewer people who could identify him the better. Thankfully, the type of people who stayed at the Vista Bell Inn wasn't the type who wanted to call attention to themselves either.

He had decided to give it another hour or so more in

front of city hall before heading over to her house to see if he might have some luck there. Since he had deposited enough change in the meter, the attendant left him alone, so time-wise he was good for a while.

Unwrapping a candy bar he pulled from an insulated lunch tote he turned on the radio while he waited, but after going up and down the dial and not finding anything to hold his attention, he turned it off. Tapping his fingers on the steering wheel and humming his own tune, he took a big bite of his chocolate bar and smiled. The term *sweet revenge* came to mind. Savoring the candy and reveling in his twisted thoughts, he suddenly paused when something, no someone, caught his attention. Sitting up in his seat to get a better look, he was mindful to stay low enough behind the window to avoid being picked up by the cameras mounted on the buildings across the street.

"Cross the street," he hissed. "Cross the street so I can get a better look."

Yes!

Today might be his lucky day after all.

***

Marshall had agreed to take Trenay home, even though he was still very much opposed to the idea. Realistically he knew he couldn't keep her in Benton Lake forever. Eventually, they would have to return to their normal lives.

Already, Marshall had mentally begun thinking about what needed to be done to ensure Trenay's safety once she was back in Columbus, assuming the police still hadn't caught her stalker. While mentally going through his list of safety measures he thought of several changes, some she was sure to argue against but there were a few she would readily agree to – new deadbolts, an alarm system, and motion-sensitive lights at the back, front, and sides of her house for starters. Much to his relief, she had agreed to most of his suggestions. He had a few more but decided to wait until later to tell her about them.

Since he was working with a pretty aggressive deadline, Marshall had to move quickly. The most important thing would be to alert Detective Prosser about Trenay's plans to return home. Next, he planned to set up small surveillance cameras around her house and he would ask the mayor for his assistance to beef up security around city hall, at least for a little while.

At his insistence, Trenay had agreed to stay in Benton Lake for two more weeks. He wanted to give the police a little more time to work her case and with any luck make an arrest so she could put this nightmare behind her. Worst-case scenario, if the police didn't make an arrest at the very least he would have two weeks to put safeguards in place to protect Trenay.

Time was of the essence and Marshall intended to make every second count.

CHAPTER TWENTY-FIVE

The festivities kicking off the annual Independence weekend celebration in Benton Lake were in full swing. Red, white, and blue banners lined the town's major streets and almost every single home proudly displayed various symbols of patriotism and pride.

Lee and Katrice had invited Marshall and Trenay to join them for a backyard barbecue. Later that evening their yard would also serve as a prime location for viewing the town's spectacular fireworks display.

Much to Marshall's surprise and relief, Trenay had agreed to go with him to his brother and sister-in-law's, which was a good thing since he didn't have a good excuse for turning down the invitation.

The tension between him and Trenay had eased up a bit over the past few days. He knew her change in attitude had a lot to do with knowing she would be going home soon. He understood going back to her house and job still made her pause, not knowing who or what could be waiting to hurt her, but in her opinion, it had to be done. It was her way of fighting against an unseen threat and more importantly, getting her life back.

To date, the police and Lee's contact on the force hadn't made much progress. Marshall tried not to worry too much about it, but he felt uneasy and more than a little nervous allowing Trenay to knowingly reenter a potentially unsafe situation. He felt that as long as the person stalking her was still out there, she wouldn't be safe. He wished she would reconsider and stay in Benton Lake a little longer. At least he was thankful she had agreed to two weeks. Unfortunately, that would have to do for now.

Aside from the main topic of Trenay returning home, they hadn't spoken about something else which continued to weigh heavily on Marshall's heart, his feelings for her. Nothing much had been said since the morning he opened his heart to her. Right now he felt as if he had gone out on a limb and the limb broke, sending him cascading into the unknown.

She had to be thinking about what he'd said even if she didn't want to talk about it. He knew he was still thinking about it every day.

Marshall didn't know what his life would be like without seeing Trenay every day. Far more than he ever expected, he liked being around her. He liked seeing her first thing in the morning, sharing breakfast, sitting on the porch in the cool of the evening, and taking walks in the woods.

Even though she missed her own home, Trenay liked Marshall's little place, his sanctuary in the woods. She had told him so a few times. The rustic beauty of the surrounding woods, the quaint home he had built from a little shack, and even the serenity of the lake. When there was a breeze she liked watching the sun dance across the water. Sometimes she just liked sitting on the bank as the quiet calm soothed her spirit as she observed nature at its best.

Marshall had never looked at the lake, the woods, or his home in the same way Trenay viewed it. He loved that she opened his eyes to things he'd never paid attention to. No matter how simple they appeared to the casual observer, she always saw something more. She gave him a greater appreciation for what he and nature had created.

Once Trenay moved back home Marshall knew he would miss their evenings together most of all. Some nights, just after sunset they would sit out on the porch, catch a cool breeze, watch fireflies, and talk above the crickets as they got to know each other at a deeper level than would ever have happened if they were back in the city.

They had also gone back to the lake a few more times in the evenings when it was cool enough and built a fire. Sometimes they roasted hot dogs for dinner and every time they made s'mores. In a way, the time they spent together was all very sweet and old fashioned. Back home their lives would have been too busy to have slowed down enough to have had anything more than an occasional dinner, night out at the movies, or drink after work.

One evening when they were sitting out on the porch talking, Marshall learned Trenay had always wanted to have a brother or sister to play with. He could tell by the way she talked about her parents and her childhood she had been spoiled, not in a way that made her selfish or entitled, but in the manner when one feels very much loved, protected, and cherished.

Marshall also found out they shared a passion – travel. He talked about his adventures during his visits to all fifty states, something she wanted to do one day, with fewer adventures. He talked about fishing in Alaska with his brothers, white water rafting in West Virginia, and riding a motorcycle through the desert in Nevada. He purposely skipped over a few of the more scandalous exploits that took place following the motorcycle trip in Las Vegas.

They both had visited France, Germany, and England. Trenay had spent her last year of college studying in London and Kenya.

She also shared with him details about a trip she had taken with her parents to Tortola in the British Virgin Islands. Her description of the island where they stayed, clear blue waters, intoxicatingly warm weather, exotic foods, and the hospitality of the island's residents, made him immediately want to book a trip there himself. It sounded like a beautiful place and he wondered if one day he would be able to visit the tropical paradise with her.

Marshall remembered when Trenay had accused him of creating a make-believe and safe world for the two of them at his cabin by the lake, and if he truly owned up to it he would have to admit she was right.

He felt almost ashamed for allowing his feelings to cloud his judgment. Ultimately, Marshall knew he had to man up and do the right thing by putting Trenay's feelings and her safety ahead of his feelings, despite his fear that as a result, she might no longer need or want him in her life.

***

Trenay was excited to meet Marshall's family. She welcomed the chance to attend the party at their house, hoping for a much-needed diversion.

Since she decided to return home and go back to work she struggled with whether or not she was making the right decision. The one thing she didn't have to wonder about was how Marshall felt about her decision. He had voiced his opinion loud and clear. He told her, in no uncertain terms and in a tone she had never heard before, that he thought her decision was premature, foolish, and a flat out bad idea.

She would be lying if she said she didn't care what Marshall thought because she did care, very much. While his opinion meant a lot, deep down she felt as if she had to do this. To stand strong and no longer allow herself to be a victim, returning home was the first step in taking back her life. This was her way of fighting back, exactly what Marshall had been telling her to do all along.

But being strong and regaining her life wasn't the only reason Trenay wanted to leave Benton Lake. With everything that had gone on between her and Marshall and the growing feelings they had for each other, both spoken and unspoken, she needed to find out if their relationship had a strong enough foundation to stand on its own, outside of their utopia.

Marshall and Trenay stepped around the back of his brother's house, into a party already in full swing. Music, people, and noise were everywhere.

Children darted around tables waving colored streamers and rattling noisemakers. There were couples seated around picnic tables, standing around the patio, and a few guys were keeping the grill master company while

Lee worked his magic.

"There are a lot of people here," Trenay exclaimed a little nervously.

She recognized Marshall's brother, Lee, as one of the men standing by the grill. Everyone else was strangers. She wondered where Lee's wife and children were so she could properly thank his wife for the invitation. She may have been nervous but she still had manners.

Marshall turned to face Trenay wanting to put her at ease. "These people are all my friends and family, people I've known for a long, long time. No need to be nervous around them. Okay?"

Trenay nodded.

Marshall took Trenay's hand, leading the way into the party.

Marshall's friends and family. This is a safe place. Relax, no need to be nervous. Easier said than done.

On top of everything else, Trenay felt an almost overwhelming and completely unexpected need to make a good impression. At the same time, she had to resist the urge to bolt back to the sanctity of Marshall's cabin. Instead, she smiled weakly, looking to Marshall for reassurance that she would be accepted, feel safe, and everything would be all right.

"Uncle Marshall!"

Trenay turned in the direction of a small, excited voice just in time to see a little boy hurl himself at Marshall.

Marshall turned too and instinctively scooped up young Taj, lifting the giggling child over his head.

Taj's excitement was infectious. Trenay forgot all

about being nervous as she witnessed the giggly interaction between Marshall and his nephew.

"And who might this handsome guy be?" she asked, smiling at the little boy who at the moment was being tickled unmercifully by his uncle.

"This little guy is the best t-ball player, soccer goalie, and the greatest big brother in the whole wide world."

Standing away from his uncle, just out of tickle reach, Taj's forehead wrinkled into a frown. "Uncle Marshall, didn't my dad tell you?"

"Tell me what, champ?"

His voice lowered slightly and Taj looked at his uncle with big, puppy dog eyes. "I'm not a good goalie. The green team got a goal when it was my turn to be the goalie. I tried to stop the ball but it was too high," he said, illustrating his point by raising his arms high over his head.

"One got by you, huh?"

Taj nodded hesitantly.

"Well, do you want to know what I think?"

"What?"

"Letting one or two balls get past you doesn't mean that you're still not the best. But it does mean that you need to practice every day and you need to eat your peas and carrots so you can grow. Then nobody will be able to kick balls over your head because you'll be big and tall."

"I will?" he asked enthusiastically.

Marshall nodded with a look of utmost assurance.

"Okay," Taj replied with childlike innocence and a look of determination on his face.

"Now, before you go, I want you to meet my friend,

Miss Trenay."

Taj turned his attention to Trenay, whom he had completely ignored up to this point. He then extended his hand for a handshake just as he'd been taught.

Smiling at the grown-up gesture, Trenay shook Taj's tiny hand. "It's nice to meet you, Taj. Your uncle has told me a lot about you."

"Okay," he said, clearly uninterested.

Unsure of what else to say, and sure Taj didn't have anything, in particular, he wanted to talk about, Trenay simply said, "Well, it was nice meeting you."

"Uh, huh," Taj replied and then turned to his uncle with a look of concern as something struck him. "Uncle Marshall, is she taking care of you?"

Caught off guard by the question and not exactly sure what his nephew meant, Marshall knelt to eye level with Taj and asked, "What do you mean, champ?"

"I heard Mommy and Daddy talking. She said that you need somebody to take care of you. Is that what Miss Trenay does?"

"Uh, Taj, honey, take these buns to Daddy."

Taj's mother, Katrice, slipped between Marshall and her son, ignoring the less than pleased look on her brother-in-law's face.

"Kids," she said with a warm smile, pushing her son in the direction of his father. "I'm Katrice, Marshall's soon to be the *ex*-sister-in-law and Taj's very embarrassed mother."

Trenay returned her smile and shook Katrice's outstretched hand while stealing a glance at Marshall. *What had he told his family about her?*

Marshall leaned over to kiss Katrice on her cheek and whispered, "We'll talk later, Sis.

Katrice gave Marshall a playful punch and turned to Trenay. "I'm glad you were able to join our party. It's really nice to finally meet you. Marshall has kept you sequestered out there at the lake for so long I thought he was holding you hostage. I know you must be going crazy out there in the boonies."

"It's not so bad. The lake and the woods surrounding Marshall's cabin are very peaceful and really pretty."

"Well, tonight you get to be around other people, not squirrels, deer, and crickets." Katrice turned to Marshall. "I'm going to introduce her to our friends. Go help your brother on the grill," she ordered.

Before Marshall could utter one word of protest Katrice had whisked Trenay away.

"I see *Operation Katrice* is in full swing," Lee said when his brother joined him at the grill.

"What has gotten into her? When did she get so bossy?"

"You know Katrice. She's the happiness fairy and she won't rest until *everyone* is happy. I can honestly say I have no idea what's brewing in that pretty head of hers, maybe a touch of matchmaking. I honestly don't know."

"So how do I make her stop?"

"Yeah, good luck with that. Haven't you learned by now? If Katrice has her mindset to do something, don't get in her way. Resistance is futile, bro'."

***

Despite her earlier apprehension Trenay discovered

the Independence Day activities at the Oliver's turned out to be a lot of chaotic fun. Katrice had introduced her to their friends and neighbors and a few employees from the bookstore. Everyone seemed very nice and to Trenay's relief, no one asked why she was visiting Benton Lake. They all probably assumed she was there on vacation with Marshall. Relieved she didn't have to concoct a story on her own she was fine with that assumption as long as no one pried any further. Not good at lying, she wouldn't have known what to tell them anyway. Frankly, the last thing she wanted to bring up tonight, on such a lovely evening, was the ugly truth.

Throughout the evening Trenay had caught glimpses of Marshall interacting with his nephew and young niece. Between practicing soccer moves with his nephew and playing with the baby, he had been busy. Taj and his sister adored their uncle and Marshall adored them.

Young Taj barely left Marshall's side the entire evening. He even insisted on sitting next to his uncle when the food was served.

Trenay wondered why Marshall never had children of his own. He would have been a wonderful father, she thought. Like most men, he probably wanted sons. She imagined he would take them fishing and hiking, doing all of the "guy" stuff men did with their sons. A scenario she could easily picture now after getting to know him, although her initial impression of him hadn't leaned toward the paternal side at all.

Once again she realized how wrong she had been about Marshall after their first encounter. But who could blame her? It wasn't as if he had put his best foot forward. Unless forward meant putting his foot in his mouth, which he had done quite eloquently.

She had misjudged Marshall on several accounts based on their initial meeting and her poor judge of character. Marshall was a good man. Actually, he was more than that, a lot more. She wondered how such a giving, compassionate, and caring man had missed out on marriage and a family of his own like his brother.

"Having fun?"

Trenay turned to see Marshall approaching, looking more happy and relaxed than she had seen him since they arrived in Benton Lake. Being around his family and friends had a positive effect on him.

Trenay nodded.

Marshall folded his arms, he seemed unconvinced. "Be honest."

"No, really, I am having fun. Your family and friends are very nice and your niece and nephew are absolutely adorable."

"I saw you playing with Lily."

Trenay smiled. "She's something else. Only a few of my friends have children, but all of their kids are older. Since I don't have any brothers or sisters it also means I don't have nieces or nephews. Until now I never thought I was missing out on being around kids but it is kind of nice. Who knew babies were so much fun? Your niece is the sweetest little thing and from what I can tell, she has you and her daddy wrapped around her tiny, adorable finger."

Marshall smiled sheepishly. "Guilty. I won't even try

to deny it. You're absolutely right. One look into those big brown eyes, and those chubby dimpled cheeks, I turn into mush."

After a few minutes of talking about the various party guests Trenay had met throughout the evening, Marshall grew quiet. "The fireworks are going to start in about fifteen minutes and I don't want you to miss them, but I need you to come with me first."

"Why?"

"I want to show you something."

Trenay nodded and allowed him to lead her away from the activity and noise from the party.

Moving from the backyard, Marshall led Trenay around the side of the house. He stopped when they reached an area partially hidden by hedges and small flowering bushes.

In the short time, it took them to walk around to the side of the house Marshall's demeanor had changed. Trenay searched his face and wondered what had changed on their short walk. She heard him sigh.

Something was wrong.

"I'm glad you came with me tonight to meet my family. It means a lot to me."

"I'm glad I came, too."

"I think they like you."

"I'm glad," she said sincerely. "They're nice people and easy to like."

Marshall looked away for a second then focused his attention back on Trenay. He reached over and traced her ear with his finger, his deep brown eyes filled with concern, yet he didn't say anything.

"Is something wrong?" she asked. She had seen him talking to his brother earlier and the two of them were deep in conversation. Until now, she hadn't thought anything of it. Had Lee found out something about her case and had told Marshall? "Did you hear something from the poli-?"

"No. No, it's not that." He didn't let her finish, not wanting any of the ugliness they had temporarily retreated from to mar their evening.

"Then what is it?" she asked, only partially relieved but still concerned. "A few minutes ago you were having fun, laughing and talking, now you look so serious."

"There's something I have to say to you. Something I think you should hear."

"What is it?" she asked, worried that she may have said or done something out of place around his family. "Did I do something?"

"Yes and no."

Trenay shook her head. "I don't understand."

"What you've done is to show me how wonderful life is when you have someone you care about to share it with. Since the first day I met you we've been on this crazy rollercoaster ride sending us up and down and in a bunch of other crazy directions. I have to admit, the first day in your office when I tried to confront you about our bid, I wanted to stay as angry with you as I'd been when I first saw the rejection. But I couldn't. You want to know why?" he asked rhetorically.

"Because you knew I was right," she remarked smugly.

Marshall smiled. "Yes, and because there was something about you. I don't know if you remember, but that day in your office you listened to what I had to say, stated your case, and dismissed me. That's when I felt there was something about you that made me want to get to know you."

"Be careful what you wish for. In this case, I think you may have gotten a little more than you expected."

"Trenay, there aren't many things I can say this about, but I have no regrets about ever meeting you or the time we've spent together this summer. I wouldn't change a thing."

He paused before continuing, looking for the right words. "You talk about me coming to your rescue, but I don't think you realize how you've affected me or how you've changed my life."

"What are you saying?"

"What I'm saying is what I said to you a few days ago. We haven't talked about it and it's killing me. We don't have very much time left before you go back home and I can't let you leave without knowing exactly how I feel. I'm crazy about you, Trenay, and I don't want to lose you," he blurted out.

Trenay stood silently allowing what Marshall said to sink in. He was right. Neither one of them had brought up the conversation from the other day. Apparently, he had been thinking about it; she certainly had been. When they were alone, it was the proverbial elephant in the room. And now the elephant stood squarely between them and could not be ignored.

Marshall stood close to her, waiting to see and hear her response. Judging by her reaction, she looked as if he had just dropped a bomb.

She tried to take a step backward to be less in his space and more in hers so she could think clearly without inhaling his aftershave or seeing the affection in his eyes or absorbing the heat as it radiated from his body. There was no retreat, her back pressed against a solid wall.

Marshall reached out to stroke her arm, but more than anything he wanted to pull her into his arms and reassure her that it would be okay to take a chance on him, on them. "Please don't let what I said scare you."

"It's just – I don't –" she stopped as she sought the right words to say.

"What? You think the way I feel about you is based on something that isn't real?"

"Yes," she said quietly. "I don't understand how you can think anything different."

Marshall shook his head and exhaled. He didn't want to be frustrated with Trenay but she certainly did not make things easy!

What would it take to get her to open her mind and heart to all the possibilities that he could see so clearly? True, their situation may not be ideal, but whose was? Would a more traditional situation guarantee success? Of course not. He knew from experience, life didn't offer guarantees, and too many times promises never materialized into anything other than mere words.

Forget ideal and perfect. What about how they felt about each other? Didn't she feel it? She had to! She wanted real? The way he knew they felt about each other was real!

As far as he was concerned his desire for Trenay had surpassed lust a long time ago and had blossomed into something so powerful that at times he couldn't make heads or tails out of it. Lately, he hadn't been able to eat, sleep, or make sense out of the simplest things. He had tried to suppress his feelings for her but how could he continue to hide what was practically bursting from his heart?

Marshall looked into Trenay's eyes, desperately searching for and hoping to see understanding and acceptance, at the very least a willingness to give them a try. He searched for acknowledgment that she wanted to reciprocate his feelings, not out of obligation, but simply because she needed to be loved and cherished, and because he needed that, too.

Far too long Marshall had pretended that sharing his bed with one woman after another was everything he needed and wanted. Who needed commitment? Who needed a loving relationship? Who needed a woman full of ambition, drive, and with an enormous capacity to love? *He did.* And once he owned up to the fact that he needed those things as much as he needed to breathe, he could be the man who was finally ready and willing to give his heart freely instead of the man who would rather flee than be hurt again.

Maybe it was time to show her how he felt instead of using words.

Marshall pulled Trenay close, leaning in to take the

briefest moment to inhale her fragrance before his lips sought hers. Softly at first, his lips covered hers.

She didn't pull away or hesitate but instead, she anticipated and freely accepted what he offered. No one kissed her like Marshall and despite the conflict in her heart, she had no control over how her body reacted to his touch, kiss, scent, and affection.

Marshall's strong hands held Trenay in place but when he realized she didn't attempt to run away that was all the permission he needed to go further. He relaxed his hold, deepening the kiss as he reached around and pulled her closer into his body.

Her mouth welcomed him, their tongues touched, their hearts pounded, their minds soared to places completely foreign to them and allowing the exploration of possibilities they had never considered. Caught up in this wonderful new realm permitted them to temporarily forget everything else.

The kiss, so full of longing and promise, rocked Marshall to his core. Never had he experienced these feelings with anyone.

Trenay's body melted into his, no longer tense or hesitant. Beneath the thin material of her top, he felt her hardened nipples against his chest, setting off tiny shockwaves flooding his body. The feel of her body pressed against his made his longing for her increase exponentially. At that moment Marshall couldn't think of one thing he needed or wanted more than Trenay. He felt practically drunk with longing.

How could she not be affected by this? Or was she?

Trenay groaned. Marshall's kiss had set off a firestorm that coursed through her body like a lightning bolt. He tasted, smelled, and felt so good she wondered if she would ever be able to let him go. Could this have been what she was afraid of? *Feeling?* Actually allowing her heart to have a say in how she felt rather than being ruled by her head? As much as she fought it, Marshall forced her to feel. Her heart came alive when she was with him. Her imagination soared. Her sexual desire awakened.

She wanted and needed what he offered. She wanted to feel. Instead of overthinking if this was the right thing to do or even what might happen next, she allowed herself to melt into Marshall's arms and against his body. At this moment, her need for him had nothing to do with repaying a debt she felt was owed but had everything to do with fulfilling her need for affection, companionship, and passion. She needed to feel him hard, hot, and throbbing inside her. To feel his strong hands caressing her breasts and his lips roaming her body would be divine. Having him take her mind and body to heights unknown would be sheer bliss.

As they stood kissing and holding each other in the still night neither Trenay nor Marshall wanted to be anywhere but right where they were, in each other's arms. It seemed as if both had needs only they could fulfill for each other.

The kisses continued, passionate, hot, and leaving the other wanting more. Marshall couldn't get enough of Trenay and she wanted to give him everything she had, right then, right there. It was as if the floodgates had been opened as they kissed each other hungrily.

"Ahem."

No response.

"Ahem!"

Annoyed by the intrusion Marshall turned; ready to pounce on whoever dared interrupt his private moment with Trenay.

"What?" he barked before realizing it was his brother who was the intruder.

Feeling more amused than threatened, Lee replied, "Uh, Katrice wanted me to tell you that the fireworks are about to start. Soooo, uh, feel free to join us or, carry on."

Marshall turned back to Trenay, instantly regretting putting her in the embarrassing situation. He pulled her close to him. She looked so beautiful, so seductive.

Damn if he didn't want to get her in his bed right then!

Marshall cleared his throat. "Uh, tell Katrice we'll be right there."

"No rush. Seems like you two have your own fireworks going on anyway," Lee remarked under his breath but loud enough so his brother could hear.

"Are you okay?" Marshall asked after Lee left.

Trenay nodded.

"I'm sorry. I didn't mean to…uh…you know. I guess I just got carried away."

Trenay smiled. "I think *we* got carried away."

Marshall placed a kiss on Trenay's forehead. He took her hand, but before leading her back to the party he reached out and stroked her cheek. "By no means is this over," he said. "I think we need to finish what we started."

Unsure of what to say and not trusting that her words would truly convey what was in her heart, she simply nodded in agreement.

CHAPTER TWENTY-SIX

Neither Trenay nor Marshall had paid much attention to the fireworks display, focusing only on their mutual longing and their bodies' hypersensitive reaction to each other. As they stood looking up at the fireworks, Marshall placed his arm around Trenay's shoulder. She leaned into his body, feeling his strength and thoroughly enjoying being wrapped up in his masculinity. Until then she hadn't thought much about Marshall's *maleness*, something she was immensely attracted to. It might sound corny if she described aloud to someone what she had assessed in her head what all of that meant. But, once she put all of the pieces together she realized there was just something about the way he carried himself, his confident walk, the ease with which he moved between conversations with his friends and family, the seductive way he smiled, the tone of his voice when he talked to her, the timbre of his laughter, and the protectiveness he provided without saying a word, but leaving no doubt that it existed. All of those things made for one heck of a package and was what she considered to be Marshall's *maleness*.

Marshall and Trenay rode back to the lake in silence, each anticipating what would happen once they were behind closed doors. Marshall pulled up in front of the cabin and killed the truck's engine.

Trenay grabbed her purse and reached for the door

handle, but stopped when she felt Marshall's hand on her arm.

"I think we both know once we walk inside I'm going to make love to you." He paused to let what he said sink in. "If I'm wrong, tell me right now."

As far as Trenay was concerned, he couldn't be more right. Having Marshall make love to her both thrilled and evoked a certain level of apprehension all at the same time. There was no doubt in her mind that his confident manner would extend quite nicely to the bedroom. Marshall would be a skillful lover, taking his time to learn what pleased her and exciting her in ways she'd never imagined.

With him, she sensed she could be open; showing a passionate side of herself, which she had never felt confident enough to exhibit. For once she could be the type of woman whom she'd only read about – the kind who pleased her man by giving and receiving unabashed passion. Her only hesitation? Exactly who would she become after tonight? How would this night change them? She wasn't the type of woman who jumped in and out of bed with men. Nor was she the type who could have a physical relationship with a man without an emotional attachment. How would being with Marshall change her?

Trenay looked at Marshall with only the light from the moon illuminating the inside of the truck. "I think it's clear. This is something we both want."

"Are you sure?" he asked praying with all his heart that she wouldn't change her mind but being careful not to pressure her.

Trenay reached out and stroked Marshall's face so

tenderly that he practically melted. She had no idea the effect she had on him and as much as he wanted her, there was something else he needed to know before committing his body and his heart to her. Something he had to be sure of. Regardless of anything else that might happen he fully understood making love to Trenay tonight would be a turning point for him. It would signal his willingness to give this woman his all – especially all of the love he had to offer.

"I just need to know one more thing," he started slowly, his voice deepened by emotion and need. "Are you willing to let me love you?"

Their relationship would change after tonight and so would she. How, she didn't know, but Trenay was willing to take a chance and deal with the outcome.

"Yes," she whispered.

The front door had barely closed before Marshall and Trenay were in each other's arms. He wanted to go slowly but the anticipation of making love to her completely shattered his last shred of resolve.

For the second time that night, he kissed Trenay with all the pent up passion and longing that had been building since the night they danced together at the hospital's benefit. He savored every second of the kiss, every touch, feeling her lips crushed against his, tongues exploring, fire igniting.

As the kiss ended, he looked down at Trenay, her lips parted, her breathing rapid, and eyes burning with passion. She looked, felt, and tasted delicious. He had waited and dreamed of this moment for so long, he wanted to savor every sweet moment. But his body had other ideas.

Lifting her, Marshall carried Trenay to his bedroom knowing at this point she wouldn't protest. He didn't bother to turn on the light but stood Trenay next to his bed. He kissed her again as the pale moonlight streamed through the window.

When the kiss ended, Trenay found herself standing barefoot, not knowing or caring where she'd left her sandals. She quickly unbuttoned and stepped out of her shorts.

"Wait," Marshall said breathlessly. "I've dreamt about this and wanted it for so long. I want to make it last."

He pulled her to him, nuzzling the side of her neck and drinking in her perfume. He nibbled her ear lobe and heard her moan. Stepping back slightly he slipped her top over her head. His breath caught at the sight of her. She was so sexy, so hot, and so desirable. Standing before him with lush breasts constrained in a lacy bra, sexy panties he knew were wet from desire, and long legs he couldn't wait to have wrapped around his waist. *So much for waiting.*

Scooping Trenay up Marshall placed her squarely in the center of the bed.

"So do I get to undress you?" she asked teasingly.

"Not this time," he said with a mischievous smile. "Maybe next time if you're a good girl."

Trenay watched him as he undressed. First, the shirt, uncovering a broad chest with enough muscles that let her know he was no stranger to physical labor. Then the shorts revealing long, strong legs. And when he removed his boxers she felt her heart leap. Well-endowed and ready for

225

action!

Marshall joined Trenay on the bed and made quick work of removing her bra and panties. His fingers tangled in her hair as he kissed her neck, then heard her moans of pleasure as he kissed and suckled her breast until her nipples stood firm.

His hands roamed her body as if he couldn't get enough of her silky skin beneath his fingers. As he explored her body with his hands, lips, and tongue, he let his fingers roam over her chest, cupping her breasts, then down to her firm stomach, and between her thighs. He teased her for a few minutes before letting his fingers plunge deep inside her.

She cried out in sweet agony and anticipation of what was to come next.

Just as he expected, she was hot, wet, and ready for him. Try as he might, he couldn't wait any longer. Marshall lifted his body and when he came down he plunged deep inside Trenay as their bodies joined in what he instinctively knew was a connection that would not easily be broken. Leaning his head back and closing his eyes he let out a groan so deep he almost didn't recognize that the sound had come from him.

"Oh!" Trenay cried out. She arched her body to take in more of Marshall, loving the delicious feeling of him hot and throbbing inside of her.

There was an ebb and flow to their movements that seemed to have been choreographed just for them. She matched each stroke and he each move.

She wanted to take everything he had to give. At this

moment, there was nothing else that she wanted more. Trenay couldn't think of anything except the exquisite pleasure Marshall was giving her. She cried out again as he thrust deeply inside her. She could feel her body giving way to something amazing, something she had never experienced and would not soon forget.

Marshall must have felt it, too, as the intensity of his movements quickened and became more intense.

Wanting to feel every fiber of this man who was giving her pleasure beyond anything she had ever imagined, Trenay brought her legs up and wrapped them around Marshall's waist.

That one move was like throwing gasoline on an already roaring fire. "Oh, baby," Marshall called out, weakly.

Together their intertwined bodies gyrated, racing to the inevitable explosive and exquisite ending yet struggling to savor the scorching intensity of the moment. Yet, ecstasy won as their choreographed movements reached the explosive ending the two of them yearned for, welcomed, and gave sweet surrender to.

CHAPTER TWENTY-SEVEN

Trenay listened to the sound of early morning rain gently hitting the window. Looking over at Marshall he continued to sleep soundly, only stirring when she moved.

It was a little after seven in the morning, she noted, after glancing at the clock. She had no desire to get up. Lying cozily in bed and wrapped in Marshall's arms felt right, as if this was the only place she wanted and needed to be.

Last night Marshall had made love to her in a way that made her temporarily forget all of her cares and worries. By filling an emotional, physical, and mental need he had left her spent, satisfied, and content. For the first time, she felt cared for by someone other than her parents and in a way far different from any parental responsibility. Falling asleep in Marshall's arms had been the last conscious thought she had before sleep and exhaustion had taken over. It was indeed a good feeling.

Not one to believe in fate until now, she had to wonder how this man ended up in her life at this particular time? Could fate have brought them together at a time when she most needed him, and he needed her? The circumstances of their meeting and ending up together this way certainly weren't ideal, but in the whole scheme of things the *whys* and *hows* didn't seem to matter very much.

How could she not love this man?

If she had ever been so inclined to list all the qualities she was looking for in a man, Marshall would have probably met every requirement on the list and likely would have added a few items of his own. In the time they had been together, he had managed to open her eyes to so much. In the process, she had learned more about herself than ever before.

With Marshall, she felt strong, needed, appreciated, protected, adored, and empowered. Before him she had only been concerned about the narrow scope of her daily life and nurturing her career, never really giving much thought to relationships, starting a family, or much else. Not once did she consider her life to be unfulfilling or incomplete, just a bit lonely.

Marshall stirred and she felt the length of his magnificent body fitted against hers.

Oh, the things that man could do with his body!

She smiled as she listened to Marshall's rhythmic breathing. She would let him sleep a little longer. After all, he deserved it. The man had rocked her world, pleasuring her from head to toe, literally! If that didn't deserve some extra Zs, nothing did.

***

Stroking his bandaged hand, he cursed when he thought about how stupid he'd been. In an attempt to keep his distance when following what he had thought to be a promising lead, he'd gotten caught in road construction traffic and lost his mark.

Taking deep controlled breaths he forced himself to calm down. Glancing at the dent he'd made in the door with his fist he eventually felt his heart rate slow back down to normal. His hand still throbbed from the last time he lost control. He needed to get a grip. He simply couldn't afford any serious physical disabilities that might hinder his plan.

Who was that man?

He had seen him before at Trenay's office but didn't pay much attention to him at the time. There were always people going in and out of her office and there was nothing especially noticeable about him that made him stand out from the others. Although, thinking back, he remembered the same man being there *that* morning, the morning he almost came face to face with her. He'd only caught a brief glimpse of him during the chaos but he was pretty sure he had been there with the mayor when everyone huddled around to protect their *best girl*.

Rubbing his hand he thought about the times *he* needed protection, when *he* needed someone to stick up for him. Bullies at school, the neighborhood kids who teased him because he didn't have the things they had. Life isn't fair for the have-nots. He had learned that lesson early in life.

As far back as he could remember his mother had worked two jobs. When she wasn't working she would be too tired to do even the simplest things. There were no trips to the park, pony rides, baseball games, or fun, only hard times.

His mouth twisted at the painful memories of his childhood and he hated Trenay, even more, knowing hers had been filled with good ones.

He didn't care how long it took or how far he would have to search, he would find her. And when the time was right, there wouldn't be anyone around but him and Trenay. No mayor. No friends. Not mommy or daddy. No one to protect her.

What would she do then? Would she grovel? Beg? Fight?

He laughed bitterly. He knew she wouldn't fight. She had never fought for anything in her life, there was never a reason to. Privilege, favor, and an abundance of resources rarely provoked an urge to fight or defend. Privilege tended to make the recipient soft, complacent, and expectant.

No, if he was sure of anything, he knew Trenay never had to fight for even the most basic thing. Why start now, even if it was a fight for her life?

CHAPTER TWENTY-EIGHT

"Can I ask you a question?"

Marshall rolled over to face Trenay with a smile on his face and lightness in his heart that he had never felt, and until now had only imagined. It was a wonderful feeling, one he wanted to hold on to for as long as possible. Yet, a small nagging thought in the back of his mind warned him it wouldn't last forever. Having Trenay like this, all to himself was only going to last a little while longer. She'd be returning home soon. Their lives would possibly head into two different directions. Nevertheless, he had decided after last night he wouldn't think about her leaving until he had to, instead he would live in the moment, savoring every minute they had together.

"You can ask me anything. I'm completely powerless. As a matter of fact, if I didn't know better, I'd say you put a spell on me," he responded with a mischievous grin.

"I'm being serious."

"So am I," he remarked softly.

Trenay leaned up in bed and rested on one elbow, looking down at Marshall. "I need to know something."

She indeed looked and sounded very serious. "What is it?" he asked, wanting to keep the concern out of his voice and hold onto the lightness he'd felt earlier.

"Last night was...special," she said, searching for the right words but feeling awkward trying to describe their night of lovemaking even though it registered way more than *special* on her emotional and physical meter. In the past, the act of sleeping with a man had merely satisfied a physical need and, if she was lucky, maybe slightly filling an emotional need, too.

Where Marshall had taken her was somewhere she'd never been and quite frankly, never knew existed. This wonderful place where need met gratification, companionship destroyed solitude, and loneliness was edged out by the closeness of someone who longed to be with her and with whom she wanted to be with equally as much. She knew if she allowed herself to think about this newfound and beautiful state of wellbeing for more than a minute, her heart and mind would refuse to accept anything less going forward.

"Yes, it was very special."

"After last night, being with your brother's family and seeing you with the kids, the way you've taken care of me and given me so much, I couldn't help wondering how I could be so lucky to have you in my life."

"No, I'm the-"

"No, wait," she said, placing her fingers on his lips. "Let me finish. I brought up last night because something has been nagging at me. I know this is completely none of my business, but I have to ask."

"I told you, ask me anything. There is no reason for me to keep secrets from you."

"Okay. Here goes. I've been wondering why you aren't married," Trenay blurted out. "Why don't you have someone special in your life? You're a good, *good* man,

Marshall. Trust me, good men are hard to find and they don't stay single very long, not unless they want to…or have been too hurt to make another attempt to change their status." Trenay stopped long enough to see if she had hit on something. He didn't appear to be upset, but he did look concerned. She continued hoping he might open up to her. "I overheard someone at the party mention your ex-wife and they said I'm nothing like her."

Marshall raised up in bed and faced Trenay. "Who said that?" he demanded, suddenly angry.

"It doesn't matter."

"Yes, it does. I don't want anything or anyone from my past to touch what we have together. You," he said, stroking her cheek, and softening his tone, "are nothing like my ex-wife. To be honest, I'm not even the same man as when I was married to her. The things I wanted then and what I want now are entirely different. I've had a lot of relationships, which amounted to very little because I didn't put much into them and I didn't expect much in return. To allow someone to get close to me meant that I'd have to have higher expectations than getting someone into bed. I'd also have to be willing to trust, something I learned from my first marriage was a dangerous thing to do, especially when dealing with someone not worthy of that level of trust or commitment."

"For a long time I blamed my ex for turning me into a – let's just say, *not* a good man – but in reality, I have to shoulder some of the blame. It took a long time for me to understand that some people aren't capable of loving anyone other than themselves. In the process, they tend to spend a lot of time and effort hiding who and what they are. But the signs are usually there. Sometimes those signs are flashing like neon lights," he said with a wry smile. "Too often when we think we're head over heels in love we choose to ignore those signs."

"She broke your heart, didn't she?" Trenay asked, feeling anger toward someone she had never met. How could Marshall's ex-wife not have appreciated and loved him? How could she not have seen what a kind, giving, and beautiful man she had? Marshall said he was a different man when he was married before, but Trenay was sure he had many of the same wonderful qualities then as he had now, the same qualities that attracted her to him. "If you don't mind my saying so, your ex-wife was crazy to let you go."

Marshall leaned back on his pillow and pulled Trenay close to him. "None of that matters anymore. She's moved on and so have I."

Trenay snuggled close to Marshall, reveling in the delicious feeling of being cherished and desired.

"Hungry?" he asked wondering if Trenay wanted to go out or cook something at the house.

Trenay giggled. "Depends. What are you offering?"

Her playful and sexy tone instantly made Marshall forget all about breakfast. He turned toward this woman with a look of total admiration, this woman who had unknowingly given him something beautiful, precious, and wonderful – permission to love and be loved.

Kissing her tenderly his heart filled with emotion as his desire for her arose.

"Trenay, baby?"
"Yes," she cooed.
"I am so in love with you."

CHAPTER TWENTY-NINE

They only had one night left in Benton Lake. Tomorrow, against his better judgment, Marshall would drive Trenay back home. He knew he wouldn't be able to convince her to stay any longer and since her case had become stagnant while she'd been away, maybe it truly was safe for her to return home. No news was good news. He prayed that was the case.

Lee and Katrice had invited them to dinner. Marshall didn't want to share Trenay on their last night together so as a compromise he agreed to an early dinner. At least he could spend the rest of the night making love to her, holding her, and cherishing their last night together at his cabin by the lake.

As they drove into town for dinner neither of them spoke very much, each knowing the other's thoughts: *Would Trenay be safe? What would happen to their relationship when they returned home?*

Marshall angled his truck into his brother's driveway next to his sister-in-law's SUV and cut the engine. He reached over and put his hand on Trenay's arm, stopping her from getting out. "Wait a minute." He leaned in and kissed her fully on the mouth, crushing her lips with his, but ending the kiss gently, leaving her wanting more. "That's just a taste of what's in store for you tonight," he promised.

Feeling giddy and all tingly inside, she nodded and smiled in anticipation.

Katrice greeted Marshall and Trenay at the door. She gave them both a warm hug and attempted to usher Marshall out to the patio to help Lee with the grilling. But Marshall had barely made it inside the house before Taj came downstairs and grabbed his uncle's hand.

"Uncle Marshall, I gotta show you something. Come upstairs."

Katrice tried to intervene. "Taj, honey, I think Uncle Marshall might need a few minutes before you pull him away."

Marshall looked from his sister-in-law who was giving her son a knowing look to his nephew, whose big, brown eyes pleaded with him.

"I'll tell you what, champ. Let me talk to your dad for a few minutes and then I'm all yours until it's time to eat. Deal?"

"Okay," Taj responded reluctantly.

Marshall went out to help Lee and Trenay followed Katrice into the kitchen.

"Where's the baby? I was hoping to get in some cheek pinching time."

"Don't worry; you'll get your chance. She's taking a late nap."

Trenay surveyed the kitchen. A small pot sat on the stove as steam escaped its lid. In the sink were two plastic produce bags, one with a variety of lettuce leaves peeking out of the opening and one filled with ears of corn waiting to be shucked.

"All right, what can I do to help?"

Katrice showed Trenay where to clean up and she put her in charge of washing vegetables.

"Pretty dress," Katrice commented. "Do you need something to cover it so you don't ruin it? I think I've got an apron somewhere."

"Thanks," Trenay responded looking down at the pretty green dress Marshall had bought for her at the beginning of the summer. Today was the first time she'd had an occasion to wear it. "I think I'll be okay."

"I'm glad you two were able to come to dinner tonight."

"Me, too." She meant it. Deciding to spend time with Katrice and her family had been an easy decision to make. Right now she needed easy. Katrice probably didn't realize it, but the way she and her husband had opened up their home and hearts to her meant a lot. Trenay would miss the budding friendship she had with them.

"So how do you feel about going back tomorrow?"

Trenay stopped what she was doing and turned to Katrice. "You know? I mean, you know why I'm here?"

Katrice looked toward the doorway to make sure no one was there. She nodded. "Yes, Marshall told me. I hope you don't mind." She hoped she wasn't betraying Marshall's confidence but she liked Trenay and wanted her to know she, too, was concerned about her safety and well-being.

"Then you know I'm a little nervous about going home."

Katrice came over and stood by Trenay. "You're

pretty brave, a lot more than I would be. But I completely understand why you're going back. At some point, you have to take back control of your life."

"I know. I keep telling myself the same thing. Deep down I know going home is the right thing to do. I haven't fooled myself into thinking it might not also be dangerous. The police don't have any new leads and we're no closer to finding out who was stalking me than we were when I first came here."

"Well, if it makes you feel any better, if I know Marshall, he's not going to let anything happen to you."

Trenay smiled. If she didn't know anything else, she knew that, too.

Going back to the stove to stir the sauce she was preparing Katrice put the spoon down after a few seconds and turned to Trenay. "You know he's in love with you, don't you?"

Trenay turned. "Did he tell you that, too?"

"He didn't have to." Katrice gave her a knowing look. "Look, under normal circumstances I would never pry, but since I opened that door, I might as well walk through. Do you mind if I ask you something?"

"No, I don't mind."

"Do you love him?"

Trenay sighed. The little she knew about Katrice told her she could trust her and be honest with her. It felt good to have another woman to talk to about her mixed-up feelings. "I've thought a lot about that lately. Part of me thinks what I'm feeling is love while another part of me keeps pointing to the fact that what I feel might be plain old hero worship. Marshall is an amazing man. He has singlehandedly taken on my problems as his own. He's put his life on hold to make sure I'm safe. He opened up his home to me, but most of all, he opened up his heart."

Katrice nodded. "I can see how that would be hard to figure out. Since we're being frank, I do feel it's my duty to warn you. Now keep in mind, I'm speaking from experience. Once these Oliver men get a hold of your heart things will never be the same." She paused. "I hope you don't mind one last piece of advice. Where Marshall is concerned, be sure the part of you which makes the final decision about your relationship takes into consideration your heart as well as his."

"So tomorrow's the day."

Marshall nodded solemnly.

"Is she ready?"

"Yeah, I think so."

"Are you?"

Marshall grabbed a beer and sat down on one of the patio chairs facing his brother. "Good question." He took a swig of beer. "I'd be lying if I said I didn't think Trenay was crazy for going back home, but she's made up her mind. Short of kidnapping her and holding her hostage, I can't do anything to stop her. All I can do at this point is to offer whatever protection I can and pray for the best."

"Do you remember my friend Wayne Bradford? He does some private surveillance and security work. If you want I can make a phone call and have him keep an eye out for trouble."

"We'll see. I had one of my guys replace her locks with deadbolts and I'll get some small surveillance cameras when we get back. I'll probably be able to take care of installing those myself. Other than that, I'll just have to keep my eyes and ears open and make sure she's safe."

"How are you going to do that and run your business?"

"I'm just going to have to make it work, little brother. Trenay's worth it."

Dinner turned out to be a wonderful combination of delicious food, good conversation, and relaxing time. Lee grilled steaks, burgers, brats, and vegetables. Katrice prepared a simple mixed green salad, corn on the cob, potato salad, baked beans, and rounded out the meal with homemade strawberry shortcake.

After dinner, Marshall and Lee played soccer in the backyard with Taj and his new soccer ball. Trenay played with the baby until it was time for her to go to bed.

When it was finally time to go home the good-byes were bittersweet. Katrice blinked back tears when she hugged Trenay and Marshall. She made him promise to bring Trenay back very soon for one of their neighborhood cookouts. Katrice even sent them home with freshly made scones.

"These go great with coffee and long drives," she said, sensing neither Trenay nor Marshall would be thinking about preparing breakfast the next morning.

Lee gave his brother the number for his detective friend and made him promise to use good judgment. The last thing he said to Marshall, out of earshot of both Trenay and Katrice, "I love you, man. Don't be a hero."

CHAPTER THIRTY

Marshall made love to Trenay with all of the passion and love he had to give until he was spent, physically and emotionally. He had hoped sleep would come easily but physical exhaustion hadn't been enough to bring him rest or peace of mind.

Throughout the night he held Trenay tightly in his arms. Her soft rhythmic breathing soothed him. Right now, at this moment, she was safe. He didn't know if he could guarantee that tomorrow.

***

The drive up highway 23 leaving Benton Lake started pretty much the same way it had getting there, with both Trenay and Lee lost in their own thoughts.

Trenay watched the passing scenery bathed in the early morning sunlight, feeling a little sad about leaving a place she had called home for several weeks.

The summer had been interesting, to say the least. In a million years Trenay couldn't have predicted the turn of events that had not only turned her life upside down but in some ways had set some things right and made her stronger in the process.

A stalker, someone she didn't know but who knew her and wanted to hurt her, had caused all of this. Yes, she had become a different person over the summer, not due to some superhuman powers she discovered, but due largely in part to Marshall.

She thought about the self-defense drills he taught her. While she wouldn't consider herself one of the Avengers, she had a new sense of self-confidence about her well-being, something she didn't have before.

Marshall had been responsible for uncovering something else – her heart. For a long time, Trenay had worked on establishing a solid career for herself. She had refused to be sidetracked by anything or anyone who couldn't help her meet her goals. In turn, she never realized just how much she had closed herself off emotionally.

In the past, dating had seemed frivolous. Relationships, a waste of time. Love, something only found in fairy tales. She had been content living her life on her terms, even if that meant living it alone. But Marshall gave her a peek into another dimension. In this new dimension, she could still have her career, independence, *and* someone to care about, without compromises. Now she only had to decide if that's what she wanted.

Trenay thought about her conversation with Katrice. Whatever decision she made, it wouldn't just be her heart on the line, but Marshall's, too.

Soon she would be back in her own house. It would be different there. She expected it would feel strange and she thought she might even feel lonely after having spent so much time with Marshall. He had offered to stay with her for a few days but she had declined his offer. It would be too easy to use his presence as a crutch. She had to make this transition on her own no matter how nervous she was to do so.

Marshall stared straight ahead, hands gripping the steering wheel, his mind racing with a thousand thoughts, all centered on the woman who had changed his life in a matter of weeks.

He wanted to ask Trenay to reconsider his offer and let him stay at her place for at least a few nights, but he would have better luck stumbling upon a leprechaun than getting her to agree with him. In typical Trenay fashion, she stood her ground and refused to budge, no matter how foolish it seemed she was being. At times he loved and hated her stubbornness. In this instance, he hated it.

They drove the remainder of the trip without saying too much to each other. The moment they reached the city limits Trenay became noticeably more nervous. She began fidgeting and tapping her foot.

While keeping one hand on the steering wheel, Marshall reached over and took hold of her hand with the other. It was cold as ice.

His heart ached for her. "Sweetheart, you don't have to do this."

"Yes, I do," she responded quietly.

Instead of going directly to Trenay's house, they stopped at the grocery store and picked up milk, eggs, bread, and a few items for dinner. It wasn't the usual grocery store where Trenay did most of her shopping but she still paid close attention to the shoppers inside and outside of the store to see if she noticed any strange activity. Thankfully, she didn't.

Driving down Trenay's street she looked around

reacquainting herself with the neighborhood and searching for signs that something might be out place. A few children were running through the sprinkler in her neighbor's yard, giggling and enjoying the early afternoon sunshine of another carefree summer day. Mr. Fillmore who lived a few houses down from her was out inspecting his near-perfect lawn for weeds. There were some teenagers she didn't recognize skateboarding up and down the sidewalk.

Nothing seemed out of place.

Marshall pulled his truck into her driveway. After turning off the engine, he waited for a second to see if she would make a move to get out of the truck. If she didn't and said she wanted to leave, he would be perfectly happy to take her anywhere she wanted to go, even back to Benton Lake.

Trenay tried to still her shaking hand as she opened the truck's door. Slowly she stepped out, keeping her eyes on her house, again looking to see if she noticed anything out of place. She heard Marshall coming up behind her. Rummaging through her purse for her keys she remembered her locks had been changed and she didn't have the new keys. Distraught, she turned to Marshall who was right by her side.

"Come on," he said gently, leading her to the front door. He pulled out a set of keys, unlocked the door, and stepped in ahead of her, giving the place a quick once over before letting her inside.

Once he let her know it was okay to enter, Trenay took a deep breath and walked through her front door for the first time in weeks. The first thing she noticed when she stepped inside her house was that everything seemed cloaked in darkness. Not at all typical of the bright open space she usually created by opening her curtains and blinds, letting in as much natural light as possible. Then again, she reminded herself, nothing would be typical again. At the very least she could open some curtains and bring some life back into her house. She made a move toward the living room but Marshall put his hand out to stop her from going any further. "Wait here for a second while I check everything out."

Trenay stood deathly still while she listened as Marshall walked from room to room opening and closing doors. She assumed he was checking behind the drapes when she heard the distinctive sound of drapery rings sliding across the metal rods.

After a few minutes, he returned. "All clear," he announced.

She tried to smile at the reassurance of learning her home was safe but the smile never reached the surface. "I guess I should have remembered that from my training. Always be aware of your surroundings, right? Good thing I'm not being graded."

The attempt at humor didn't go unnoticed. Marshall knew she was trying and he wanted to remind her to be patient, but he didn't think she wanted to hear that message again. "This is your home, Trenay. You're safe here. But from now on you'll have to take an extra step to make sure that's always the case."

Her eyes dropped and she let out a weary sigh.

He knew how she felt, but as much as he wanted to make everything okay, he also knew from this point on she had to rely on her strength, not just his. "Come on, let's put the groceries away." Marshall took her hand, leading her into the kitchen.

"I called Cristina. She wanted to know if you wanted the cats back tonight or tomorrow."

"What did you tell her?"

"I told her tomorrow. I also told her you wouldn't be back to work until Monday. That'll give you tomorrow and the rest of the weekend to get settled. I hope that was okay."

Trenay nodded.

Marshall placed the last few grocery items in the refrigerator and folded the bags, putting them away to use for later. He'd even remembered to get paper and not plastic. Next time he would buy some of the canvas reusable bags he saw near the checkout.

"All right, let's take your bags upstairs and get unpacked."

Trenay led the way to her bedroom carrying one of the two suitcases that had initially been packed for her to take to Marshall's.

Placing the other suitcase beside the bed Marshall left Trenay alone to unpack. When he heard her come from the spare bedroom where she stored the empty suitcases he joined her back in her room where he found her sitting on the side of the bed, staring off into the distance, deep in thought.

For the hundredth time that day, he felt an ache in his

heart so strong he nearly became overcome with emotion. He loved Trenay and wanted to protect her but he had to be careful not to allow his strength to overshadow hers. He didn't want to become what Trenay had accused him of – her rescuer. That wasn't what she needed right now. He had to find the right balance or possibly risk facing her resentment.

Marshall walked over to the bed and sat next to Trenay. "At any time you feel as if you can't or don't want to do this, just say the word. We can go back to Benton Lake at any time."

Trenay turned to him and smiled weakly. "You're so good to me."

"You're easy to be good to," he said, returning her smile.

She let out a long, slow sigh attempting to release as much tension as possible. "Marshall?"

"Yes, baby?"

"I'm tired," she whispered, leaning her head against his shoulder.

Kissing her tenderly on her temple, he held her for a moment before gently guiding her down on to the bed. He removed her shoes and placed them at the foot of the bed. Then he removed his shoes and joined her. They lay facing each other, not speaking but each drawing what was needed from the other.

Fighting an overwhelming need to cry Trenay closed her eyes knowing that if she allowed one tear to fall, others would quickly follow and she wouldn't have the strength to stop them. Listening to the sounds outside her bedroom window of children playing, lawnmowers, and laughter she stopped fighting the fatigue which permeated down to her soul.

Marshall pulled her as close to him as possible, holding her, stroking her hair, and protecting her until eventually, she drifted off to sleep.

CHAPTER THIRTY-ONE

Good, she's back. I wonder if she knows how much she was missed.

Driving slowly enough to get a reasonably good look at the house but not so slowly he would arouse suspicion, he continued to access the situation.

That truck. Hmm…he wondered how long *he* would be hanging around. Hopefully not too long. Depending on how involved he was in Trenay's life, he might end up as collateral damage, which at the moment seemed a distinct possibility. Putting a few random pieces together, he had surmised that the owner of the truck was someone important in Trenay's life. He may have even been the one who had been hiding her. He wasn't very smart. *If he knew what was good for his girlfriend, he would have kept her hidden. Their bad luck; his good fortune.*

Trenay's absence hadn't been a complete waste of time. It had actually been time well spent, allowing him to perfect his plan and make adjustments where necessary. Now the execution of the revised plan would be even more fulfilling than the original version. He laughed, in spite of himself, at the clever play on words – *execution.*

Reaching the end of the street, he thought about making one more pass by Trenay's house but quickly thought better of it. Anonymity had been his most important advantage; jeopardizing his anonymity now would be stupid and reckless.

He had decided to let Trenay get settled back into a routine. He wasn't sure how long that would take. When the time was right, he would know it. Until then he had decided it would be best to lay low. It would be sweeter that way.

He turned on the radio, tapping his fingers to the catchy rhythm of a song he would normally not have paid much attention to, but today was a good day and his mood had suddenly brightened at the reappearance of dear Trenay.

If she knew what was good for her, she'd expect the unexpected.

Yes, a week should be about right, two weeks tops. She would easily fall back into her familiar humdrum life. Then, when she least expected it, when she once again felt all was right with the world...*Wham!* The sound of his fist hitting the steering wheel made a dull, heavy sound, punctuating the sentiment.

Just then, the car behind him hit their horn, startling him. Annoyed, he flipped the driver the bird before turning on to the next street.

He felt almost giddy thinking about how everything would play out. From the very beginning, he had likened his plan to a theatrical play. Just getting Trenay all alone would be the exhilarating opening. He would take his time with her, letting each scene reveal more and more about himself and his motive. Taking his time and not rushing the plan/production would be important. He knew Trenay. She would be nervous. He would have to calm her down so she would listen and come to understand what this was all about. He wondered if she would feel sorry for him then. He hoped not. It wasn't pity he wanted. Oh, but there was so much more he wanted from her than mere pity.

Once he had her undivided attention, he would introduce himself, not in the typical way strangers met, but in a more intimate way. She would learn who he was by his story, his long, sad story, and he'd spare no detail. The best part about all of this is that she would have to sit quietly and listen to everything he had to say. After all, where would she go? She would truly be a captive audience.

After the grand introduction and then going into a detailed account of his life, which she would see contrasted sharply to hers, he could finally release all of the anger, hurt, and disappointment he'd carried with him his whole life. Finally, he would be free.

Then, the final act. He closed his eyes and imagined it like so many other times before, each detail carefully thought out and planned. The precision with which his plan would be carried out gave him chills. *Yes,* he thought, *the finale.* At that moment, nothing or no one would be able to stop him. It would be perfect. It would be…*poetic.*

CHAPTER THIRTY-TWO

Trenay sat straight up in bed when she heard the doorbell ring. Her heart pounded in her chest as she looked from side to side at her semi-familiar surroundings, fighting to remember exactly where she was.

Home. I'm home.

She forced herself to calm down, taking a moment to steady herself before getting out of bed. It had gotten dark outside and inside her bedroom. She switched on the lamp beside her bed and looked at the clock on her nightstand. Pushing the blanket off her legs she sat up on the edge of the bed.

"Answer the door," she urged herself quietly when she heard it chime again. Afraid to move, she simply waited. Maybe whoever was at the door would go away.

Then she heard muffled voices downstairs, one belonged to Marshall. She breathed a sigh of relief. Afraid he had gone home she instantly felt better knowing he hadn't. *Get it together, girl!*

Trenay took a deep breath and forced herself to get up. She went into the bathroom and looked at her reflection in the mirror. *You're stronger than you think.* Marshall's words echoed in the back of her mind. She hoped he was right.

After splashing water on her face and running her fingers through her hair, she joined him downstairs.

"Wow, what's all this?" she asked looking at the Styrofoam containers lining the kitchen counter.

"Dinner. Grab a plate and dig in. I ordered a little bit of everything so I don't want to hear you're not hungry."

Doing as she was instructed she took small amounts from each container.

"What happened to cooking?" she asked between bites. "Not that I'm against all of this, but wasn't that the purpose of stopping by the grocery store earlier?"

"We'll cook tomorrow."

"What's in the bag?" she asked, nodding toward a small paper bag on the table.

"Dessert," he replied, wriggling his eyebrows.

Trenay ate everything on her plate and even went back for seconds. She had been too anxious to have anything more than Katrice's scones and tea earlier for breakfast and hadn't eaten anything since.

"Thanks. Everything, and I mean *everything*, was good. Now I'm too stuffed to move," she remarked.

"I'm glad you liked it."

"Now what?"

"Now we clean up."

Trenay and Marshall made quick work of tidying up the kitchen and putting the leftovers away. Once all the food had been put away and the dishes washed, they settled on the couch in the family room to watch TV.

Trenay snuggled up next to Marshall on the couch and drifted in and out of sleep. Marshall held her close, listening intently to the sounds inside and outside of the house – every car door slam, barking dog, and floorboard creak.

Earlier while Trenay slept he had spoken with Detective Prosser and confirmed that he would send a patrol car by at random times to make sure everything appeared okay. Marshall had also spoken to the neighbors on either side of Trenay, informing them there had been some break-ins in the area and asked them to keep an eye out for someone who didn't look familiar and to call him or the police if something seemed odd. He didn't want to be specific and mention the stalking incidents; instead, he simply gave enough information to ensure they would be on alert.

When it got close to midnight, Marshall reluctantly decided it was time to leave. Trenay needed to get some sleep. As much as he enjoyed having her rest in his arms, she was exhausted and needed to get some real sleep, in her bed. He prayed she would be safe and could sleep peacefully in the house by herself.

As he stood by the front door, preparing to leave Marshall thought once again about extending an offer to spend the night, but thought better of it. He had to give Trenay the space to stand on her own two feet. "When I close the door, lock it. I'll wait until I hear you click the locks before I leave."

"Yes, sir," she replied, trying to make light of the situation.

"I'm serious," Marshall said firmly.

Trenay nodded, stifling a yawn. "I know. Don't worry. This place will be locked tighter than Fort Knox. Now go. You need to get your rest, too."

Marshall kissed her and waited for her to close the door. He heard her lock the deadbolt and the bottom lock and slide the chain into place. Turning toward the street he looked to see if there were any cars parked along the street that seemed as if they didn't belong, not that he was familiar enough to tell otherwise, but he did his best with the little he knew.

Satisfied she was secure, Marshall walked to the back of the house and surveyed the backyard. Everything appeared to be okay.

For a few minutes, Marshall sat in his truck in Trenay's driveway before starting the engine. He would have sat there all night if he had to. Instead, he waited. She had left the light on downstairs as he'd instructed. Her bedroom was toward the back of the house so he couldn't see the light from that window.

He waited another minute or so, looked around the neighborhood once more, and slowly pulled out of the driveway, all the while whispering a prayer of safety for Trenay.

***

Trenay lay in bed staring up at the ceiling. Listening to the low hum of the ceiling fan she thought about all of the things she needed to do before returning to work on Monday. Tomorrow Cristina would bring Felix and Oscar home. It would be nice seeing her two favorite furry friends. She hoped they weren't too traumatized by her absence or their sudden change of routine and residence.

The house needed a good dusting and the carpet needed vacuuming. It didn't even smell like her house anymore. Once she worked up enough nerve, she wanted to open up all the windows to let some fresh air in.

She also needed to go by the post office and pick up her mail. Either Cristina or Marshall had put a stop on mail delivery when she was gone. Almost all of what she received any more in the mail amounted to a bunch of junk, especially since most of her bills were handled electronically, but she still wanted to see if anything important had been delivered.

Her car had been sitting idle for several weeks and would probably need a jump and maybe a trip to the car wash.

She turned on her side facing her bedroom door. Trying to focus on any and everything except the one thought that refused to go away wasn't easy. No matter how she tried to put on a brave front, it didn't amount to anything more than that – a brave front. Admittedly, it would have been easy to stay in Benton Lake with Marshall but at the same time unrealistic to think she could live that way forever. She had a job that she loved and a life she needed to get back to.

Marshall had made her feel safe and protected and for that she was thankful. Now, to feel the same sense of security she'd felt with him, she would have to rely solely on herself. No matter how much she tried to convince herself otherwise, doing so might prove to be the hardest thing she'd ever done.

CHAPTER THIRTY-THREE

The clock at the bottom corner of the computer screen read one-fifteen. Trenay had been moving slowly all morning and even slower that afternoon while trying to get back into the routine of work, but finding it rather difficult. Friends and acquaintances from the mayor's office to the janitorial staff had been stopping by to welcome her back. Most of them knew the circumstances surrounding her absence but were sensitive enough to not bring it up.

After clearing out her email box she finally mustered up enough *oomph* to review some files Cristina had left for her.

Picking up one file after another her struggle to concentrate continued. Maybe she had come back to work too soon. No, she thought. Better to dive back in than to sit at home and be afraid. At least at the office, she could be around other people.

Checking the time again on the computer screen she noticed the new email icon flashing. Opening up her email, she smiled when she saw a message from Marshall. The subject read "Dinner? To cook or not to cook? EOM."

Trenay smiled, remembering the reference. *Eat out more.*

While she was typing a reply, Cristina walked in.

"You're smiling! It's good to see you're happy. Did

somebody email you a joke?"

"Kind of," she replied and hit the send button.

"Well, I've got something to tell you and I promise it's going to be better than any email joke."

"What?" she asked, skimming through the pile of mail Cristina had just placed on her desk.

"Guess who's retiring?"

"No clue."

"Come on, you're no fun. You could at least try to guess."

"Okay. The old guy who does the weather on channel 4."

"No. Better. Councilman Ryan!"

Trenay put down the letter she was skimming over and stared up at Cristina in disbelief. "What? When did this happen?"

"The old snake tendered his resignation last week, citing health concerns. The mayor hasn't appointed anyone yet to replace him for the remainder of his term but I'm pretty sure it will be someone more progressive than that old goat."

"Wow. That is good news."

Cristina stood looking down at Trenay with a wide grin on her face.

"What?"

"There's more," Cristina replied, barely able to contain her excitement. She whipped out a letter she had been hiding behind her back, shaking it in Trenay's face.

Trenay took the letter and began reading. "Oh my goodness," she exclaimed after a few seconds.

"I know! Keep reading."

"Our office is being honored for our efforts to advance energy efficiency and renewable energy information and applications to a broad and diverse audience throughout the state," she read.

"I know!" Cristina squealed.

"Oh my goodness," Trenay said again, this time waving the letter in the air. "This is one of the highest honors we could receive. Cristina, do you know what this means?"

"Yes, an all-expenses-paid trip to Washington, D. C. for you and your assistant."

"Yes, but it means more than that. We can expand our program with the grant money as a result of receiving this honor. This means we can help more businesses, smaller ones who may not have been able to make the necessary transition to becoming more energy efficient. Or, better yet, maybe we can earmark this money to rehab homes in the neighborhoods that desperately need the kind of resources we can provide."

"Oh yeah, that, too."

Trenay pushed the pile of mail aside and opened up some files on her computer. Before long she was typing fast and furiously. "Cristina, when will Mayor Hanover be back in the office?"

"Tomorrow afternoon."

"Good. Schedule a meeting with him, Randy from the Office of Urban Affairs, and someone from the Planning Commission. Oh, and see if the Building Commissioner is available, too."

Cristina jotted down notes on a scratch pad while Trenay gave her instructions for records she needed to be brought up from the file room, applications to be reviewed, and meetings to schedule.

On her way out of the office, she turned to her boss and smiled. Trenay had become completely engrossed in her work and seemed like her old self again. "I'm glad you're back," she said.

Trenay stopped typing and looked up at her friend. Smiling warmly she replied, "So am I."

CHAPTER THIRTY-FOUR

That's right. Live your life. Get comfortable and into a routine. Little by little, things will fall into place. You'll become complacent, ignoring little changes, not paying attention to your surroundings, or even to the people who are watching your every move.

From this point on it's just a matter of time…

***

"Excited?"

"Very."

"But?" Marshall asked sensing hesitation in Trenay's unspoken words.

"Really, I'm excited. My mind is racing with all of the good we can do with the grant money that comes with this honor."

Marshall sat a plate of food in front of Trenay and took a seat across from her at the table. She tried to sound convincing but he knew better.

"This is going to pass, baby."

Trenay stared down at her plate. Sitting back in her chair she looked across at Marshall, whom she knew understood how she felt better than anyone else and like her was powerless to wave a magic wand and make the world right again. "I know it will. Don't get me wrong, I'm very proud and excited about the honor our office has received, but…" she paused, searching for words that might truly convey how she felt.

"But the uncertainty of…the case…makes it hard to enjoy this success."

Resting her elbows on the table, she tried to smile. "Either I'm that transparent or we've been together so much that you know what I'm thinking before I say it."

If only that were true, Marshall thought, as he watched Trenay pick at her food.

If he could read her thoughts he would know how she felt about him…about them. He would know if she longed to be in his arms as much as he longed to have her there. He would know without her having to say if she needed a hug, a kiss, or simply wanted to sit quietly in comfortable silence. To be able to read her thoughts would allow him to know exactly what she needed and when.

Without using words he would know that she understood how difficult it had been for him to leave her on her own the night they returned from Benton Lake.

The biggest advantage of all to knowing Trenay's unspoken thoughts, and the one thing that would mean everything to him, would provide an answer to the single most important question he was afraid to ask: *Did she love him, too?*

CHAPTER THIRTY-FIVE

Nearly three weeks had passed since Trenay and Marshall returned from Benton Lake. During that time, Trenay checked in regularly with Detective Prosser to see if he had any new leads. He still did not.

Even though he didn't say it outright, she had a feeling her case had been moved to the back burner, and maybe rightfully so. Every night on the news she heard one story after another about a robbery, murder, or assault which had taken place somewhere in the city. Surely those cases took precedence over hers, especially since there weren't any new leads, nor had there been any more incidents.

Forcing herself to regain control of her life, little by little Trenay had begun to return to some of her favorite places – the coffee shop where she liked to buy herbal tea and muffins, the dry cleaners, and even the park where she liked to take brisk walks. Although ever vigilant, she made sure to pay close attention to her environment.

Tea and walks in the park weren't the only things that had become part of her return to normality. Since they'd been back she and Marshall had fallen into a bit of a routine, albeit a nice one. Most evenings he would either come to her house for dinner or she would go to his. She liked his house in the city almost as much as she liked the cabin at the lake. She felt safe and comfortable in both places, probably due more to Marshall's presence than anything else.

The time she spent with Marshall was nice. She looked forward to seeing him in the evenings and talking to him occasionally throughout the day. He always made a point to ask about her day. He listened when she talked about the various projects she was working on and she liked hearing him talk about his projects and the guys working for him. Marshall was as passionate about his work and the people who worked for him as she was about hers. Meeting up with him a few times on job sites, she had a chance to see him in action. Marshall was the kind of boss who got things done. He had a lot of respect for his crews and it showed in the way he interacted with them and treated them as valuable assets, not as a means to a financial end. And the respect was mutual.

She was coming to appreciate that Marshall had that effect on a lot of people. She was no exception. She had a great deal of admiration for Marshall, amongst other things. While they didn't talk about their feelings for each other anymore, one thing she knew for sure, he loved her. Everything he did demonstrated to her how he felt, not in an overt or boastful way, but a more gentle and thoughtful manner. Even if he had never said the words 'I love you', she knew he loved her and she felt it with every gesture, word, kiss, caress, and look.

Before they left Benton Lake Marshall had confessed his feelings for her. He told her he loved her. Facing the uncertainty of what they would deal with when returning home, he only wanted her to know how he felt. At the time, he hadn't pressured her to find out where she stood.

It wasn't as if she didn't think about her feelings for Marshall. On the contrary, she couldn't ignore them. Other than work and her case, that's was pretty much all she thought about. Marshall was on her mind morning, noon, and night, and more often than not, in her dreams.

Marshall was easy to be with and easy to love. Yes, she did love him. She hadn't told him so, but she had no doubt what she felt for him was a deep and ever-growing love.

Tired of feeling as if her life was in limbo, she wanted more than anything to move forward. She wanted to forget about past events, almost as if they never happened. She wanted to pretend that life was normal again. Over and over she tried to convince herself of that, but it hadn't completely worked. The dark cloud of uncertainty and underlying fear still hung ominously over her life. And before entering into a more meaningful relationship with Marshall, something she did want, or even exploring the opportunity to do so, she needed to be sure she had the freedom to move forward. She had to know that beyond all doubt, what she feared was gone from her life for good. But until the police confirmed it, all she could do is pray that when and if this unstable person came back into her life, she would be ready.

CHAPTER THIRTY-SIX

Marshall scrolled through the pictures on his phone until he found the one he wanted; Trenay, sitting on the bank at the lake watching the sunset. She looked happy and completely at peace.

Trenay had discovered he'd taken the picture of her when they had returned from the lake that night. Once she saw it she didn't seem to mind but she did comment about her hair being messy. To Marshall, she simply looked beautiful.

The day the picture was taken had been one of those days when everything seemed perfect, or as perfect as it could be. Earlier in the afternoon, they'd practiced self-defense drills, later had an early dinner, and then decided on a whim to take a walk down by the lake. It had been hot most of the day, but the evening had cooled off enough to enjoy spending time outside. The breeze off the lake made the temperature more tolerable and provided enough energy to stir the leaves on the trees. Crickets chirped, bees buzzed, and a flock of Canadian geese headed off to wherever they rested for the evening. Marshall and Trenay had sat quietly, observing it all and marveling at the beauty in simple things.

Now those carefree days were in the past and Marshall wanted more than anything to spend another evening as private and uncomplicated as that one had been.

Zenobia cleared her throat.

Looking up Marshall abruptly shoved his phone off to the side of his desk. "How long have you been standing there?"

"Long enough for me to see you're in desperate need of my services."

Embarrassed he'd been caught engaging in something as unproductive as daydreaming, Marshall feigned annoyance. "If they aren't admin services I'm not interested."

Undaunted, Zenobia continued, "Oh, but I think you might be interested in what I have to offer."

"Why's that?" he asked, clicking his mouse and pretending to scroll through something important on the computer screen.

Taking a seat across from her boss, Zenobia heard him sigh heavily. "Oh come on now, Marshall. You know I have never steered you wrong and I'm not about to start now."

"Get to the point, Zen," he said tersely, jotting down a note about nothing important but wanting to seem busy.

"Like my granddaddy used to say, I know you like the back of my hand. You might be able to fool other people, but not me."

Exasperated, Marshall stopped writing and looked up. "Zen, what are you talking about?"

"Trenay! And the fact that you are so head over heels in love with her you can't see straight."

Zenobia had seen Marshall at his best and his worst. Right now wasn't exactly his best. She knew him and she could help if he let her. He needed to hear what she had to say whether he wanted to or not.

Marshall put his pen down and glared at his assistant. He wanted to be angry with her for prying, but he knew she was only looking out for him. What could he say in his defense? Absolutely nothing. He couldn't fool Zen. She was right; she did know him, better than almost anyone, although he would never give her the satisfaction of admitting it. Over the years as closely as they had worked together and with Zenobia putting in just as much blood, sweat, and tears into building up the business, she had become more than his assistant. Truth be told, he didn't know what he'd do without her and he hoped he would never have to find out.

Marshall closed his eyes briefly. Maybe it was time to talk about his feelings. Maybe then his heart wouldn't be so heavy. "Okay, Zen, you're right. I'm very much in love with Trenay."

"So what are you going to do about it?"

"What *can* I do about it?"

"Have you told her how you feel?"

"Yes."

"Okay, let me be more specific. Have you told her you love her?"

"Yes, once."

"And?"

"And she didn't say it back."

"Hmm…that could mean a few things, not necessarily no. Words don't always tell the tale. And we all know actions sometimes speak louder than words."

Marshall shrugged. "So the saying goes."

"Does she act like she loves you?"

"Zen, I-I don't know," he replied, annoyed. "What signs should I be looking for? See if she doodles hearts around our initials on a piece of paper? Check to see if she's written *Mrs. Marshall Oliver* inside her science book?"

"No need to be sarcastic."

"Look, in a way this love thing is kind of new to me. And to complicate matters, as if we need more complications, some nut was stalking her, breaking into her home and where she worked, sending her into an almost paralyzing state of fear. For a while when we first got to the lake the woman barely left her bedroom. I had to practically drag her out of the house. Now, she's back home but I can't say everything is back to normal because I don't know if normal is even an option anymore. I love Trenay more than I have ever loved anyone. I go to bed at night thinking about her. I wake up thinking about her. I drive to work thinking about her. I drive home thinking about her. I'm at a point where I'm afraid to imagine what life would be like without her."

"Have you told her that?'

Marshall rubbed his hand over the back of his neck. "Not in so many words. And I don't know that I would say all of that anyway. She might think I'm nuts."

"She's probably afraid, Marshall."

"Well, that makes two of us."

"Look, I think you need to give her the benefit of the doubt. I guarantee Trenay is thinking about you almost as much as you're thinking about her. If I had to make a guess, I'd say she is afraid to move forward because she doesn't know when or if this crazy person is going to show up again. Before making a move with you, she probably wants to make sure the relationship is on a firm foundation and not one that can be rocked at a moment's notice by something or someone she has no control over."

Marshall nodded. Everything Zenobia said made sense. He only wished their circumstances were different.

Zenobia stood ready to leave.

Marshall tried to smile but the ache in his heart prevented it. "I know I must sound like a lovesick teenager. You're a good listener and a good friend. A little nosey and a bit pushy, but I still love you. Thanks for not making fun of me and thanks for the advice, Zen."

"Anytime, boss. By the way, my *other* services are available whenever you're ready."

Marshall looked puzzled.

"I'm your girl when you're ready to pick out the ring," she replied with a wink. "If you haven't noticed, I have impeccable taste."

CHAPTER THIRTY-SEVEN

Tick. Tock. Tick. Tock. Time's up...
***

Trenay watched from her living room window as Marshall backed out of the driveway. He needed to be in Cleveland to check on a project that had gotten severely delayed due to an order mix up with one of the suppliers. Marshall had been hesitant to leave and had tried to convince Trenay to make the overnight trip with him, but she had a very important meeting the next day with a newly formed neighborhood association. She had targeted a neighborhood on the south side of the city to receive funds from the grant money her office had been awarded. The grant money would be used to rehab several abandoned houses and turn them into multi-unit apartments and single-family homes. This project, she felt, would be the shot in the arm the neighborhood needed to begin to get back on track.

After Marshall left, Trenay settled in for the evening and tried not to think too much about him being away. As instructed she had diligently checked all of the doors and windows before he left and she checked them once more after he was gone.

Deciding the best way to keep her mind occupied was to concentrate on work. Pulling out the architect's plans for one of the houses selected to be rehabbed she studied every detail. The house was a three-level brick home with a large front porch. Each floor would become a separate rental unit, which would include one bedroom, one bath, and a small kitchenette and dining area. Shared laundry facilities would be located in the basement as well as an additional space for storage. She liked the layout on paper but knew she would love to see the finished project.

Earlier in the day, she had driven down the street where three of the houses were located. Over the years absentee landowners had abandoned many houses in the area. Sadly, whenever that happens criminal activity and lack of pride for the neighborhood seem to follow. While there were still several well-kept homes on the block, more was needed.

It made Trenay sad to see children playing on the sidewalks and at the same time exposed to the drug activity she was sure took place in some of the abandoned houses. She prayed this project would be enough to restore its pride and bring back a sense of responsibility to care for each other.

Trenay arrived early at work the next morning. As hard as she tried, she hadn't slept well, tossing and turning most of the night. So the next logical thing to do – in her mind – was to get up and go to work. She wouldn't be meeting with the neighborhood association until after lunch, which left her plenty of time to review the architect's drawings once more and to tighten up her presentation.

Sitting at her computer she heard Cristina in the outer

office. It must have been a good night. Her assistant was singing.

"Do I even want to know?" Trenay asked, graciously accepting the cup of tea and muffin her assistant had brought in with her.

"You might want to know, but I can't tell," she teased. "All I can say is tall, dark, handsome, and *yum*. Feel free to let your imagination run wild."

"Tall, dark, handsome, and 'yum'? Where do you meet these men?" she asked, laughing. "Never mind, some things probably should remain a mystery."

Cristina shrugged and winked. "What's that?" she asked, sipping her aromatic coffee concoction.

"The architect's drawings for the south side neighborhood rehab."

Cristina nodded. She knew the neighborhood well and did her best to avoid being anywhere near it at all costs. "Far be it from me to be the wet blanket, but I hope you realize that even though you're excited about this project, not everyone else will be. There are people in that neighborhood who simply want those abandoned houses torn down. They don't see the value in trying to fix up old, dilapidated eyesores."

Trenay nodded. "I know. I'm sure someone is going to bring up the fact that any money coming into their neighborhood should be spent on police protection and anti-gang or anti-drug initiatives."

"I have to say, I think the same thing. It's a pretty depressing area. The only people who are there now are the ones with nowhere else to go."

"But don't you agree it's important to provide affordable housing?"

"Of course I do. But cheap rent doesn't mean I want to come home and see dope boys and prostitutes in my front yard. I say get rid of the crime, then work on the affordable housing part."

Trenay placed her cup on the desk and looked thoughtfully at her friend. The things she was hearing from Cristina was what she'd have to prepare to be asked and have a good answer for that afternoon. "I know this isn't the silver bullet, but we have to start somewhere."

Cristina nodded. That's what she loved about her friend, the eternal optimist. "All I can say is good luck and watch your back."

CHAPTER THIRTY-EIGHT

Trenay had just pulled into the parking lot of the neighborhood center when her phone rang. Fishing it out of her purse she saw it was Marshall calling.

"Hi. How's it going?"

"Fine, I guess."

"What's wrong?" she asked, sensing things weren't exactly fine.

"I'm just frustrated. A major supply order was canceled and no one seems to know who canceled it. I probably wouldn't be so upset if we could move forward without the materials, but we can't. This kind of mistake is going to set the project back four to six weeks."

"Wow. I'm sorry. Is there any way to make up the time?"

"Not without working sixteen-hour days and killing my crew in the process. I'll have to follow up with Zen when I get back. She went to Las Vegas for a mini-vacation and won't be back until Monday. I guess in the meantime there's not a whole lot I can do. I'm going to meet with my stakeholders tomorrow and try to smooth things over and see if the supplier can put a rush on the materials we ordered."

Trenay rolled down the windows to let a little air in the car. "So you won't be back tonight?"

"Is everything all right?" Marshall asked, picking up on

her change in tone.

"Yes, of course, everything's fine," she said a little too quickly to sound convincing.

This would be the second night she would have to spend alone. Yes, she slept at her house by herself most nights, but Marshall was never more than a phone call away. Well, she wanted to stand on her own two feet. Now she would have to. Besides, what other choice did she have? She certainly couldn't ask him to make the three-hour drive back that night only to have to turn around and drive back to Cleveland tomorrow. Surely she should be able to handle one more night alone.

"Are you sure you're all right?"

Trenay could hear machinery in the background and someone calling Marshall's name. "Yes, really, I'm fine and everything is okay," she said, infusing as much confidence into her voice as she could

"Look, baby, I've got to run. If there aren't any more screw-ups I should be home tomorrow evening. One thing before I hang up."

"Yes?"

"There's something I want to talk to you about when I get back tomorrow night."

Someone called Marshall's name again and the sound of machinery seemed to get louder making it hard to hear him.

"What is it?"

"I'll tell you when I see you. Sorry, I gotta run. I'll see you tomorrow. Okay?"

She barely had time to answer before the line went

dead.

***

After about forty-five minutes Trenay began to wrap up her address to the crowd. "Ladies and gentlemen, I want to thank you for coming out this afternoon. I've left some cards on the table in the back. If you have any other questions or concerns, please do not hesitate to call my office or send me an email."

Trenay breathed a sigh of relief. The small room in the recreation center held a near-capacity crowd. She was pleased to see a decent number of residents from the area in attendance. As expected, many of the residents had voiced some of the same opinions and concerns Cristina had mentioned earlier – police protection and seeking an end to gang and drug violence. Thankfully, many of the residents understood the link between vacant properties and criminal activity. They agreed that fixing one might bring an end to the other. Trenay knew she wouldn't likely get one hundred percent consensus, but she would work with whatever cooperation she could get.

This meeting would be the first of many, but at least she was off to a good start. Folks from the neighborhood knew someone cared enough to want to make things better for them. And that was a good start.

Trenay gathered her things and prepared to leave but was stopped by a man carrying a steno book, pen, and small recording device.

"Ms. Bradley, my name is Bill Overstreet. I'm a reporter with the *South Side Voice*."

Trenay knew the newspaper well, in all of its

geographical varieties – the *West Side Voice,* the *East Side Voice*, and the *King-Lincoln Voice*. Each of the newspapers had a small readership and featured stories about the neighborhood schools, marriage, engagement and anniversary announcements, spotlights on area businesses, and other local happenings.

Hello, Mr. Overstreet," she replied, inadvertently looking at her watch.

"Please, call me Bill."

"Bill," she repeated. "It's nice to meet you."

"Likewise. As you might have guessed, I'd like to talk to you about this project and run the story in our paper."

Trenay checked her watch again. She wanted to get back to the office and finish a report the mayor needed for an upcoming presentation. On the other hand, it might be wise to talk to the paper, no matter how small their readership was. Any positive information she could get out to the residents, the better.

She chose a compromise. "I would love to sit down with you, but I really need to get back to my office." She fished around in her purse and pulled out a business card. "Under normal circumstances, I'm not this pressed for time. It's been kind of crazy at my office and my schedule has been pretty busy," she offered, feeling a need to make a plausible excuse.

"Oh, I completely understand. Do you think we could meet soon? I'd like to get the facts out to the residents before people start to speculate about things that aren't true."

"Of course." Trenay took her phone out of her bag

and pulled up her calendar. "I can meet you tomorrow afternoon. I have a couple of hours open after two or we can meet Friday morning before eleven."

"Tomorrow afternoon works."

Relieved that she had been able to schedule time with the reporter, Trenay asked Bill to call her office to give her assistant the details of when and where they would meet.

Driving back to the office Trenay tried to think about the presentation she was to prepare for the mayor, but she couldn't stay focused. No matter what she did to mentally steer herself back to work matters it was Marshall who dominated her thoughts. His being away would be something she needed to get used to. He couldn't always be at her beck and call or spend every evening with her, as much as she thought she might like if he did. He had a business to run and a life of his own. Admittedly, she had gotten used to seeing him every day and spending time with him in the evenings.

Marshall was good to her and for her. He had seen her at her most vulnerable and not once had he taken advantage or pitied her. She knew she was stronger, better, and happier because he was in her life and she couldn't think of a single reason why he shouldn't be. She missed him, more than she thought she would.

Trenay pulled into a parking spot and turned off the engine. Instead of getting out and heading straight to her office she leaned her head against the headrest and thought about the "warning" Katrice had given her. *Once those Oliver men get a hold of your heart things will never be the same.* Her heart wasn't the same. Truer words had never been spoken.

CHAPTER THIRTY-NINE

Trenay checked her email one last time before shutting down her computer and heading out to meet with the reporter from the neighborhood newspaper. Cristina had left earlier to go to the Recorder's office to do some research and wouldn't be back in the office until tomorrow. Trenay had decided she, too, might as well head home after the interview. She hadn't heard from Marshall but assumed he would still be back tonight.

Bill had asked her to meet him where a few of the abandoned houses slated for rehab were located. He wanted to run pictures of her standing in front of one of the houses along with the article.

Deciding to not take work home that evening, Trenay flipped off the lights in her office, shut the door, and left for her meeting. She hoped the interview didn't take too long as she was eager to get home and see Marshall.

Some of what she saw on her drive to the south side of town looked familiar from a few days ago - small to medium-sized, two and three-story houses, beauty shops, dollar stores, and liquor stores in great abundance. From experience, Trenay knew the character of this neighborhood and all the neighborhoods that made up the city couldn't be judged by outside appearances alone. This one like so many others was home to families who worked and played hard, celebrated life's ups and downs, and who simply wanted the same things everyone else wanted regardless of money or status – they wanted a decent place to live to raise their children and they didn't want to live in fear. She wanted the same things for them.

Trenay continued to drive until she came to a section of the neighborhood with which she was unfamiliar. She didn't know if she should turn left, right, or keep straight. Stopped at a four-way stop, she checked for the address Bill had given her. Punching the location into her GPS she patiently waited for the device's helpful voice to give her directions.

Making a series of turns she followed the directions given by the GPS and soon arrived at her destination. Pulling up behind an older model car that had seen better days, she parked and cut the engine. Giving the area a quick once over she became immediately saddened by what she imagined had once been a thriving neighborhood. Only a few houses now stood as a testament to that fact. Broken down cars, trash littered yards, and poorly kept houses now made up the neighborhood Trenay hoped to soon bring back a little of the spark and pride it once had.

Bill got out of the car toting the same type of notebook he'd been carrying when she first met him. He also had a small camera bag. His forehead glistened with sweat in the late summer heat. Trenay was pretty sure his car didn't have air conditioning and she wondered if the windows even rolled down.

"I'm sorry I'm late," she apologized. "I thought I knew how to get here but I ended up having to use my

GPS."

Bill smiled, "No problem. We all get a little lost sometimes and we need help finding our way. I'm just glad you made it here safely."

Despite his smile, Trenay detected a bit of an attitude. She didn't know if it was the heat or her being late that annoyed him more. While Bill rambled through his camera bag she checked her watch. Five minutes late. Not enough to warrant an attitude. She knew all too well the importance of punctuality. Except for this one time, she was typically quite punctual. She valued her time and others equally.

"If you don't mind, I'd like to start with a few questions. Then I want to get a few pictures of you in front of one or two of the houses on this street. Ready?"

A group of curious teenagers who looked like they were on their way to play basketball eyed them for about twenty seconds but quickly lost interest when one of the boys pulled out his cell phone to share something with the rest of the group.

Trenay nodded and Bill turned on a handheld voice recorder and flipped open his notebook. She smiled at a woman who had come out of her house to see what they were doing. Seemingly satisfied with what she witnessed as a non-criminal activity, she went back inside.

"First, can you provide a brief description of the program your office is initiating?"

Trenay talked a little about the grant money her office had been awarded. She explained how the money would be used to rehab several homes in the area to spark a neighborhood revitalization effort.

"Why not just tear these houses down? They've been abandoned for years."

"If the properties aren't a hazard to the health, safety, and welfare of the neighborhoods, then it only makes perfect sense to turn them into livable and affordable units instead of one more vacant lot that will eventually become overrun with weeds, garbage, and pests. At any given time there are over 6,000 vacant and abandoned homes in this city alone. Admittedly, some of these structures are beyond repair, but many are still structurally sound. Turning these properties into affordable living spaces is a win-win for everyone."

Bill asked Trenay a few more questions about the involvement of the mayor, and the other city offices while he jotted down some notes. After about twenty-five minutes, he wrapped up the interview.

Clicking the recorder off and tucking it inside the camera bag, Bill gave his next instructions.

Trenay followed him up the steps and on to the porch of a three-story brick house. The first-floor windows of the structure had been boarded up years ago but pieces of plywood were now missing from most of them. The windows on the second and third floors had been broken out with very little glass still intact.

Bill wanted to take a picture of Trenay standing on the porch in front of one of the boarded-up windows. She did.

After that house they walked halfway down the block to another house; this one is in slightly worse shape than the previous house. All of the windows had been broken out, garbage littered the front yard, and the front door was missing.

Bill walked up to the house, stepped onto the front porch, looked from side to side, and stepped back off the porch. He walked around the side of the house and after a few minutes, rejoined Trenay out front.

"What?" she asked, wondering what Bill was looking for.

"I know this is a little unorthodox," he began, "but do you think I could get a picture of you inside the house?"

Bill must have been outside in the sun a little too long. Why on earth would she want to step inside an abandoned house? God only knew what creepy, crawly things were nesting inside, not to mention the potential of stumbling upon a homeless person using the house as a temporary shelter, or worse. Seriously, putting this much time and attention into setting up a shot for a story that maybe sixty people would even bother to read seemed like overkill. And for that, she would put her safety at risk? *Not today, buddy.*

"I think we might be able to find a more suitable shot out here," she advised.

Disappointed and annoyed with her reluctance to indulge his journalist whim, Bill settled for a few shots of Trenay standing in the yard amongst discarded bottles, cans, old tires, and other debris.

"Thank you very much for taking the time to meet with me today." Bill had already packed up his camera bag, notebook, and pen and now stood leaning against his car with a puzzled look on his face.

"You're very welcome," Trenay responded, hoping he hadn't thought of another ridiculous shot to run with the story. She had had enough. "If there is anything else you need, please don't hesitate to contact my office."

Finally, Trenay thought as she watched Bill pull off. He seemed a little weird, but at least the interview had ended without any more odd requests.

Trenay leaned against her car and pulled out her phone. She had been dying to check to see if Marshall had left her a message, but she didn't want to further annoy Bill. Scrolling through her messages she smiled seeing a message from Marshall.

Got tied up in a meeting. I'll be home tonight, but very late. If you wait up, I'll make it worth your while. He had added a smiley face.

She missed him. Despite everything else, Marshall had been a constant in her life and she had to admit, she liked that. For once she didn't feel as if she needed to justify how she felt about him or worry about the timing of their relationship. She even readily admitted, to herself anyway, that they actually had a relationship.

Marshall loved her. Did he know she loved him? As ridiculous as it sounded, she rationalized that she hadn't said it because she wanted to wait for the right time. Maybe the right time was now. Yes, she thought, she needed to let Marshall know how she felt about him now. Why wait any longer?

Preoccupied with finding her keys and thinking about finally revealing her feelings to Marshall she never saw the man walking up to her car until it was too late.

CHAPTER FORTY

"Well, I'll be."

"What's going on, Pross?"

It had been a busy crime day. Robberies, assaults, a hit-and-run, and two bank robberies. Detective Prosser had been away from his desk most of the day but finally had a chance to follow up on a hunch he had concerning the Bradley stalking case. Glad he did as it seemed likely his hunch was paying off.

"I think I may finally have a lead in Trenay Bradley's stalking case," Detective Prosser responded, staring intently at his computer screen.

"I thought the case had gone cold."

Detective Prosser nodded "Yeah, but cold doesn't mean my investigation stopped."

"So whatcha got?"

"First things first." He grabbed a piece of paper and jotted down some notes. "I need to get in touch with Miss Bradley. If my suspicions are correct, I think we may have found our man. I just pray we find him before he finds her."

CHAPTER FORTY-ONE

As the fog began to clear, Trenay felt the remnants of a bizarre and disjointed dream slowly fading away. Her head felt heavy and when she tried to force her eyes open it seemed to take an extraordinary amount of effort. Why couldn't she wake up?

Trenay struggled to shake off the heavy veil of grogginess as the sound of slow and steady footsteps penetrated the silence. When the footsteps stopped she tried to hear something that would give her a clue as to whether she was experiencing a dream or some odd reality.

"Good, you're finally awake. I was afraid you were going to miss out on all the fun."

Sitting on the floor in the corner of a room she didn't recognize, across from a man unfamiliar to her, she blinked slowly, straining to adjust to the dusty sunlight. As her mental fog continued to dissipate she struggled to focus. Although unclear about what was happening, bit by bit she began to realize this was not a dream.

"Hello, Trenay."

How does he know my name? Something seemed very wrong. Her instincts went on high alert and she immediately sensed danger. She tried to move but her hands and feet were bound.

"Oh, you're not going anywhere. You might as well stop trying."

Bound by her hands and feet while feeling the effects of what she believed to be a drug wearing off, and being held in what looked and smelled like an abandoned house, she began to quickly put the pieces together.

The man leaned down. "You are a smart girl, aren't you? I can see your mind working to figure things out."

Understanding dawned. "*It's you*," she said, her voice laced with fear. "You're the person who was stalking me. You're the person who broke into my house and came into my office."

"True, but I wouldn't call what I was doing stalking. I don't like that word. Let's just say I was getting to know you."

"Why?" she asked. "Who are you?"

The man sat on the dusty floor and faced Trenay. "Don't I look familiar?" he asked, almost comically.

Familiar? She had never seen this man in her life. Who was he that she should know him?

"Come on, Trenay. Think. Get a good look." He turned his face to the left, then right.

Fearful but curious, she did as she was told. Searching his face, she tried to associate him with work, her circle of friends, and business associates away from the office, but she came up with nothing. Should she have known him? Had she seen him before? Around her office? Her home? At the store?

Confirming what he had suspected, he asked, "You don't know, do you?"

No, she didn't know him. No one she knew would do this; no one she knew would ever make her feel this way.

One thing she did know for sure, this man, whoever he was, meant to harm her.

Abruptly, the man stood and walked across the room. He looked over at something covered by a dirty, greasy tarp, then glanced away quickly. Taking a seat on an overturned milk crate he leaned his back against the wall opposite Trenay. For a while he only stared, appearing to feed off her fear.

Trenay tried to think through what was happening and what she could do. *Be aware of your surroundings.* A few seconds. She had been distracted for only a few seconds. She knew better. She had learned to be careful and watchful. Marshall had taught that. *Marshall,* she thought. She needed him, but she had no way of letting him know where she was or what was going on. She remembered he said he wouldn't be back until late that night. *He won't know anything is even wrong until later.* Choking back a sob she looked at the man again. He continued to stare at her, his face void of emotion.

The light in the room began to fade as the sun set for the evening. She didn't know how long she had been in the room or even where she was being held. The last thing she remembered was something hard being shoved into her back and someone telling her he had a gun. He made her get into the backseat of the car. She had barely caught a glimpse of the person talking before she felt something being sprayed into her face. The next thing she remembered was waking up inside this room.

The man pushed away from the wall and sighed heavily. "I have waited a long time to meet you, Trenay.

To meet you *formally*, I should say. I have followed your career and your rise to fame, such as it is." He smiled. "I guess you could say I have literally followed you, too."

"I do have to say you have certainly turned out to be a creature of habit and very predictable. You have a small circle of friends. You don't hang out with your co-workers except for Cristina and the twice a month lunch with His Honor, the Mayor. I've watched you over and over again buying your daily muffin and picking up the occasional pizza from Antonucci's. It's funny but you even shop at the same grocery store, go to the same dry cleaners, and pretty much keep to a regular routine."

Trenay felt a cold chill snake down her spine. She remembered the pictures.

"I do have to say, when you disappeared earlier this summer, I thought I'd lost you. By the way, where did you go? You weren't with your secretary and Mom and Dad are out of the country, and as we both know you don't own a little cabin in the Poconos or have a condo in Miami. So where were you?"

She couldn't tell him where she was. Marshall had done a great job of keeping her away from danger. He had promised her no one would find her at the lake and he had been right. With everything this man had revealed about her and the places she had been the one thing he didn't know about was Benton Lake. Even now, facing the unexpected, she needed to guard her secret place.

"You're not going to answer?" He shrugged and pushed himself up from the milk crate. "I guess in the whole scheme of things it doesn't matter. I know where you are now and it's right where I need you to be."

"Why? I don't know you and I have never done anything intentionally to hurt you. Can you just tell me who you are?" she asked again, hoping he would reveal his identity and what he wanted. Maybe then she would be able to reason with him. There had to be a way out of this. *There had to be.*

He walked over to her, squatting down, he paused before answering. "Where are my manners? It's time I properly introduced myself. My name is Steven, Steven Michael Turner to be exact. I'm your brother."

CHAPTER FORTY-TWO

Marshall swore beneath his breath. *So much for getting back early and surprising Trenay.* Traffic going 71 south had slowed down to a crawl. Between a major road construction project shutting down one of the three lanes and what he assumed was likely an accident further ahead, he knew he didn't have any other choice except to wait it out. At least if he could make it to the next exit he might be able to take a detour, although the idea of driving through several rural towns and possibly getting stuck behind a slow-moving, horse-drawn Amish buggy on a one-lane road held even less appeal than sitting and waiting for traffic to clear.

Despite the unexpected traffic delay, he was glad he'd been able to straighten out the mix up with his supplier. The project wouldn't completely recover from the loss in productivity over the next several weeks and would likely slide past the deadline by a few weeks, but he had at least smoothed everything over with the stakeholders.

His supplier, on the other hand, didn't get off as easily. The owner of the company stated their computer system had been hacked. Several of their customer's orders had been deleted, not just Oliver Construction's. Had it not been for the longstanding relationship Marshall had with the supplier, he would have dropped them on the spot and never given them another dime in business.

Despite the traffic construction and slow traffic, Marshall's mood began to mellow when he thought about going home. He couldn't wait to see Trenay. When they last spoke he told her he wanted to talk to her about something. He didn't elaborate at the time because he needed to talk to her face-to-face. He wanted to talk about them, their relationship.

Time to lay it on the line…again. He felt as if he needed to let Trenay know just how important she was to him and how much he loved her. This time he needed to know what her feelings were for him. He needed to be sure she loved him. He didn't want to speculate anymore. Once he knew for sure they could move forward, wherever forward took them. He didn't care, as long as she was there with him.

Traffic began to clear and as Marshall navigated his truck through the construction zone and slowly picked up speed, his phone rang. Hoping it was Trenay, he saw Detective Prosser's number display on the caller ID.

"This is Detective Prosser, Mr. Oliver. Is Ms. Bradley with you?"

"No," Marshall responded. "I'm driving back from Cleveland. She should be at home. Is something wrong?"

Silence.

Alarmed, Marshall asked again, this time with more urgency, "Detective, what's wrong? Is Trenay all right?"

"I've tried reaching her at work, on her cell phone, and home phone. We have a break in the case and we need to ask her some questions," the detective replied, trying his best to keep the concern out of his voice. "We've identified a possible suspect in her case."

Marshall listened, wanting to hear the detective say the person was in custody or at the very least being watched. He needed to hear Detective Prosser say the situation was under control and there was no need to worry. Instead, he heard him say they had officers out looking for Trenay. Detective Prosser tried to put Marshall's mind at ease and assure him it would only be a matter of time before she was located and brought to safety.

Sensing more than a little concern in Detective's Prosser's voice immediately set off alarm bells for Marshall. He picked up speed, moving in and out of lanes as the traffic congestion eased.

There was a pause on the line. Marshall could hear people talking but it sounded as if someone had their hand covering the phone's mouthpiece.

After a few more seconds, Detective Prosser came back on the line. "I'm sorry. I was getting an update from one of the officers."

"What is it?" he asked. "Did you find Trenay? Is she okay?"

Clinging to the hope the police would find Trenay before the stalker did, Marshall forced himself to remain optimistic. Trenay was smart, resourceful, and strong. Over the summer he had taught her everything he knew about self-defense and had shown her the best ways to protect herself if faced with a dangerous situation. But right now none of that put his mind at ease. He only prayed she wouldn't have to use any of what he'd taught her.

Marshall continued to listen as other people talking to Detective Prosser faded in and out. He tried to be patient, but couldn't. "What's going on? Did you find her?"

As Detective Prosser came back on the line Marshall could hear the obvious concern in his voice. But it was the words he said next that sent a dagger of fear straight through to Marshall's heart and shattered the remaining optimism he had been clinging to.

"I believe Ms. Bradley is in grave danger."

CHAPTER FORTY-THREE

Trenay watched the man who had revealed himself as her brother with a combination of fear, curiosity, and skepticism. She didn't want to care who he was, but at this point, she couldn't help wondering if what he'd said was true.

Steven puttered around the room, covering the windows with dark trash bags and setting up what looked to be a small camp light. The sun had set, leaving the room dark and almost completely void of shadows. He fumbled around with the lamp's batteries and after a minute or so managed to get the light working.

In the dim light of the room, Trenay tried to see if his face revealed any clues as to who he really was. She wracked her brain trying to make a connection or to see some type of resemblance to either of her parents.

Her father stood well over six feet. Steven was also tall, which didn't prove anything. Her mother had deep brown skin, the same as Steven's; again, yet another similarity that didn't prove anything.

This man, who looked to be early to mid-forties, had acne scars on his face, a receding hairline, a small paunch, and a space between his front teeth. Both her parents had slender builds, perfect teeth, and her father still had a full head of hair, which he kept closely cropped.

How could this man be her brother? He didn't look

like them, sound like them, or act like anyone in her family. Her parents had never mentioned another child. As far as she knew neither of them had been married to other people. Wouldn't they have told her about a previous marriage or relationship? *Wouldn't one of them have at least shared that she had a brother?*

Trenay wanted to cry, but with every ounce of resolve she could muster, she did her best to remain calm. She didn't know exactly what Steven had planned for her, but she knew it wasn't anything good.

Leaning wearily against the wall with her hands and feet still bound, her body began to get stiff from sitting on the hard floor. Her throat had gotten dry in the hot, dusty room. "May I have something to drink, please?" she asked, nodding in the direction of a bottle of water that had rolled out of a plastic grocery bag.

Steven finished covering the windows and turned the lamp up a little brighter. He picked up the bottle, unscrewed the cap, and brought it over to Trenay.

She held up her hands. "Can you untie me?"

"You can hold the bottle just fine."

"You've got these ropes so tight; they're cutting off my circulation."

"Too bad," he said, shoving the water in her hands and spilling some of it on her.

Trenay took several long swigs of lukewarm water as Steven watched her. She looked away, not wanting to make eye contact with him or show just how desperate and afraid she felt.

How was she going to get out of this? Looking down

as spilled water mixed with dirt on the floor turning ugly and brown she closed her eyes for a second and sighed. If she could only get her hands free. She had hoped he would loosen the ropes enough that she could wriggle her hands free, but he must have been thinking the same thing.

"So, little sister, I guess you're wondering why I brought you here."

Taking several more sips from the bottle Trenay placed it between her knees. Turning her head from side to side and moving her legs around as much as she could, she did her best to stretch her shoulders, back, and legs that now ached from sitting in the same position for such a long time.

"I can see you don't believe I'm your brother. That's understandable. It's pretty obvious no one ever told you about me."

"My parents have always been open and honest with me about everything. They've never said anything to me about having other children."

Steven smirked. "Obviously."

"The real question is why my brother would stalk me, break into my house, drug me, tie me up, and hold me hostage?" she asked angrily. "Maybe you're lying and you're not related to me at all. Is this about money or are you trying to get your fifteen minutes of fame?"

She saw him wince.

Steven walked to the other side of the room, his back to Trenay. Staring at a piece of ripped wallpaper he stood silently for a moment, taking his time before offering a response.

Afraid she had made him angry she braced herself. Perhaps she had pushed him too far, but maybe she had also found a window of opportunity. Still afraid but thinking instinctively she took advantage of the momentary distraction. Struggling against the ropes she tried desperately to free her hands. She had to get free. There was no doubt in her mind that this man was unstable. She had no way to predict what he was capable of.

She heard Steven exhale heavily. Still wriggling her hands she felt the ropes give a little. He turned to face her and she quickly stilled her hands.

"No, Trenay, I'm not lying." Steven walked to another corner of the room and sat on the milk crate. He leaned his back against the wall and stretched out his legs. For a while, he just stared at her with a blank expression. He didn't appear to be angry or sad, just indifferent.

The silence was uncomfortable, but Trenay didn't dare say anything else. Sitting with her hands and feet bound, she wouldn't be able to fight him off if he became angry and lashed out.

Steven pulled a pack of cigarettes out of his pocket. Before lighting one, he held out the pack to Trenay.

"I don't smoke," she replied.

"I know. I was just being polite."

It didn't take long for the thick haze of cigarette smoke to mix with the suffocating hot air in the room. Trenay coughed and her eyes burned from the smoke.

Steven ignored her discomfort and continued taking long drags from the cigarette until there was nothing left but the filter. Stamping the cigarette out with the heel of his foot, he seemed more relaxed. Pushing away from the wall he checked his watch and sighed.

"It's getting late," he announced. "It's about time we wrap this up."

What did he mean? Trenay was too afraid to ask.

Steven appeared calm, moving toward her with purpose. His mood had shifted. Trenay felt a sob rising in her throat as terror paralyzed her. A tear rolled down her face and her heart thumped inside her chest. Although he never uttered a word, Trenay finally understood the true purpose of bringing her to the abandoned house. Steven was going to kill her.

CHAPTER FORTY-FOUR

"My mother was Sylvia Turner. She was nineteen years old when she had me, just a kid. Our father, Mr. Alvin Bradley, was twenty-three."

"*Our* father," Trenay repeated. "We have the same father?"

Steven nodded.

"That's a lie! My father is responsible and honorable. He would never have had a child and abandoned him."

"Well, I guess the man you know now and the one who knocked my mother up when he was twenty-three didn't share the same *honorable* intentions."

"That can't be true," Trenay said quietly. Why would her father have a child and never acknowledge him or love him and watch him grow up? None of this made any sense to her. The man Steven was talking about sounded cold and distant. That wasn't the man she knew.

Her father loved her unconditionally. She had no doubt he would do anything to protect her. Growing up she had never felt anything but safe, secure, and cherished. Her father doted on her and spoiled her. It was obvious to anyone who knew them that she and her mother meant the world to him.

If anyone knew her father, she did. This man claiming to be her brother – her father's son – didn't know him at all. He simply had to be mistaken.

Trenay looked over at Steven.

"I'm afraid it's the truth. You see, little sister, growing up I didn't have quite the same charmed life as you. We were poor. My mother's parents kicked her out when she told them she was pregnant. They weren't exactly thrilled to be grandparents. So Mom moved us to southern Florida and tried to raise me on her own. Not easy to do when you're working one crappy job after another, trying to make ends meet and not having enough money for even the simple things."

Southern Florida. Her father had gone to school in Florida and her parents had lived there before she was born. *This had to be another meaningless coincidence.*

"You wouldn't know anything about that, would you? Trying to make ends meet. Money problems. From what I can tell dear old Dad has been pretty successful and provided quite a cushy life for you."

"How do you know what kind of life I had?"

Steven shrugged. "Once I tracked down our father, I did a little digging into his life. I wanted to find out the kind of man he was. I guess what I needed to know more than anything is what kind of man would leave a helpless woman to raise a child on her own. But what I found out was a whole lot more."

Trenay shifted slightly, still trying to get free while Steven was distracted telling his life's story and pacing around the room, but something he said made her stop. "What do you mean?"

"Your parents got married a year after I was born. Not too long after that, they moved out of the state. Dear Old

Dad's job transferred him; they had you and settled into a cushy suburban life. Ballet and tennis lessons, vacations in California, Florida, and Europe, private schools, and top-notch college education, even a family dog named Leo, all compliments of a father who traded one family for another."

Stunned, Trenay listened as Steven recounted intimate details of her family's life.

"Your life compared to mine," Steven said shaking his head, "night and day."

Now he stood facing her. The look in his eyes no longer masked what he was trying to hide. In the dimly lit room, there was no mistaking the sheer hatred emanating from his eyes.

Steven was beyond disturbed. He hated and wanted to punish her for something she had no control over. Even if what he said was true she didn't know what kind of satisfaction he would get from hurting her.

"Steven, I'm sorry for how you grew up, but there is nothing I can do about that."

Furious he grabbed Trenay by her hands, pulling her to her feet. "My childhood was robbed because the one person who should have loved me, protected me, and cared whether or not I had food to eat or clothes to wear, decided to pretend that I didn't exist."

"But I didn't have anything to do with what my father did or didn't do to help you and your mother."

"No, but you're who I'm going to use to make him regret his decision."

CHAPTER FORTY-FIVE

Cristina hung up the phone. With tears in her eyes, she turned to Marshall. "He said he doesn't know where she is. He left after their meeting and that was several hours ago."

Marshall swore under his breath. *Where could she be?* He was quickly running out of places to look for Trenay. Then he had an idea.

"Where was Trenay's meeting with the reporter?"

Cristina tried to remember the address or at least the area. "It was on the south side," she said, trying to remember the address. "I took the call and set up the appointment."

"Call the reporter back. He probably remembers."

Cristina made the call. "I got it!" Handing Marshall the piece of paper with the address of the house Bill Overstreet said he'd left Trenay.

Marshall grabbed the paper and bolted for the door. "Call Detective Prosser and give him the address. Ask him to meet me there."

"Wait. I want to come with you."

With one hand on the doorknob, Marshall stopped. "I need you here in case Trenay tries to get in touch with you."

Cristina started to protest but Marshall stopped her before she could say a word. "Cristina, please. I don't know what I'm going to find. The safest place for you to be right now is here."

Marshall checked his phone. Still no call from Trenay.

Speeding across town to an area that was unfamiliar to him, he prayed he would find Trenay safe and sound. In his mind, he hoped she'd had a flat tire and couldn't reach him because her phone died. Or maybe she had decided to go someplace else before heading home after her meeting and had lost her phone in the process. As much as he hoped it was one of those scenarios, he knew it was something else.

Using his GPS he was directed down one street after another until he came to the street where Trenay had met the reporter earlier in the day. It was almost ten o'clock and except for a few kids playing basketball under a streetlight in front of one of the few houses that didn't seem abandoned, there was no other activity.

Marshall looked up and down the street hoping to catch a glimpse of Trenay's car amongst the handful of cars parked on both sides of the street or some other clue that would lead him to her. His heart sank when he didn't see the car or anything else that would help him.

Once again, he tried calling her cell phone, but just like all of the other calls, it went straight to voice mail.

Desperate and running out of places to look, Marshall decided to drive around the neighborhood to continue his search, all the while praying for a miracle.

"Please don't do this," Trenay pleaded.
Steven seemed oblivious to her pleas.

"I don't understand how any of this is going to help you," she continued.

Steven stopped what he was doing and charged across the room. "You're not supposed to understand. I need this," he yelled. "I hate my father and I hate anything and anyone he loves. Knowing how much killing you is going to hurt him is all I need."

Standing on legs that were now trembling, Trenay watched helplessly as Steven pulled a gasoline can from underneath a tarp. She nearly fainted when she realized what he was going to do.

"Steven, don't do this," she begged again. "I'm sure my father never meant to hurt you or your mother. Why can't you believe that? Talk to him. Let him explain his side of the story."

"*His side of the story!* Are you serious? What could he possibly say at this point to erase all of the nights I went to bed hungry or when my mother and I had to light candles because the electricity had been turned off? What words would make up for my mother and me living in a tiny apartment that was barely big enough for one person, let alone two? Unless Alvin Bradley can turn back time, there is nothing left to say."

Through her tears, Trenay desperately plotted an escape knowing there was no reasoning with Steven. But, the situation seemed bleak.

Think! What had Marshall taught her that she could use? There had to be something. *She had to fight. Her life depended on it.*

For weeks, Marshall had drilled it into her head to

fight. She couldn't allow herself to be a victim. At least if she was going to die she would die fighting.

Maybe if she could keep him talking long enough, she could think of a way out.

"Steven, you're right. If you kill me it will hurt my father."

Steven pulled out a stack of newspapers and began scattering them around the room.

"That's the plan," he responded absently, continuing with his work.

"How are you going to let him know you were responsible?"

Steven stopped and turned toward Trenay. "What do you mean?"

"You went through the trouble of finding me, bringing me here, and killing me," she said, her voice sounded strained. "Won't it mean more – to you – if my father knew who you were and why you killed me?"

Steven shrugged and continued shredding and scattering the newspapers. "Just knowing your death will bring him pain for the rest of his life is enough for me."

Disheartened that she couldn't throw him off, Trenay leaned against the wall for support. She had to think of something else.

After scattering a fair amount of newspapers around the room Steven gathered up his bag and picked up the gas can. Giving the room a once over, he walked over to Trenay. Grabbing her firmly by the shoulder, he forced her back down to the floor.

Searching his face for a glimpse of regret, hesitation,

or maybe even compassion she saw none. As Trenay watched Steven unscrew the cap on the gas can and splash the flammable liquid around the room, the fumes suddenly ignited something inside of her.

No! She refused to let Steven win. *Fight! Your life depends on it.*

After he had saturated the newspaper with gas, Steven walked over to the doorway and paused. Turning toward Trenay he smiled, lit a match, and threw it inside the room.

"Good-bye, Trenay."

Struggling to get her feet free as flames sprang up from the newspaper, Trenay felt the ropes give enough that she could almost slip her foot through.

Steven, standing just outside of the doorway seemed mesmerized by the smoke and flames.

Trenay continued struggling against the ropes. She was almost there. If she could just get her feet free.

Hearing the commotion inside the room Steven turned just as Trenay lunged at him with the full force of her body knocking him into the hallway. Realizing she had landed squarely on top of Steven who seemed stunned and disoriented, she quickly scrambled to her feet. Looking around for an escape her eyes watered and burned from the acrid smoke pouring out of the room Steven had set on fire. Seeing the stairway just down the hall, she did her best to keep low to avoid the smoke but at the same time maintain her balance. Crawling along the floor toward the stairs with her hands still bound proved to be a struggle, but with every inch, she came closer to freedom. Just as she neared the landing a firm hand grabbed her ankle preventing her from going any further.

"No!" she screamed, fighting through smoke and tears. Trenay began kicking wildly. Steven must have hit his head when she lunged at him and he fell. His reaction was slow but his grip was unrelenting, but so was her will to live.

Seeing the bright glow from the flames growing brighter and brighter with each passing second, Trenay knew she had very little time. Her kicks barely had any effect against Steven's strong grip. She could feel him pulling her back; back into what she knew would surely be her death.

Fight!

Kicking relentlessly she fought to get free, she fought for her life. The crackling of wood became louder and the acrid smell of smoke burned her nostrils as flames escaped the room and crept up along the outer walls and up to the ceiling. Then, suddenly she remembered. A defensive move Marshall taught her suddenly came to mind. In one swift motion Trenay flipped over to her side and with her free foot, she thrust with as much force as she could muster, connecting with the side of Steven's head.

Trenay heard Steven moan and he loosened his grip enough for her to break free. Crawling until she was just a few feet from the landing, she struggled to get to her feet. Turning to see her captor lying on the floor, dazed and confused, she was seconds away from freedom until suddenly everything faded to black.

***

Marshall drove up one street and down another. There

was no sign of Trenay anywhere.

Pulling over to the side of the street, he checked his phone one more time. Still nothing.

Where could she be? Marshall had never felt such fear or hopelessness. Sensing Trenay was in danger but being unable to find her and help her tore at his heart and soul.

If only...what? he thought. What could he have done differently? He couldn't keep Trenay under lock and key. He couldn't be with her twenty-four hours out of the day.

Marshall leaned his head back and closed his eyes. He had to find her. Refusing to think the worst he pressed on. Somewhere, somehow, he would find her. And this time he would never let her go.

CHAPTER FORTY-SIX

Off in the distance, an odd glow lit up the night sky. Fire. *A house fire.* It didn't seem far away, maybe just over a few streets. Marshall put his truck in gear and drove in the direction of the fire.

Parking a little way down the street, he quickly joined the small crowd of onlookers who had gathered across the street from a dilapidated three-story house that seemed to be burning from the top down.

"Does anyone live there?" he asked an older woman staring at the burning house.

She shook her head and replied, "Nothing but junkies, rats, and cockroaches. I'm glad it's burning down. Now, maybe the city will do something about it. Id' rather see an empty lot than that old eyesore."

"Wait," Marshall, said, looking at some of the other houses on the street, some occupied but most of them not, "If no one lives there and the house is abandoned, the utilities should be shut off."

The woman pulled her housecoat tighter around her ample frame and replied, "Probably."

"Have you seen anyone go into that house today?"

The woman shook her head. "I don't think so. I did see a man kind of hanging around the past few days, but I thought he might have been the owner finally taking responsibility for his property. I had a good mind to go

Alicia Wiggins

over there and tell him how sick I am of looking at these raggedy houses day in and day out. What's wrong with people letting their properties get all torn up like this? It makes the rest of us who are trying to have a decent home mad. How would you feel having drug dealers, prostitutes, and homeless people doing their dirt right in your own backyard? I'll tell you; you wouldn't like it."

Marshall was only half-listening to the woman as the sound of sirens pierced the night air.

"I saw some people today," said an old man standing near the woman.

Marshall turned his attention to the man. "Here? At this house?" he asked, desperate for any bit of information that might help him find Trenay.

"I saw a man and he had a woman with him. I figured they were a couple of crack heads looking for a place to crash for the night."

"A woman?" Marshall repeated. "You saw someone go into *that* house with a woman?"

"I think so."

Marshall didn't wait to hear anything else the man or woman had to say. He bolted across the street.

"Wait!" someone shouted from the crowd. "You can't go in there! The fire department is almost here."

Ignoring the warning, Marshall ran up to the porch and tried to open the door. Something was blocking it. Pushing against the unrelenting structure he leveraged his weight, giving it his all until he felt the door budge. Pushing until there was an opening wide enough to squeeze through, he entered. The fire hadn't reached the lower level but he could smell smoke.

"*Trenay!*" It was hard to see in the dark house. "Trenay, are you in here?" he called out again.

Marshall looked around the dank surroundings, running from room to room calling her name and looking into each room for a sign she might be there. After exhausting his search on the ground floor, he went to the stairwell as smoke began to drift down. "Trenay!" he called. Still no answer. Taking two steps at a time, he quickly came to the second floor, peering down the narrow hallway and squinting against the smoke. He frantically searched the three rooms on the second floor but came up empty-handed. Running back to the stairs he paused momentarily before heading to the third floor. Fearing the worst, he could see flames and thick black smoke. The third floor was close to being fully engulfed.

Running up the stairs into what he felt was the worst possible scenario, he squinted as his eyes and throat burned from the smoke. The stairs were old and unstable but he pressed on. Then, suddenly, he stopped. His heart leaped in his chest and he gripped the rickety railing for support. Lying just a few feet from the landing, he saw her. Trenay's lifeless body.

***

Racing to the hospital the vehicle's siren screamed with a sense of urgency, letting everyone in its path know, this mission was a matter of life and death.

With every fiber of his heart, mind, body, and soul Marshall prayed it wouldn't be the latter.

CHAPTER FORTY-SEVEN

The room was bathed in a strange pale light. It wasn't her room or another room she'd ever been in. Everywhere she looked Trenay saw people but was unable to make out their faces or what they were doing. The people all seemed to be moving in slow motion and their voices were muffled. When she tried to speak to ask them where she was and what was going on, no words came out.

Trenay felt strange, her body heavy and unable to move. It seemed as if she was in a fog or a dream. But even in a dream, there would be something familiar. In this dream, nothing and no one looked or sounded familiar.

Then she heard it. Her name. Someone was calling her. She tried to focus but her eyelids felt so heavy and she struggled to keep her eyes open. Again, she tried to answer, but the words never made it to the surface. Turning her head toward the sound, she saw a figure but couldn't make out who it was. She heard her name again but this time it was further away. Straining to follow the sound of the voice proved to be too much effort. What little strength she had left slowly dissipated and even though she tried to fight it, her body gave in as she drifted into a dreamless sleep.

***

Marshall stared off into the distance, oblivious to the sound of the machines monitoring Trenay's breathing, blood pressure, oxygen level, and heartbeat. Trenay's parents, family, and friends had drifted in and out of her hospital room over the past several days, but he could barely remember anything that was said or done during that time.

Trenay was in a coma.

What he wouldn't give for one more day back in Benton Lake. He smiled. Moonlit walks, sitting by the lake at sunset and making s'mores, picnics, making love until they were so exhausted they had no other choice than to fall asleep in each other's arms. They had so many wonderful memories from their time spent at the lake and selfishly, he wanted more. Was that too much to ask? He didn't think so. All he wanted was to spend the rest of his life with the woman he loved with all of his heart and soul. That's all he wanted. But she needed to pull through. She needed to wake up. One more fight. That's all he required of her and he would take it from there.

CHAPTER FORTY-EIGHT

Trenay reached up and took the steaming cup of chamomile tea Marshall offered her. After she took it he leaned down, kissed her on the top of her head, and joined her on the porch step.

"Cold?"

"Not really," she replied, staring out into the darkness.

"Are you okay?" he asked, sensing a hint of melancholy in her voice.

Trenay sipped from her cup and snuggled in a little closer to Marshall. "Honestly?"

"Yes."

"In that case, I'd have to say yes. For the first time in a long time, I can truthfully say yes and feel deep down that I'm okay."

Marshall let out a slow breath and put his arm around Trenay's shoulder, taking comfort in her closeness.

"I'm glad we decided to come here early," she replied, leaning against Marshall and looking up into the night sky.

"Me, too. Although I wasn't a hundred percent sure the weather would cooperate. Typically this close to Thanksgiving we're shoveling snow. For it to be mild enough to sit out here on the porch and look up at the stars without freezing our toes off is a nice surprise."

Trenay nodded. "I can't believe it's almost Thanksgiving," she said softly.

Marshall had been thinking the same thing. In retrospect, time had passed quickly since *that* night.

After finding Trenay that late summer night in the burning house Marshall had learned to look at things differently and to appreciate everything he had, particularly Trenay.

Once she came out of her coma, Trenay had to recover from smoke inhalation, burns on her back, and a broken arm. Just a minute or two more inside the burning house it could have been much worse.

By the time the fire department had arrived, Marshall had made it out of the house with Trenay in his arms. No more than a minute or two after reaching the front porch, the third floor collapsed. Marshall later learned the firefighters had fought a losing battle in attempting to save the house. Between the gasoline Steven had used to start the fire and the house's wood-framed construction, it quickly burned to the ground.

After fire investigators sifted through the charred rubble, it was later confirmed that Steven had perished in the fire.

The word *nightmare* couldn't sufficiently describe the ordeal Trenay had suffered because of him. When Trenay's parents arrived at the hospital after learning of their daughter's ordeal, Detective Prosser had explained to her father about Steven Turner's claim that he was her brother and Alvin's son.

Alvin Bradley was sick knowing that because of him his daughter had suffered under Steven's psychotic delusions. As it turned out Alvin Bradley did know

Steven's mother. She had worked as a waitress at a greasy spoon where he and his buddies would sometimes end up after a night of drinking.

Alvin never dated her and at best the two of them only shared a few brief conversations. However, Alvin did remember that a lowlife friend of one of his buddies taking an interest in her. At the time none of that neither interested nor concerned Alvin. He moved on, finished school, and later took an internship in another part of Florida.

Alvin swore to his wife and daughter that he had never had a relationship with Steven's mother and the forged signature on the birth certificate solidified his claim.

All of that was in the past and for the first time in a longtime Trenay and Marshall were no longer under the dark cloud of fear and uncertainty that Steven had been responsible for bringing into their lives.

"Speaking of Thanksgiving, I feel like I need to warn you, Katrice goes all out for the holidays. Next to Christmas, I think Thanksgiving is her favorite time of year. The big turkey, brown sugar glazed ham, mounds of stuffing and mashed potatoes, homemade rolls, pies, cookies, cakes, the whole nine yards."

Trenay smiled. "I'm looking forward to it. Will your dad and Miss Vonda be there, too?" Trenay had met them when she was in the hospital, after the fire. They had come to check on both her and Marshall, which Trenay found particularly touching considering the little they knew about her had come from their sons and Katrice, having never met her in person.

"Yes, and my brother Shaun is supposed to be here late Wednesday evening."

"Sounds like it's going to be a good time."

After sitting for a few minutes simply enjoying the night sky and cool air, each lost in their private thoughts, Marshall broke the silence.

"Can I tell you something?"

"Can I stop you?" Trenay replied knowing quite well that she couldn't.

"That night when…you know…I was driving back from the job in Cleveland, I wanted to –" Marshall's voice trailed off.

Concerned, Trenay sat up. Turning to face him, she tried to read his expression, but couldn't, even with the light from the pale moon.

"You wanted to what?" she asked, feeling comfortable enough with this man to share any burden or concern he had. After everything they had been through, he could tell her anything. No matter how big or small, they could handle it, together.

"I wanted to and still want to tell you something important." Marshall appeared nervous and suddenly very serious. "Trenay, what I wanted to tell you that night is the same thing I've wanted to tell you for a long time but because of everything that's happened, I've had to wait. Well, I can't wait any longer." He paused. "I need to and want to spend the rest of my life with you." He let what he said sink in while he gathered the courage to continue. "You don't know how happy I would be waking up beside you every morning and falling asleep every night with you in my arms. I want us to sit out by the lake with a roaring fire making s'mores and take long walks through the woods. On every special occasion – birthdays, anniversaries, Valentine's Day, Flag Day, or just because – I want to make banana pancakes for you and serve them to you in bed. I want you to keep reminding me to put stuff in the recycle bin. One day it'll sink in. And when we're old and gray, I want us to take walks around the lake with our canes and walkers and at night sit out here on the steps and look up at the stars. But, the one thing I want most of all is for you to never forget how precious you are to me. I am so in love with you that the thought of spending the rest of my life showing you just how much I love you is what gets me out of bed in the morning. You're the reason I can't seem to stop smiling and why I feel like I can move heaven and earth if you asked me to."

Trenay looked up at Marshall, hearing the heartfelt words she already held in her heart. She had no doubt he loved her. Everything he said and did was a testament to that love and she felt truly blessed to have him in her life.

"Trenay, be my wife, for no other reason than because you love me, too."

Trenay's eyes glistened as she fought back tears.

"I almost lost you and the thought of you not being in my life was enough to make me realize that I couldn't take a chance on losing you again. So, I'm putting it all on the line, baby. Again!"

"Wow," Trenay said, smiling through her tears, "you have put it all out there. You're getting good at that."

Marshall took Trenay's hand. She looked down just as

he slipped an antique diamond and sapphire ring onto her finger.

Looking into his eyes, she replied, "Marshall, it's beautiful." Peering down at her finger adorned with the beautiful ring, she knew it was her turn to put it all on the line. "I know you may not know this but I've loved you for a long time. The problem was that my heart and my head weren't on the same page. That's why I had such a hard time telling you how I felt." Trenay sighed. Feeling free to express how she felt about Marshall, she continued. "I made every excuse not to love you. Call it fear, apprehension, or just plain stupidity; I wasted a lot of time fighting my feelings for you and trying to decide if it was real or not. All of that is over now. I have to admit there are times when you make me crazy, angry, happy, excited, and five or six other different emotions all mixed in, but I wouldn't trade what I have with you for anything in the world because it's real. The bottom line is I can't imagine my life without *you* in it. And I don't want to."

Marshall wiped away a tear rolling down Trenay's cheek. "So is that a yes?" he asked softly.

"Yes," she replied, smiling broadly, "especially if you really promise to make banana pancakes every year on our anniversary."

Overwhelmed with relief and joy, Marshall jumped to his feet, lifting Trenay high in the air and bringing her back down to kiss her with a love so strong it couldn't be more real. "Yes," he replied. "That's a promise I plan to keep."

The End

ABOUT THE AUTHOR

Alicia Wiggins began her writing career in the late 1990s. She loves creating realistic characters who often find themselves in precarious situations on their way to happily ever after.

Alicia is a graduate of Central State University and Franklin University. She spends her days immersed in numbers and spreadsheets and her nights fully engulfed in drama and romance. When she's not writing, Alicia enjoys traveling, reading, watching cheesy horror movies, and spending time with her family (including her beloved cat).